MYRA MIGHT SURVIVE

THE SERIAL SURVIVORS
BOOK 2

LIZ HAMBLETON

EDITED BY
BETH HUDSON INK

COVER DESIGN BY
K.B. BARRETT DESIGNS

LIZHAMBLETONBOOKS LLC

*To all the girls who were taken advantage of for being too nice.
Remember, Karma rarely misses.*

CONTENT WARNING

Before you read…

Myra Might Survive contains adult subject matter that may not be for everyone. If you are uncomfortable with explicit on-page romance, this book is not for you.

There are mentions of violence, the foster care system, and undead zombies that have sludge for blood. It's gross.

Be mindful when you read.

CHAPTER
ONE

Myra

Tips for surviving the apocalypse.

Number one. Share your food. You'll always find more.

Well, not always, but humans can go a long time without food. Weeks even. A person can get used to hunger, and the emptiness eventually goes numb, or at least it does for me. It's water that gets tricky. After three or four days without it, organs start to shut down, and you get confused and delirious, dropping dead around day six.

There's no greater feeling than tearing off a piece of bread and handing it to someone desperate to eat. That feeds me more than calories. We live next to a massive river, so I'm not worried as long as water is near. I'll find a meal eventually.

Number two. Give away your stuff if someone truly needs it.

Blankets, tampons, and hair ties aren't necessary, and I can go without them. The temperature's dropping, and while some can't handle the cold, nobody likes working with hair in their face. Periods are a nuisance, but I can do my laundry and figure it out.

I always say, "Treat others how you would like to be treated." I've never needed much, and that hasn't changed since monsters started roaming the earth. We're all terminal anyway, so why hoard what little is left?

Okay, so after you have no food, blankets, or toiletries, you need to, erm…

Oh, right. Number three! Learn to swim!

That's a big one, and unfortunately, I'm not following my own advice.

You see, the infected, zombie-like creatures roaming around outside are *not* good swimmers.

Not that I'm any better.

If I could safely find a houseboat and plant it out in the middle of the river, I think I'd be okay. They'd waddle to the shoreline, bloated bodies pumping black sludge for blood, gray eyes staring into nothing, until they spotted me and broke into a dead sprint, toppling into the water to drown. That seems to be their only weakness, but unfortunately, it's also mine.

I've never been in a pool long enough to learn. Once, I jumped a neighbor's fence with some kids from school to go skinny-dipping. It wasn't a neighbor, not really now that I think about it, because it wasn't my house next door. The Tenards lived there, and I had a room.

Wait, no.

I had a bunk with two other foster kids, not a room.

Anyway. Not my house, my neighbor, or my pool, but there I was, bottoms up over a decaying fence, getting a splinter in my right booty cheek.

I knew I couldn't swim, but I didn't think it would be too hard to figure out. Plus, the other girls had stolen a bottle of alcohol from Grandma Tenard and were meeting some boys there. When I said I would go, it was to keep an eye on them and make sure no one got hurt.

Turns out, I was the one needing looking after. I sank like a stone and woke up in the hospital two days later to an angry foster family and my social worker.

I shake my head to free myself of the memory and continue my mental list.

"Tip number three," I mumble to myself. "Must learn to swim."

"Myra." Lincoln snaps his fingers in front of my face a few times. "You're in space again."

"I wish." I force a smile and take the can of beans he hands me.

Sometimes there's no place to go except inside my head, and I'm great at thinking about lists and tasks. Taking action is where I falter.

Honestly, I'm the last person who should be writing a survival guidebook. By some miracle, I'm still alive, but only because I was at the right place at the right time and had some good luck.

I suppose these would be some good tips for staying alive in a crowded habitat with dozens of strangers. Years of foster kid life and co-mingling with new families gave me some skills in that department, and I'm adept at going along to get along.

The room buzzes around me, suddenly too loud after Lincoln's brought me back to reality. I tip the can back and let some beans slide into my mouth, watching the drooping Halloween decorations sway from the ceiling. It's been almost a month since that dreaded October 31st, but no one's clamoring to redecorate.

I chew slowly and lick my lips. "Honey baked. Wow. Pulling out the fancy stuff," I say. "Here you have some."

He swats the can away and taps on the bottom, urging me to eat more.

"Nothing but the best for you," Lincoln says with a grin. "And it's your last meal and all."

He's joking, but my stomach sinks. My face gives away my dread, and Lincoln wraps his arm around my shoulders. He's younger than me, but who isn't around here? Still, his strength and confidence ease my tension, and my shoulders relax.

"You won't have to swim," he promises. "The council has looked this over a hundred times."

"Oh, you're right about that," I tell him. "I won't swim. I'll drown."

Flashes of memory come back. A girl with black hair dives in first. Some kid is doing a cannonball into the water with his briefs still around his ankles. My foster mother refusing to enter my hospital room the next morning, screaming at the social worker that I wasn't worth the check.

Lincoln's reassuring me for the hundredth time that I won't have to swim when they set off their explosion, but that's not the only reason the council's plan of attack upsets me.

We're safe here, nestled within the rooms and offices of the dam wall. It's a little cramped, and sure, some of us are sleeping in the maintenance closet, but it offers a nice humming sound that puts you right to sleep.

We were lucky to be trespassing when the world ended, and luckier, we were able to break into the control station of this dam, sealing ourselves off from the rest of the world. It's not perfect, but if I were anywhere else, I'd be a goner, and so would so many of the people here.

It doesn't matter what I think, though. They've decided, and all I can do is sit back and hope it's the right choice. Lincoln goes on about the greater good, but I've tuned him out, shoving cold beans down my throat so my stomach will stop growling. We are starving, but the council doesn't want to hear alternative solutions. They won't change their minds.

Lincoln's girlfriend, whose name I can never remember, makes her way over to us. I feel so bad about forgetting who she is, but names never stick with me. Why make a point to remember people if you leave them in a matter of weeks? It's a poor habit from childhood that I can't seem to shake.

I do my best to appear happy to see her, even when she pops her hip and scowls at us. Jealousy seeps from her every movement, but she pretends she's confident, making rounds through this place as if nothing is wrong.

Not that I blame her for the show.

Lincoln is a flirt, and I've caught him making out with other girls when she's not around. That's their business, not mine, but I wish he would cool it so she would take it down a notch.

Lincoln doesn't bother removing his arm, even when I raise my shoulder into his armpit and try to pull away. It's like he's trying to be rude to what's her name.

Gah, what is her name?

"Hi, Myra," she says, her voice dripping with disdain.

I may not have learned how to swim in any of my foster homes, but

I figured out how to read people. Especially women. We're equally wonderful and terrible to each other, and right now, this girl whose name I can't remember is leaning towards terrible.

"Hiya." I hide my mouthful of beans behind the can, trying not to be rude. "You look nice today."

She rolls her shoulders back and smirks. "Are you ready for Friday?"

What the H - E - double hockey sticks is her name?

Ashley? Beth? Crystal?

"It's got to be a waterfall explosion," she goes on. I'm still reciting names in alphabetical order as she continues. "I know you're afraid of water. Lincoln said you can't swim."

Donna? Eileen? Farrah?

"Give her a break, Bobbi."

Lincoln to the rescue!

"I'm not afraid of water under the right circumstances," I tell her. "I would kill for a bath right about now. You know what I mean?" I chuckle at myself and almost choke on a bean, coughing a few times while Lincoln pats me on the back.

Bobbi sighs, disgust written all over her face. She tries to pretend we aren't living in filth and hates the idea of not being the most attractive female around. There are only a dozen women, so it's not quite the crown she thinks it is, but good for her to have a hobby.

In truth, I think all women are beautiful, with or without a regular bath, but I don't think Bobbi agrees.

"I don't know what you're talking about," she sneers. "I take care of myself every day."

Bobbi's hair is brushed and braided. She carries around some toiletries, some of which I gave her, and uses them when she thinks no one is looking. I keep some toothpaste with me at all times, but I left my lip gloss and mascara behind on Halloween.

"You're a better woman than I," I say, wiping my mouth with the back of my sleeve.

"Than me," she corrects me.

"Oh, right. Thank you."

She's wrong, but there's no need to be rude.

Lincoln's already standing, ushering her to move along. She gives him a kiss that lasts too long, making him, and anyone watching, uncomfortable. It takes a considerable effort not to upchuck my honey-baked bean dinner.

He pulls away when she tries to whisper something into his ear, and I wonder if he likes his girlfriend or is just afraid of being murdered in his sleep. It's a solid fear, and I don't blame him. We're all under a lot of stress, and it wouldn't take a lot for a woman to snap. Bobbi sways her hips as she walks away, and I let out a slow exhale, grateful the exchange is over.

Lincoln turns to me, arms crossed, and sighs. "She's not wrong about the—"

"I know. I know," I interrupt him. "Do you think my intense fear of drowning would stop me from blowing up a dam that will flood a hundred miles in minutes? That would be silly. Fire away."

"Do you trust me?" Lincoln asks.

"Sure," I say and rise to stand. "We're friends."

His eyes flash with something strange. Displeasure perhaps? He's disappointed in my answer, so I try again.

"I don't have a reason not to trust you," I offer.

Not it, either. I'm still disappointing him with my answer. He breathes in through his nose and out through his mouth, slow and even.

"I need to hear you say it," he says.

His arm snakes around my middle, and I turn to look for his girlfriend, whose name I already forgot again. If she sees him touching me, I'll be the person sleeping with one eye open. There's nothing for her to worry about, but the optics are not good.

"I trust you," I say, my voice an octave too high. It's not a lie, exactly. I'm not someone who inherently distrusts people, is all. I believe that others are naturally good.

He grabs my chin and turns me to face him. That flash of unease is there again, but it fades when my eyes meet his.

"I do," I repeat, keeping my voice calm. "Trust you."

He releases me, and I take a step back.

"Good," Lincoln says, pleased.

A familiar expression spreads across my face, one I've used a million times. It's how I look at people when I want them to believe me, when I'm apprehensive or unsure of their intentions, but find myself at their mercy.

It's how I get others to trust me.

I haven't used it in this place. Not yet, but there's something about this exchange that tells me Lincoln needs to know I'm on his side.

I've known him for a month, and in that time, he's never grabbed me like this or demanded obedience. It's odd, but all I can do is adjust and change with the environment I'm in.

He flashes me a grin, and I add to my mental list.

Tip number four for surviving the apocalypse.

Know who's in charge, and never let them doubt it.

CHAPTER TWO

Lincoln insists he should walk me to my sleeping bunk, and I'm not in a position to decline.

A few teenagers from the night watch walk toward us and wave. They don't look Lincoln in the eye as they do me, and I find myself analyzing this, wondering if I've missed something about him.

"Hello," I say as they approach, fairly certain the redhead is named Lydia, but I don't chance it. I've been teaching them history in my spare time, and they enjoy the lessons.

When education isn't forced or used to pit kids against one another, it's enjoyable. I haven't asked if it's something we could continue on the outside, but I hope it doesn't end. Everyone needs a purpose, and teaching is something I can offer.

Unless it's swim lessons. That I cannot do.

"You know you're safe with me," Lincoln says.

"Oh, okay." I'm unsure how to respond or what he wants to hear, so I keep my responses light.

He takes the empty can from my hands and chucks it in a nearby trash can.

"I'm this way," I say. "I'd better get going." Sleep is always a wonderful escape, and I don't need him to tuck me in. "You better go after… her," I blank on his girlfriend's name again, but Lincoln doesn't appear to notice. "She's probably waiting for you down the hall."

"You know I've offered you lessons," Lincoln replies, ignoring my hint about his girlfriend.

"Lessons?"

"The infected can't swim," Lincoln reminds me. "We could go out to the river at night. It would be safe-ish."

The idea of Lincoln and me out in the dark together, bobbing in the water, sopping wet, doesn't sit right. My stomach gets queasy, and a lump forms in my throat.

"Safe-ish is not a word," I joke. "Your girlfriend would love to correct your grammar on that."

Ever since she found out I was a teacher, she's begun a one-sided battle to prove I'm stupid. If that helps her, I don't mind, but I wish she would find something better to do.

"She won't be a problem much longer," he retorts.

I'm too nervous to ask what that means, and my stomach sinks. Every second of this exchange is torture, and I'm desperate for it to end.

"Offer is always there," he adds, veering down another hallway. I exhale, knowing my escape is imminent.

"No thanks," I say. "I trust you will keep me dry when the time comes."

A teenager walking by gives me an awkward look, which I rightfully deserve for that comment.

"I didn't mean…" I trail off, unsure what to say to him. Everyone around here is constantly thinking about sex, so of course, his mind went there. It's the last thing I'm concerned with, but I should've known better.

I turn on my heel and groan, unsure of what just transpired between Lincoln and me, and wondering how much it matters. We will blow this place to smithereens in a few days anyway, so best not to dwell.

"Lights out!" someone yells.

The generator's humming stops, and darkness fills the space. It takes a minute for my eyes to adjust, and I make it to the wall, feeling until I get to the doorframe. The long corridors and hidden rooms of this place once felt like a maze, but in the weeks since the infected came, we've memorized our way around.

This place we call home was once full of offices and labs, a space for people to work. Cabinets hold brochures, manuals for the dam, and donation envelopes – all of it relics from another time.

The best and worst thing about our sanctuary is its seclusion. We're safe, hidden inside the cement hull that holds the river at bay, but it's isolated. That presents its own list of dangers, with lack of food being the largest. With nearly fifty of us, hungry and crammed together, we're all feeling the strain.

I won't sleep tonight even though my belly is full for the first time in a week. I've volunteered for so many night shifts that I can't get my circadian rhythm back. My body never knows if it's coming or going, and by the time I make it to my pallet on the floor, I'm spinning with thoughts.

The dread of what's coming keeps my mind whirling, refusing to let me rest. Add in the moaning and assorted sex noises echoing through these close quarters, and I'm in for an all-nighter. Apparently, taking a night off isn't an option, and at this rate, someone's bound to end up pregnant, if they aren't already.

I miss the beginning of the apocalypse when people had some sense of privacy. Now they poop in a bucket while you're mid-conversation and think nothing of it.

The end of the world has been full of fun new adventures.

I keep trying to sleep, tossing and turning on my little cot, but I know I've been awake for hours when the moon's light slices across the ceiling.

My back pops as I stretch, giving up on sleep. The earlier rustling has faded to soft snores, never true silence with ten of us crammed in here. I picked this room for its rare window, and after a lifetime of sharing space, the crowd doesn't bother me much.

Some people took a while to adjust to our cramped way of life. The noise alone can overwhelm them, and then there's the smell. It's not like we're all walking around with toothpaste and deodorant in our pockets.

I never had my own space, and even in adulthood, I had roommates. I suppose I got used to the communal lifestyle because living alone never crossed my mind. There were a few good homes over the years, but I never lucked out finding a family as a baby, and then I got older, and well, everyone wanted a puppy.

"You're double digits, kid," my social worker would tell me. "Twice the number and twice the problem."

She wasn't very nice, but there's a ninety-nine percent chance she's dead or a monster because karma rarely misses. I think about an infected person changing her, her veins bulging, dark liquid pouring from her mouth and eyes, and I shiver.

No, I don't wish that fate on anyone. The idea of spending one's existence as a bloated ogre with black sludge for blood makes my skin crawl and my stomach churn.

Tonight, my thoughts feel unbearable. They press on my chest, a heaviness from all these people depending on me not to freak out when I need to do my part. I could say I'm just as worried about them, but that'd be a lie. What's strange is I'm not scared of the plan failing. I'm scared of what happens if it succeeds.

There are fifty of us here, but there could be thousands in the way of the flooding we'll cause by blowing up this dam. Yes, it will wipe out the infected along the way, but who else could we hurt? All for what? Safe foraging followed by the hope that we stumble across another refuge.

The council says everyone is dead, but they don't know. They can't possibly be sure, and in my heart, I know they don't care.

What if I didn't do it?

I don't have much to lose, and I never did. I don't have any parents, and I never created a family for myself over the years. No kids, and my longest relationship lasted about six months. I switch schools every few years, never too close to a co-worker or a town.

Next month, I turn twenty-ten. That's what one of my foster parents used to say about her birthday, and I chuckle at the thought.

She'd make macaroni and cheese with real cheese, and I'd fight an infected for a bowl of that tonight.

Thirty.

I'm the oldest person here.

That's because at midnight on Halloween, most thirty-year-olds are asleep after a busy night of trick-or-treating with their kids. That or they go to a party with other thirty-somethings that ends at a reasonable hour because, well, we're thirty and we're tired.

Thirty-year-olds don't trespass on state property to check on their students who might be making poor decisions and participating in underage drinking by a large body of water.

I grumble to myself and sit up in bed, dragging my feet along the floor until I find my shoes. Feeling along the walls in the dim light, I make my way to the stairwell.

It's fifteen flights up to the lookout at the top of the dam, and I curse myself for being unable to sleep with every step.

Darn conscience. A lot of good it's done me over the years.

Lincoln's on watch tonight, his girlfriend likely curled up in the twin bunk she insists they share. Stepping outside, the wind whips my hair around my face, and I have a flicker of regret for giving away all of my hairbands.

The moon is full, and I see there are maybe a dozen people stretched along the walkway, all of them staring out at the nothingness below. It's usually two or three, but we're getting closer to when the infected circle back.

We've learned to track their movements, to know when they're coming. They're like a horde of giant zombies, though I'm pretty sure brains aren't on the menu. One touch is enough to turn you, black blood flooding your veins until it spills from your mouth and eyes within minutes. It's a vile way to die, though death is rarely dignified.

Their walking patterns aren't their only flaw. After enough time has passed, they burst into a heap of dark sludge. And then there's the drowning. Sometimes we spot them bobbing in the water, bloated and swaying, waiting for the inevitable pop. When I think about it, they're not as terrifying as they seem. Maybe all we have to do is outlast them.

"You're in space again, Myra," Lincoln says to me for the second time today. I crouch down beside him, hanging my legs over the wall and wrapping my arms around the metal bars that keep us from falling to our death.

He traces a finger along my cheek. "What are you thinking about?"

We are at least a hundred feet above the river, but I squint and search for something to convince him we can't go through with the explosion.

A flicker from a fire.

A rustle in the brush.

Something.

It's beautiful how the moon reflects on the deep water that reaches out to the thick trees along its edge. I imagine all the families that would fish here or paddle a canoe, but there isn't a trace of anyone. This land, so serene and exquisite, stretches as far as I can see.

And we're going to destroy it.

"Do you think they would die off eventually?" I ask.

We've seen the numbers get smaller in the last two months. Witnessing them pop like disgusting balloons was a real treat.

Lincoln's fist closes around one of the bars, and he squeezes the metal. "We'll starve first."

I nod in the darkness. A kid says, "Hey," as he passes. I wave, recognizing him as another person who comes to my classes.

"We could hunt," I offer. "When the infected is furthest from us, which is..." I look at my wristwatch that stopped ages ago. "Right about now. I saw deer by the river just yesterday."

"They could smell you and change their pattern."

"You don't know that," I argue.

Lincoln sighs and shakes his head, pushing back from the railing in frustration. My eyes trail over him, watching how he tightens his jaw in the moonlight. He turns his gun over, running his hand down the barrel, studying the weapon. "You won't drown, Myra. I'll keep you from those fucking bloats."

"Bloats?" I ask.

He smiles. "The name fits, right? They look like grey marshmallows, all bloated and shit."

"Better than… the infected." I use air quotes with my hands. "I can see the name sticking."

"Right," he agrees.

I'm not sure of Lincoln's age, but I would guess early twenties. He's lost some of his youthfulness due to the end of days. It tends to age a person.

"Anyway, we're already close to starving," Lincoln says. "Fishing nets are bringing less and less back."

"I know," I agree. "But we've got guns and there are deer right there."

"Guns make noise, Myra."

I tighten my grip on the bars, pulling myself closer to the edge. A cloud passes, making it too dark to see the drop or the massive pool of water below our feet, but I know it's there. I know the danger it can cause, the damage it will do, and how it will kill.

Lincoln places a hand on my shoulder, and I fight the urge to flinch. He's been my friend all along, just acting a little off today, that's all.

"What's going on in that head of yours?" he asks. "Why are you against the plan?"

"Because it's murder. People who survived will be killed when we blow up this dam. People who fought this hard and this long to make it, and we're going to take their lives."

"No one else has survived, Myra."

I look at him, studying his young face as the cloud passes, examining the angle of his jaw and arch of his eyebrows. He's firm with his expression, sure of himself, believing the lie the council is spewing. He must. No one can be that callous.

"How can you be sure?"

He sets his gun beside him and moves closer to me. "We would have seen something from up here, and there's been nothing. Nothing for a month."

I'm silent, knowing whatever argument I make will be refuted. He's decided, and there's no changing his mind.

"You said you trusted me."

"I do," I say.

"So, you'll do as you're told, then."

There's an edge to his voice, and my skin prickles.

"Myra?" he questions. "Are you going to be a problem?"

"Not at all," I say.

The words send a jolt of adrenaline through my veins, my face flushing red, and I wonder if he sees it in the night. I'm not the type of person who makes promises I can't keep, and even though I want to believe the words as they escape my lips, my body knows the truth.

I'm lying.

CHAPTER
THREE

"Even the shallowest part of the water is a hundred feet deep," Dillon yells. "That is an exorbitant amount of feet. "

My brother paces in the distance, nervously shifting his weight, arms crossed tightly at his chest. He's still half asleep, awakened when he heard me sneaking out of our cabin.

He's a thinker who, when presented with a crisis, will still take the time to write out every potential stumbling block and alternate solution. Then he'll waste time weighing the pros and cons before taking action. The problem with thinkers in the apocalypse is that they'll fucking starve to death before doing anything.

I will not let my brother starve.

"Dammit, Dillon," I argue. "What other options do we have? Everything is dead. The weather's getting colder."

"Exactly, Cade," he interjects. "Fish are less active in winter. They won't bite."

"Which is why I'm diving."

His pace quickens along the shoreline, walking back and forth along the river we've loved our entire lives. We've fished here since we were in our mother's stomach and every summer after.

"They're twenty, maybe thirty feet deep at the most," I shout. "I'll just drop the net and see what pulls up tomorrow. What do we have to lose?"

"Your life, Cade!"

"That's an exorbitant exaggeration," I counter.

"That's not how you use that word!" Dillon fumes.

He shakes his head and scratches his beard, his mind churning with a way to stop me. "You'll scare them away. This plan makes no sense. Just let me think," he pleads.

I jump into the water, tired of this conversation and desperate for a fish dinner. Surfacing, I see Dillon raise his hands in frustration, no doubt cursing me under his breath. I'm impulsive, yes, but I get things done.

"Throw the net," I order.

Dillon trudges back to our supplies while I tread water. It's fucking freezing, colder than I remember for this time of year. Not that I have a clue about the date. It's wild how quickly we lose track of time when nothing anchors us to the outside world.

I know the apocalypse came on Halloween, and we kept track for a while, but then everything started to blur together. It's been maybe a month since the world fell apart, but I can't be sure. By the feel of this water, it's been longer, or we've been cursed with a short autumn.

This isn't the first winter I've taken a swim in this river. We had a yearly tradition of doing a polar plunge every morning in January. Dad would say it awakened the spirit.

Woke me the hell up when he threw me in the first few times.

We even did it while I had the flu one year. I've jumped in with a cast on my arm wrapped with garbage bags and duct tape. I'm not afraid of this river, but I am scared we'll starve.

"Careful of the weights. Don't let it get tangled up," I remind Dillon. "Damn. Hurry up, man."

The kayaks are already floating away, and I need to secure them with this net. It's not a perfect system, but I've done it before. There are pockets of the netting where, if fish swim forward, they can't escape. I'll need to hang it from the kayaks and let the bottom sink. It will be a net blanket, and the fish will get all wrapped up.

Hopefully.

If I can get a few Striper in here tonight, it's worth the trouble. All the deer are spooked, and the occasional squirrel or rabbit isn't enough to feed us for long. Dillon's too fearful to leave the cabin, and I can't blame him. The thought of their misshapen bodies, leaking a trail of oil as they run towards us, makes my heart pound harder.

When the infected come around, we secure ourselves in the basement bunker. As far as we can tell, they can't hear, smell, or find us, and it's worked thus far.

"How cold is it, Cade?" Dillon asks.

"I can't feel my fingers or my dick. Throw the net over, will ya?"

"If you can't feel your fingers, how are you going to catch it?"

"The net, Dillon! Now!"

I love my little brother, but his lack of urgency baffles me. Being indecisive is one thing. Leaving me in a freezing river while he questions my plan is another.

He tosses the net, and I catch it even though my hand is numb and it's getting dark. Swimming toward the kayaks, I'm shaking, and my teeth chatter. I realize I've never swam far in winter, only jumped in and got the hell out.

No worries. I can still do this. It's not like we have a choice, and I won't let my brother know he may be right. That's a fate worse than freezing to death.

The kayak closest to me bobs up and down as my strokes get closer, but I manage to secure one side of the net with little trouble.

"How are you going to keep the kayaks spread apart?" Dillon yells. "They might just drift together."

He's right, but I don't give a fuck. Maybe they'll stay apart long enough to catch a fish, and maybe they won't, but if we don't try something, we fail either way. If this doesn't work, I'll have to venture further out into the woods or try to make it into town. No doubt there's something to scavenge or kill, but it's far more dangerous, and the idea turns my stomach.

"Cade?" Dillon calls.

"I hear you, I'm just choosing not to answer," I shout.

"The water looks like it's getting choppy. Can you feel it?"

It's chopping because I swim like a lumberjack, and making it to the other kayak proves difficult. My limbs, numb and clumsy, push it further out with every stroke. Every time I get close enough, I feel the net slip from my grasp, and I have to clamber for it and pull it back up.

"Cade, I don't think this is working. You could be turning hypothermic."

My teeth chatter too hard to answer him, not that anything I say would make a difference. Years-old sibling rivalry gives me enough gusto to swim a little faster, and I reach the second kayak after many failed attempts. Holding onto the side for a minute, I try to catch my breath.

These kayaks are for fishing, and I'm grateful for that when I manage to hoist myself on top with one push. It doesn't topple over, but the air hitting my wet clothes sends a sharp stab of cold deep into my bones. It was instinct to get out of the freezing water, and I didn't realize I'd done it until I found myself breathing hard into the seat, my shaking hand twisted in the netting.

"Why didn't you just paddle our kayak out there?" Dillon asks. "Instead of swimming."

That would have been a brilliant idea.

I underestimated the cold and acted impulsively, yet again. Maybe if I kept some sort of calendar, I would know the river's temperature, but I'm here now, and the only thing I can do is react.

Damn him for being right about thinking things through before jumping.

"I don't know, man." My voice cracks and shakes. "Does it matter now?"

Sitting up, I rip off my wet shirt and rummage through the pockets of some stranger's boat. This is probably one of the houseboats' kayaks that got loose. We wouldn't have something this nice, and there must be some supplies in here we can use.

There's plenty of tackle, a vest, and a spotlight attached to the back of the chair. I feel around for the on switch, my hands inundated with painful pins and needles as the blood flow returns. The moon is bright, but it's still too dark to see well, and it takes minutes before I find the button and flick the light on.

It's blinding.

Pointing it at Dillon, I can see my brother's shoelaces, the color of the bricks under his feet, and that angry expression on his face.

"Off!" Dillon yells.

Infected people are not drawn to light, at least I don't think. He's worried about neighbors. People who we once called friends might murder us for the meat on our bones. The first few weeks after the apocalypse, we had four attempted break-ins from men my father thought were buddies. It's a good thing he wasn't around to see what they had become. Human or inhuman, those people were unrecognizable.

There's an eerie quiet to the world lately, something that makes the hair on the back of my neck stand up. In the first few weeks of November, we saw people regularly, but lately, there's only silence. Everyone is dead or has ventured out to find supplies and food, never to return. It's part of Dillon's theory and why he doesn't want to leave the cabin.

The only people to come back are infected.

I flick the light off, my vision struggling to adjust to the sudden darkness. The kayak lifts on one side, a wave hitting from the east. Strange because this river is normally glassy, especially these days. You could skip a rock across it until it fades from sight.

The kayak jolts upward, something bumping it from below, and I pop up to my feet, every molecule in my body firing to life. The cold leaves my chest, replaced with an uneasy awareness.

"Cade?"

"Shut up," I yell back.

The water ripples on the surface, tiny waves reflecting in the moonlight. Soft splashes lick on the sides of the kayak as it rocks under my feet, and I crouch lower to keep my balance.

That's when I see them.

Floating pillows in the current, pale skin drifting face down in the water.

Some of the infected are only a few swim strokes away, and I look past them, further east to where the river bends right.

There are hundreds.

"Don't move!" Dillon shouts.

I feel around the boat, refusing to sit here until I'm infected and become one of those things. The oar is clipped to the side, and I yank it free, gripping it with two hands.

Dillon's jogging from side to side, his hands in his hair.

"Go inside!" I scream at him.

They aren't crawling up into the kayak or reaching for me, but soon, I'll be surrounded.

Slamming the oar into the water, I hit something hard and push myself off. Lifting the oar, it sticks, something pulling on the flat paddle. It looks like fabric, pale and shining in the moonlight.

It's skin.

I fling it off and try again to push away from the few infected that are bobbing around my vessel.

There's a splash, and I feel wet against my left side. More are coming, making waves in the river and shaking the kayak. I'm on my knees, but these things are known to be flimsy. Too much fight, and I'll flip.

"You have to go downriver!" Dillon screams. "Try to cut it and get back to shore."

He's right. If I keep fighting this current, I'll end up in the water covered in their black ooze. I have to flow with this mess and try a diagonal approach.

"Get into the fucking bunker, Dillon. Now."

"They're dead," he argues.

"Now!" My voice echoes. A flicker of light catches our attention. It's several houses down, but I would guess someone has lit a candle or turned on a flashlight. Dillon's still stuck in place, his feet planted on the shoreline.

I turn the kayak so I'm no longer fighting the wake of these things. There's another splash across my legs as I paddle, but I don't stop, trying to keep ahead of the mass of bodies floating my way.

"I'll jump in the goddamn river again if you don't get your ass inside," I scream at Dillon.

That gets him to listen, and he turns on his heel and runs back to the cabin. If it's just him, there is enough food for ten days, twenty if he stretches the rations.

The kayak lurches forward, something or someone wedged under the back, and I paddle hard and fast to get free. Our cabin disappears from sight, and after a few minutes of paddling without hitting anything, I feel behind the seat for the light.

The river isn't silent. It's filled with sounds of bumping bodies, my heavy breathing, and the rush of water that slaps against the shoreline from their weight. I pause, hesitating before I turn on the light. The wind slices through me, cold and hard, sending pinpricks of pain across my skin.

I take in a deep breath and turn it on, pointing it at my feet while I listen. They aren't talking. The steady moans and groans that go back and forth between those who are infected don't sound from these corpses. Nothing swims in my direction, no monster clawing its way into the kayak.

They're dead.

They have to be dead.

I've never seen one alive in the water, but we never stuck around to check. Not after witnessing bullets pass through the infected while they charge toward prey, limbs swaying from their bloated bodies as they run.

We thought they were invincible until we noticed a few drowning.

Lifting the spotlight, I point it around my kayak and find nothing but dark water. Waves still push me further away, too strong to fight.

Daring to stretch the light further out, I see the mounds of grey skin coming towards me. My eyes are playing tricks on me when one explodes before my eyes, then another. They pop like balloons, spreading black ooze over the surface of the water. An oil slick of death stains the pale skin of the surrounding infected.

Damn, I hope Dillon got to the bunker.

"He did," I tell myself. He's slow to decide, but once he does, nothing can stop him.

I turn around and search the woods, letting the light penetrate the trees. There is no movement, only an empty, dead forest, a skeleton of what this place once was.

Even if I could make my way back to shore, I couldn't climb the steep sides to exit the kayak. I'll have to head farther south, where the shoreline levels with the water. I'm not jumping in with their blood circling. Who knows what that would do, and who would I be when I make my way back to Dillon?

With my head start, I'm able to paddle with purpose, but I'm unsure where I'm heading. Dillon and I rarely came this far fishing, and all our friends were on the opposite side of this massive river.

My body shakes from the cold, but I do my best to push harder, warming myself from the inside out.

"Why don't you listen to people smarter than you?" I mumble. "You wouldn't be in this mess if you let Dillon work the problem. Oh, but then you'd starve waiting for him to decide."

I'm talking to myself, which happens a lot lately, hoping the distraction helps me forget the temperature or the fact that I have a half-day walk back at best. I've lost track of time paddling along, but I know I've gone far.

The slope of the ground by the water's edge is getting lower, and soon, I'll be able to run ashore and hop on land.

"I could check out some of these houses," I say. "Without Dillon to argue with, I could find us some food. I'm out here anyway."

A light hits the water, and I jerk my head in its direction.

"What the fuck?" I whisper and crouch down. A pointless effort in this shallow piece of plastic, but I try my best to hide.

It flashes again, the rays of white coming from somewhere higher.

Much higher.

"Fuck," I grumble.

I'm at the damn dam wall.

I must have been moving at the speed of light to get this far.

There is movement from the top, people controlling the lights that surround me. There's no place to hide, so I wave and hope for the best.

"Hey," I shout. "Hello, I—"

Bang! Bang! Bang!

Water splashes all around me.

Gunfire pelts the river from high above, landing far too close to be considered a warning.

I can either die for sure or take a swim and risk ending up as a zombie.

Fuck, I hate it here.

Lights circle my vessel, and before I give it any more thought, I dive.

CHAPTER
FOUR

The sounds of gunfire cut through the air as I walk back to bed. So fast and sharp, I wonder if I'm imagining them. I'm exhausted, my body strained under more stress and anxiety than I ever thought possible, but I'm sure those were shots fired.

Pop. Pop. Pop.

Again, I hear it, and before it registers how bad of an idea it is, I turn around and run towards the sound. The door to the dam's walkway opens, and several kids on night shift pour into the hall. I recognize a few from my classes, and I reach for their elbows and shoulders to get someone to tell me what's going on, but they don't stop. Something in their faces isn't right, an expression I can't nail down, and my stomach sinks.

Pop. Pop. Pop.

It's louder this time, a haphazard mess of bullets that never ceases. That's what happens when a bunch of teenagers are armed with weapons. They can't wait to use them.

I make my way through the crowd, the crisp night air sending goosebumps over my body when I step outside. It's windy this high atop the dam's ledge, and sometimes I feel so close to the clouds I wonder if I can touch them.

We always keep a watchful eye on the world below, but there's been nothing for weeks, and never this much shooting. There hasn't been a lot to see besides death walking its rigid march around the river, always making the same circles and always waiting to find someone to turn.

Lincoln comes into view, flashes of moonlight casting over his enraged face. "What the fuck are you doing?" he yells. He's holding someone by the shoulders, shaking their body like a rag doll before shoving them to the ground.

I hold onto the railing, steadying myself, my body shaking from nerves, but I dare to look down at what danger lies below. Lights cascade over the side of the wall, reaching out to the dark water and trees along the shore. The circular beams dance back and forth, searching for something unseen by me.

Lincoln continues yelling. "I can't fucking believe this."

A few more gunshots ring out, but I don't see where they land. Pulling myself away from the world below, I turn back to Lincoln.

It's William he screams at, a young man who attends my classes. He looks terrified, his hands up to protect himself from Lincoln's wrath. I move toward them, bracing myself to hear more gunfire, but there is only the wind and Lincoln's anger.

"You fucking idiot. I can't believe how stupid you are."

William's a bit of a rule follower, emphasis on follower, and I can't imagine he would do something to incite this kind of reaction. He's timid and thoughtful, always staying out of trouble. I've never caught him slipping away with women or heard about him drinking the homemade moonshine everyone knows makes the rounds here.

"Lincoln, please. What's going on?" I plead.

Lincoln grabs William by the elbow and throws him against the bars that keep us from plummeting to our deaths below. I feel the metal tremble around my hand, and adrenaline spikes through my veins.

William's face is stricken with panic, and he reaches out for me when I get close enough. He's a teenager like so many of them here. A child, really, and my heart breaks a little.

"Answer me!" Lincoln spits at him. "Do you realize what you've done?"

I put myself between them, using my body as a shield. Dumb but effective in the moment.

"Stop, Lincoln," I beg. "He's just a kid."

Something in Lincoln's demeanor changes when he lays eyes on me, his focus shifting enough to make him pause. He still looks over the teenager with disgust, but the imminent danger is gone.

"Go, William," I say, impressed with myself for remembering someone's name. Maybe I'm better in a crisis than I give myself credit for.

William pauses, unmoving, so I shove his shoulders. He doesn't budge. I'm at least a hundred pounds lighter, and the momentum sends me stumbling backward until I'm flat on my bottom. I get right back up and bark at him once more, this time using my best school teacher voice. "Get outta here. Move it!"

Lincoln grumbles in frustration. That, or he's laughing at my feeble attempt to push William away. The kid takes the opportunity to exit, running toward the stairs and almost falling as he makes his way down and out of sight.

"Are you okay?" I ask Lincoln.

His chest heaves with heavy breaths, and I brace myself to take a tongue lashing or worse. His response is a grunt, his fists clenching and unclenching at his sides. A sharp gust of wind makes me unsteady on my feet, and he reaches forward to help me, pulling me close where I can feel his breathing slow until I know he's calm. His grip around my waist eventually relaxes, and so do I.

Crisis averted. Well, except for the gunfire. That still qualifies as a mini-crisis.

"What happened? Is anyone hurt?" I ask. "It sounded like a lot of shooting. Did someone attack us?"

Lincoln releases me, takes two large strides toward the ledge, and leans over the bars. He waves me over, and I scurry toward him, grabbing the railing before I dare to look over the side.

I haven't felt this much adrenaline in my veins since the night I accidentally chugged four energy drinks. That was fun. I thought I was being responsible with soda water until I saw my heart visibly pounding through my chest.

Swallowing hard, I look down, unable to make anything out at first. The lights are moving too fast, scattering over the water and making me dizzy. Other lookouts are searching for something, but my vision can't focus long enough to see what.

"He shot at him," Lincoln grits out.

"At who?" I turn around, looking for someone bleeding, and realize everyone is hanging over the side like us, their focus on the water below.

"Protocol is we wake up Simon," he says.

"And tell him what? What is going on?"

"There!" Lincoln points. "Hey. Five o'clock. There!"

Beams of light congregate over the water, illuminating something that bobs on the surface below.

"Is that...?" I squint, leaning farther over the edge, my heartbeat drumming against the metal. Another foot won't make the view any clearer, and I'd give anything to have my glasses again. I handed them off in my first week here to a girl who needed them more than I did. "Is that garbage?"

"There was someone in that boat," Lincoln says.

"Oooo, a boat!"

Sure enough, floating in the water is an empty kayak, the smallest, most pathetic boat I've ever seen.

My excitement begins to rise. This means there's another person alive, and survivors are out there living among us.

But, where are they?

"The boat is empty," I groan. "And William... shot at it? Why would he do that?"

Lincoln white-knuckles the metal bars and shakes his head. "He's young. Got spooked."

"By an empty kayak hundreds of feet below us?"

Lincoln grabs my arm, his patience waning with me, and I can't blame him. I'm full of questions and shooed William away while he was mid-yell. He drags me to one of our larger spotlights, shoving the guy using it aside and grabbing the two bars that control a bulb that's bigger than my torso.

Other lights still scatter around the water, making my head spin as I try to follow what they're after. The infected, or bloats as Lincoln calls them, can't operate things like a kayak, and they certainly can't fit inside one. I almost giggle at the thought.

"By that, Myra."

He casts light further out onto the river, and I watch as what looks like large grey balloons float toward the barrier wall.

"That's not…" I trail off, my brain not computing what it's seeing. I once read that if something ahead of you isn't moving, it's actually heading straight for you. Does that apply to tornadoes and zombie-like creatures? The balloons appear still but grow larger by the second.

It's bloats.

Hundreds of them.

This wall of monsters tumbles over itself, almost multiplying in number as it closes the gap between us and them.

"It is," Lincoln says. "Got to be a thousand of 'em."

"He was probably so scared," I mumble to myself.

"Didn't mean he should have shot," Lincoln grits out.

"No, not William," I say. "Whoever was in that kayak."

I think about that person paddling for their lives away from a wall of infected monsters. And then we go and shoot. It must have been horrible.

The floating bloats begin to bounce along the dam wall, and like all the others we've seen, they aren't swimming. They're dead, or more dead than they were before.

It's hard to gauge the level of death with the undead. If a walking bloat was a one out of ten dead, then these bloats might be an eight out of ten. Exploded bloats, I categorize ten out of ten. Very very dead. It's all a little confusing, but that's my spectrum of bloat death.

What's most unnerving is how many there are.

Lincoln's guess is right. It looks like a thousand, but it's too dark to count.

"What is this?" I ask. "Did someone take out bloat town?"

"I've never seen that many at once," Lincoln says. "William must have thought… I don't know. They were charging us or something. I need you to check on him?"

"You want me to leave?"

Part of me wants off this walkway and far from the never-ending sea of infected, but I can't pull myself away.

"There!" someone screams. "By the red truck."

There's a broken-down F-150 just inside the treeline. We've all seen it so many times that every person knows where to point their light. A flash of something moves within the trees, and I gasp. Glasses or no glasses, it was a man. I'm sure of it.

Something stirs inside me, a small whisper I can't ignore.

Don't let him die.

The person disappears into the woods, leaving shaking branches and falling leaves in his wake. I let out a shuddered breath, stepping back from the railing and holding myself in the cold night air.

"Did you see that?" My voice shakes.

Lincoln remains unmoving next to me, his jaw slack as he stares out into the woods.

"The water is freezing," I add. "Do you think… Did he get shot?"

Lincoln shakes his head. "He's dead if he hit that water."

I know what he's thinking. Within the tower of bloats swaying below us, some of them must have popped, leaving their sticky, dark blood behind in the water. But we don't know for sure what that means. The infected were alive, or less dead depending on your bloat death scale, when I've seen them turn people. Bloat blood may be harmless.

"What if he's not? We don't know for sure…" I trail off, lost on how to finish my thought.

Lincoln ignores me, bringing his radio to his lips. "Everyone shut up," he yells. "I need to call this in."

Metal creaks from one of the lights, footsteps come to a halt, and the wind whips my hair around my face. Everyone waits for what happens next.

No one has seen a person since our first few days here, and the buzz of excitement mixed with fear is palpable.

"We have a male on foot. He's right up on the northwest entrance."

The radio crackles. "An infected?"

Lincoln holds the radio to his lips and pauses before he answers. "If he's not yet, he will be. He was in the water with a thousand infected."

"You can't know that," I argue and reach for the radio. "He didn't look infected. I saw him running!"

Lincoln straight arms me, my limbs too short to get the device from him.

"We'll respond accordingly," they answer.

"What does that mean?" I cry out, but I already know. Simon and the rest of the council are not mature enough to make decisions outside of point and shoot. They have all the guns, so we're all at the mercy of their subpar leadership.

"This is a person," I insist. "He needs help."

Lincoln pockets the radio and orders a few lookouts to keep an eye on the trees, ignoring my pleas and denying what we both know is true. Wrapping an arm around my middle, he walks us back to the stairs.

"Bloats don't run like that, and never alone," I argue. The steel door swings open, and my one-sided argument echoes into the stairwell. "This means there are people out there, Lincoln. We can't just leave them to die. We can't just kill them."

"I need you to check on William," he orders.

Somehow, I've become the team mom to this band of youthful survivors. I loved being a teacher, but I also loved sending them home to their parents. I'm not a mother, and I don't know what to say to the kid.

"What are you talking about? We need to help that man."

Lincoln continues to stonewall me, pulling my body tighter against his as we weave through the hallway.

"What if he comes to the door and needs help?" I ask. "They'll shoot him if they think he's infected."

I fight his grip, desperate for him to listen. "There are others. We can't blow up the dam."

This sets Lincoln off, a frustrated growl escaping from his lips. I'm shoved into a corner, the walls pressing on my arms from either side.

He's never laid a hand on me before, but the way he looms overhead makes it impossible to ignore how trapped I am.

"You are not stopping the explosion, Myra!" His breath is on my cheek, every word angry and forced. His hand lifts to my neck, fingers pressing into the sides, my pulse quickening against them. "Why are you looking for any excuse not to do the one thing that can save us?"

I'm careful when I speak, making my words soft and my voice low. "There could be another way. We could just—"

"Because last I checked," he cuts me off, "any time we bring up the plan, you have some bleeding heart reason to kill us all instead."

He's not wrong.

Not about my objections or my bleeding heart.

"I-I'm sorry," I stutter.

The grip on my throat gets tighter, restricting my airway, and I claw at his arm, my fingernails digging into the skin, begging him to pull back. I cough, but no sound escapes while hot tears slide down my cold cheeks. Raising one arm, I try to turn and swing it down on his forearms to break his grip.

It doesn't work, but something breaks him from the trance, acknowledgment of what he's doing, perhaps. He releases me, taking a few steps away until his back hits the opposite wall. I bring my hands to my throat, lightly pressing the tender spots while oxygen burns into my lungs.

Gasping, I open my mouth to speak, but all I can do is gulp air while Lincoln watches. Dark spots flutter in my vision, and behind them, Lincoln stands, expressionless.

Does he care that he hurt me, or was I being taught a lesson? Either way, the message is clear.

This dam is going, and anything in its path, including me, is collateral.

They don't care that survivors will drown when they blow it up. It doesn't matter to them because they want to live more than they want to be human.

Maybe murder is a part of humanity, but we've been too civilized to admit that.

"Listen, Myra—"

"I'll g-go," I cough a few times, needing a moment to regain the ability to talk. "I'll go check on William and the others," I say, pushing away from the corner. Swallowing hard, my neck throbs, sure to be bruised and sore tomorrow.

My footsteps reverberate down the hallway, getting faster as I race away from him. I glance back to find him still rooted to the same spot, eyes fixed on his feet.

He's not looking when I turn right instead of left, and that will buy me enough time to put my bleeding heart into action.

CHAPTER
FIVE

A layer of black slime covers my jeans, leaving a trail behind with every step.

I'm a human snail.

Deep into the woods, I have some cover, but through the leaves, I see the dam's wall and all the infected that pile up. They jostle against it, the current drawing them to the cement boundary, and the mound of them vibrates as they pop, a disgusting end but better than the alternative.

Will I be the alternative?

I still feel like myself, except I'm freezing. It's dark, and I'm too dirty to see if black veins cover my skin, so I keep moving and hoping for the best. Dillon and I have seen someone turn. It looked intentional, one infected holding another while they convulsed for less than a minute. Like a dog bite, short but focused, and that person is gone as soon as they're released.

Once I find a clearing that's far enough away from the gunshots and river of death, I lie back and catch my breath. When I can no longer hear my heartbeat pounding inside my chest, and the adrenaline of being shot at wears off, I admit to myself how utterly fucked I am.

It's freezing, and all I'm wearing are soaking wet jeans. I'm stuck on the wrong side of the river with hundreds of infected in my path. There are no residential properties close; only the hatchery, which I can smell from here.

Dead and rotting trout left unattended for a month are no guarantee that the place is unoccupied. It's not like people are cleaning up after themselves these days.

Yes, I am one fucked snail.

I rule out getting infected as a small stroke of luck. It's a quick turn into a pudgy zombie, and I've been wandering around the trees for a good half hour, bathed in their pseudo blood, not feeling any different.

The moonlight cuts through a break in the branches overhead, their dying leaves falling whenever the wind blows. I take the opportunity to look myself over and find no protruding veins or bloated flesh.

There is another surprising development.

I've been shot.

There's a small red circle on both sides of my forearm. Through and through is the best outcome for this shitty situation, but there's still a hole in my body. I watch it bleed, trickles of red mixing with the dirt, grime, and sludge of the river.

I'm grateful to bleed red, but "Fuck," I mutter to myself. "Dillon will never let me live this down."

My heart sinks with the thought of my brother all alone and thinking I'm dead or worse, turned. He's all I've got in what's left of the world, and I didn't listen to him when it mattered. Of all the half-brained plans I've gone through with, this is the worst.

Lights continue to scan across the water and peek through the trees. People are operating them on the dam's crest, and they are looking for me. I'm no danger to anyone, but who knows what they think or what they're after.

The dam's operating center isn't a bad place to take shelter. Operated by the Army, they would have rations and weapons. It's quite brilliant, considering the infected don't seem like great swimmers, and they have the high ground.

Very high.

It's soaring above me, and I know they can see for miles, making escape difficult unless they decide to give up.

I'm one person, not some brigade coming to siege the castle, but they don't know that. Maybe they were firing at the oncoming infected and not me, but I can't be sure.

Did they even see me? Really? I'm one small kayak amongst a thousand bloated bodies.

Doing my best to wipe away the remaining black blood that's stuck to my pants, I decide there are two choices, both terrible.

Walk all night along the edge of the river, hoping I don't run into more crazies with guns or some infected, then swim across when I get to our cabin.

Or… try to talk to these gun-toting fuckers.

It would be an obvious choice if it weren't for the fact that I'm shivering uncontrollably, and I've been fumbling through these woods like a toddler learning to walk. Grime and dirt are all over my pants, and I'm scraped up on my arms from running into trees. I'm dizzy, the world tilting slightly on its axis, and there's a nagging voice begging me to sleep.

The first stages of hypothermia are well underway. Add blood loss to the mix, and soon, I'll be too confused to find my way home.

"Fuuuuuuck," I say again to no one.

Mom would be so pissed.

Not so much about the cursing, but she was always getting on me about stopping and taking a breath before making big decisions. Her advice stopped me from enlisting in the military because I saw a sign, and getting multiple tattoos in terrible places, and it kept me alive in my formidable teenage years. Her voice is still in my head, but I didn't listen tonight.

A light makes its way into the trees, blinding me, and I flatten myself in the dirt, hoping I'm hidden somehow. This destroys my theory that they weren't shooting at me. Why keep beaming your spotlights into the woods when all the infected are making a wall against your house?

Exhaustion hits me like a brick now that I'm lying down. It makes my eyes heavy as I rest on a bed of dead leaves coated with mud. This is not good, but I don't have the will or strength to do anything about it.

The lights continue, and I see them through my closed eyelids. Forcing myself to flutter them open, I watch as they dance around the ground, getting closer and closer.

This is the time to get up and run, find somewhere deeper into the trees, but my limbs feel like lead. They must have some highly sophisticated shit to beam this far past the river.

I make a promise to myself that if they keep me alive, I won't tell them anything about Dillon or what food we have left. They can pull out my toenails, but I won't be saying a word. That's the least I can do after leaving him all alone.

My body shakes, trembling from the cold, and I curl into myself, but it doesn't stop.

Remove your wet pants, you idiot.

Wrap your gunshot wound.

Get up and run!

Except I can't will myself to move. My heart beats hard and slow, a steady thumping in my ears. I swear the beats are taking longer to thrum, ticking down to my end.

This isn't the worst way to die. It's falling asleep, except I thought death by hypothermia would be more comfortable. Don't hikers on Mt. Everest say they felt warm when they were close to the end?

My dad's voice echoes in my mind.

Your little brother is your responsibility, son.

That gets me moving, at least enough to sit up. I straighten my arms and push against the dirt, forcing my body to lift. My injury burns, warm blood pouring from the limb, but I make it to my knees.

A beam of light shines in front of my hands once I get one foot on the ground. I get myself to standing, wobbly and trembling, and lean against a tree for balance. The light moves with me, hitting my chest.

It's far narrower than the beams from the dam. A flashlight, maybe; handheld, but powerful.

"W-who's t-t-t-there?"

Dammit, I can't even talk. My jaw trembles uncontrollably, and what little I can make out in the darkness wavers at the edges.

Leaves and twigs crunch beneath timid footsteps, and I slump against the tree trunk, feeling myself lower back down to the earth.

"No, you don't," someone says. A woman speaks, her warm hands wrapping around my torso.

"Oh, no. You're so cold. Oh, no. Oh, no."

She flings one of my arms around her shoulders, causing the flashlight she's holding to fall. The light bounces against her before it rolls away.

"H-heyyyy," I say.

It's the best line I can manage with my mind fuzzy and my body falling against hers. I can't remember the last time I saw a live woman. It may have been my mother, all dressed up for a Halloween double date with my dad and some neighbors.

There's some comfort in knowing they died together.

"Can you please try to stand up?" she begs. "Oh, no, that's blood."

More footsteps rush forward, and someone's gloved hands lift me to standing, or so I think. Everything feels sideways.

"This is a bad idea, Myra," a voice says. It's a man, or rather, a boy. He sounds young, and his words tremble with worry.

"William, please. I need your help, and you can trust me," the woman, Myra, says. Her voice is soothing and calm. "If anyone asks, you were never here."

The young man groans in response and whispers something back at her. She doesn't respond, doing her best to move me into a position where I can walk. Myra and William clearly aren't on the same page, and I feel like I'm not even in the same galaxy.

We take a few steps, but I can't be sure in what direction or how many, with my body numb from the neck down.

This escalated quickly.

My mom said men die first because they make poor decisions. I can't recall a moment when that woman was ever wrong. If I see her again, that's the first thing I'm telling her.

"You need to take some clothes off," William says.

"Excuse me, sir!" she retorts.

I want to chuckle, but I'm not sure if this conversation is even happening. This could all be a hallucination in death, my brain tricking me into thinking someone's come to help. These people could be figments of my imagination brought on by hypothermia.

Focusing on breathing, which grows increasingly difficult with each gasp of breath, I question why everything hurts so much if I'm dead. I could swear I thought death was supposed to be white robes and pearly gates and far fewer bodily fluids.

William, if he's real, hoists me to a fully standing position, my knees locking into place, as he pulls me against him, taking most of my weight.

"Myra. Take off your sweater and jacket. Now."

He's quite stern for a young buck, and it's a weird time to get a chick naked, but whatever gets your rocks off, my friend. I'll be dead by the time you blow your wad.

I feel her warmth move away, and the William person drags me back to use the tree for support. As I flop against the bark, he tells Myra to toss over her clothes. My wet jeans flop to the ground, my senses so dull I didn't feel him remove them.

"Okay, over here," he says, still fumbling me around. "Myra, get closer. Both of you, now."

Hot skin hits mine, the woman giving a small squeal when she presses against me. Cloth grazes my face, some sweater he's pulling over both our heads, and we are cheek to cheek, both of us wrapped up in the fabric.

Smart kid. Skin-to-skin is the best way to warm up, and he's using the sweater as a cocoon around us. I hear some ripping of the fabric as her soft body adjusts into my side.

Once we're settled, a searing heat tears through my chest, sending a surge of blood thundering through my veins.

"You okay?" she asks.

I feel her mouth move when she speaks, and I try to nod. Maybe I am, but I can't tell. My movements are disjointed and out of body. I still feel like I'm floating above all of this, but some feeling is returning, and I want to believe this is real.

"Let's walk," William orders.

They both hold me up, and we move. I count the steps, keeping myself as alert as possible.

One. Two Three.

"How are we going to get him back inside?" Myra asks.

Four. Five. Six.

"Penny may have offered some… assistance with the door," he says.

Seven. Eight. Nine.

"Oh, she is so sweet."

William groans. From what they're saying and the attempted murder earlier, I don't think I'm welcome inside their fortress.

Ten. Eleven. Fourteen.

"Okay, and then what?" he asks.

Wait, fourteen doesn't come after eleven.

"I don't know. I'll get him to the schoolroom," Myra offers. "I'm the only one who goes in there."

What the fuck is after eleven? Man, I am so going to die.

"We will get him there," William corrects her. "You can't carry him on your own."

Is it twenty? That's not right.

"Thanks, William."

"Just remember, the evacuation is happening soon. You can't leave him on a sinking ship. You need a plan B. Hell, you need a miracle. Lincoln's going to flip his lid if he finds out about this."

I've lost count, but before I can remember my kindergarten-level math, everything spins, and the world goes dark.

CHAPTER SIX

Myra

William's pacing. Impressive, considering this room is smaller than my bedroom in my last apartment, which is the size of a closet. Both spaces are host to an impressive number of roaches and my bad decisions.

"You'll talk to Lincoln?" he asks me for the tenth time.

I run my palms down the front of my pants and lean over. My back is killing me from carrying this guy's weight for the past hour, and I worry that if I sit down, I may never get back up.

"Yes, William. I told you I would, and I will," I say.

He flinches from my response and stares at his feet. I'm annoyed and maybe a little hangry. That tiny can of beans wasn't enough considering the marathon I just ran, or rather stumbled through. I'm not an obstacle race type of girl.

"He wanted me to talk to you. I don't think he's that mad."

"You don't know what he is," William counters.

I let the words linger in the space between us. Partially because I do not have the mental capacity to handle this conversation, and also, I don't want to know.

"I'm sorry," I apologize. "I'm juggling a few things right now." I point to the stranger we've placed on the floor. "But I will make sure to talk to Lincoln."

"Tonight?"

"Seriously, William. I will do it," I promise.

"Please, Myra," he begs. "Talk to him tonight. You don't know how he can get."

Oh, I'm starting to get the idea.

Standing straight, my body aches in all the wrong places. Even my hair hurts when I yank out my haphazard ponytail. Me, the apocalyptic survivor. What a joke.

I've made so many mistakes tonight, and it's only a matter of time before someone pays the price. It can't be William.

"Are you scared of him?" I ask.

William rubs the back of his neck, his eyes averting mine. "I don't want to be on his bad side." There's fear laced in his words, and my stomach turns sour.

"What can I do to help?" I ask. "I'll talk to him, but is there anything else?"

"No, Myra. Don't put yourself out any more than you already do."

I want to protest, but I am neck deep in trouble with this stranger, so I nod and give my best impression of someone confident that everything will be just fine.

William rushes out, and I shut the door behind him, resting my forehead on the metal.

"Oh, you've really stepped in it this time," I mumble to myself, refusing to turn around and face the fallout. My shoulders rise, and I groan. "And what's crawled up Lincoln's pooper?"

It's true that no one here is in much of a good mood. We're all starving, and since I'm not involved in the sexcapades, I don't see the rare flickers of happiness. Still, until tonight, no one had ever laid a hand on me or raised their voice.

It's been bearable until the plan to murder countless survivors and the hallway choking stuff. Lincoln wasn't the person I thought he was, and when someone shows me their true self, I believe it.

Turning around, I lean against the steel and fumble to check the lock. I yank the handle up and down, but it doesn't budge.

No one should be able to barge into this scene, not that anyone's interested in our makeshift schoolroom. I tried sleeping here before, but the pipes on the south side rattle and clang, jolting people awake at all hours. Maybe it will wake this guy up, and we can get a proper introduction.

Satisfied I'm safe for the evening, I slide my back against the door, lowering down until I'm sitting on the dusty cement, staring at some stranger we've wrapped in old blankets.

He's a man burrito.

A man I don't know.

An incognito burrito.

He moans, sounding pained. "I know, burrito man. You are in quite a state. I'm hurting all over, too."

This guy doesn't know I've sweated buckets and worked muscles I didn't know existed to get him here, but I must admit he looks worse.

I crawl over to him because, yes, I'm that pathetic and exhausted. Part of the blanket is sticking out, and I pull it over me and lie down.

"Sir, I know you're cold and possibly dying of hypothermia," I sigh.

This feels pointless talking to someone unconscious, but I've come this far. Might as well keep walking into ridiculous territory.

"I am sorry about that, but listen. Please don't wake up and freak out. Please don't wake up and hurt me or rape me. But for the love of whatever deity you pray to, please wake up. If I went through all that to lug a corpse into this place, I'll be so mad."

I scoot closer, trying to get more of the blanket over my freezing limbs, when I slide my hand into something warm and wet.

"That better not be pee," I grumble.

I rip my hand from underneath the blanket and gasp.

Blood.

Tearing the fabric off of him, I search his body for the source of the sticky liquid. He's almost naked, and I'm growing frustrated that I can't find anything.

"Is it your blood?" I ask no one, but the puddle at his side continues to grow. "Okay, it has to be yours."

Taking the edge of the blanket, I pull upwards with all my might, forcing the burrito to unravel. He flops onto his back, and the wound stares me in the face. A gaping hole in his forearm, no doubt from one of our bullets.

I do my best not to vomit.

It does not work.

I swallow it.

There were a multitude of reasons I chose to teach high school back before this sudden apocalypse.

Teenagers can have intellectual conversations. Their parents no longer think they are angels, so conferences were much smoother. But if you asked me the most important reason, it was that the vomit-to-kid ratio was next to zero. A time or two, some girl would bathe in strong perfume and make some of her peers gag, but that's the closest I got to vomit.

I do not do vomit.

A close second is blood.

"Get it together, Myra," I tell myself.

There must be something in this room that can help, and I ignore my queasy stomach and search. This is a schoolroom and not the clinic, but I'm afraid to leave him like this. What if Lincoln stops me in the hallway, wanting to have another rousing conversation about ethical explosions, and my man burrito bleeds out?

I can't risk taking him with me, not that the aches in my body would allow it.

Yanking open a few drawers, frustrated that I didn't keep myself more organized, desperation creeps in. Sifting through papers, dozens of plastic pens, and about a million paperclips, a silver stroke of luck comes into view.

Duct tape.

I pull at the end and hear the beautiful rip before I kneel next to the stranger. Looking at the open tape and back to his bloody arm, I wonder if this is a good idea. I've heard of doctors using superglue on the battlefield. One could argue that duct tape is superglue adjacent.

But he looks dirty.

Dirt equals infection.

I shouldn't seal dirt inside a wound with duct tape.

My thought process is broken and mechanical, and given my little medical training, the best I can do is clean him up and hope for the best. I soak some fabric scraps with Dawn dish soap and wet them with water bottles.

If it's good enough for ducks covered in oil, it's good enough for humans, right?

I have no idea, but I also don't have much of a choice.

Collecting my pathetic amount of supplies, I return to the patient.

"I am sorry about this," I whisper to him, but he doesn't respond. He doesn't move or do much of anything. The bullet went straight through his arm. Shoving the rag in the gaping hole seems wrong, so I scrub with some force instead.

Still, he doesn't stir.

"Be glad you're asleep because this would hurt something awful," I say to the sleeping man. "One time I had to go to the dentist without enough numbing, and boy oh boy, I felt that in my soul."

His heavy arm is difficult to maneuver. It's dead weight and a lot of it. This guy isn't abnormally large, about six feet, I would guess, and I would argue that he's fit, if not a little thin. Who isn't lacking in calories these days, but as I look over the rest of him, I feel a rush of heat.

He's a man.

It's more than anatomy that makes me flush. There's something masculine and virile about his maturity.

This place is full of underage drama kings and queens. Most of them are over eighteen, but their frontal lobes are far from formed. It's like living in a frat house but smellier, and I'm always reminded of how old I am.

I'm ancient to the majority, well past my prime. Considering the world's population has plummeted, and I doubt there are many elderly left, maybe I am an old lady.

Not to mention I'm acting like everyone's mom, watching out for them and finding anything they need, even if that means I go without. There's a part of me that enjoys caring for others, but I miss talking with another real live adult.

I miss that full frontal lobe, darnit. It makes a heck of a difference.

His arm is wrapped in a significant amount of duct tape when I'm done. I hope it's not so tight he loses a limb, but tight enough to keep him from bleeding to death.

Life is about balance.

Literally, in his case.

He still has the blanket under him, so I wrap him back up like a burrito, tucking the fabric under one side. His skin feels cold, as if the river's icy water sank its teeth into the man and won't let go.

"I hope you make it, burrito man," I whisper.

I lie down beside him, watching the gentle rise and fall of his chest beneath the blanket. It must be something like what new mothers feel, a constant trickle of fear that the next breath might not come.

Except I would be a terrible mom because, after a few slow blinks, I can't open my eyes again. The weight of exhaustion is too heavy, and I let myself give in to sleep.

I fear I'll dream of the bloats along our home's wall. The infected invade my thoughts when I'm not careful, but there are stronger worries that rise to the surface of my mind.

Memories of this stranger's ice blue eyes.

The way he looked at me under the harsh fluorescent lights of the hallway as we brought him inside. It was a brief flicker of life before he slipped under again, and he spent it fixated on me.

They won't leave my mind, and I'm scared I'll never see them again.

CHAPTER
SEVEN

Myra

I'm not sure how long I slept before a blaring intercom jolts me awake. It doesn't do the same for my friend here, who sleeps like the dead.

Oh, golly, is he dead?

My eyes fly open, the sound of their lockdown orders piercing my thoughts. His back is against my chest, and I still myself, waiting for the intake of breath.

A large inhale expands his ribs and presses him against me. I realize I've wrapped an arm around this guy, making myself the big spoon.

Should I move?

Yes.

Do I?

Not for a full sixty seconds.

Counting slowly, I allow a whole minute of inappropriateness, so relieved that he's alive. Then the guilt seeps in.

I apologize to the sleeping man. He didn't consent to the cuddle, and even though it was out of an unconscious effort to prevent death by hypothermia, it was wrong.

At least he feels warmer, and we're out of the woods with that problem. I check on his arm, pulling it from the blanket and gently touching the duct tape. There's no liquid underneath from what I can tell, but ripping it off will be all sorts of terrible.

"Geez, I've molested you, and now you're going to get an unintentional arm wax. Sorry about your luck," I say, curious if he's hearing any of this. What if he's in a coma and completely cognizant of the world around him?

I will die of humiliation if that's the case.

The speaker system blares again, half-broken words spew out, but I know what they're saying.

All cit—- of —- Wall. — —- — lockdown until —- infected are — —. Do not — — to ex— the building. ——- ——- cafeteria moment—.

They could have said it like it is instead of trying to make it formal.

We are stuck behind locked doors because there's a bloat mountain outside, and we've all watched Game of Thrones and don't feel like the dead are ever really that dead. Which, given what's been going on lately… understandable concern.

Forgetting my watch doesn't run, I check it again and whimper. It's got to be dawn or close to it. With infected bodies exposed in daylight, nearly everyone will rush upstairs to see what's happening. This is the best time to try and scavenge the clinic for burrito man while making sure my face is seen.

My muscles protest fiercely as I stretch, begging me to stay beside the stranger and force a cuddle, but I know I can't. Not only did I promise William I would talk to Lincoln, but they ordered something about the cafeteria. Everyone will need to congregate together to hear the self-appointed leaders of this place give us direction. If I'm not there, someone will find me. That someone might be Lincoln.

But what if incognito burrito wakes up?

I roll to my back and scan the shelf of supplies. There are pads of paper for me to write a note. He was speaking English earlier, and given the area, I'm fairly certain he can read.

"I don't wanna get up," I whine.

Burrito-boy lets out a few low moans, and I give his shoulder a small shake.

"Can you hear me?" I ask. "Hello?"

Nothing.

"Do you happen to like burritos?" I smile to myself. "You… sir. You — no-named man."

He is quite the man.

It wasn't only playing nurse that got me a little hot and bothered. During our hike in the woods, our bodies touching and rubbing against one another, I may have had some daydreams.

It was at night, so would that be night dreams? Oh, my, it qualifies as a fantasy. I'm so naughty, but that was the most action I'd gotten since before the apocalypse.

Pausing to count, I think about how long before.

When was the last time I went on a date?

When was the last time I was topless with a man?

Well, I had my bra on last night, and it's not like he consented. He wasn't conscious, and technically, I kidnapped him. It was for his own good, but he could think I tried to steal him, lock him up, and use him for my pleasure.

Wow, Myra. You've read way too many romance books.

I have violated this man in so many ways, and I make a mental note to apologize once he's awake.

It's not fair that I develop a crush just because I'm starved for adult connection in this place. It would be so nice to have a voice of reason to keep the kids in check around here. They want to blow up the largest dam in the south, and I'm too much of a chicken to stand up to the Lord of the Flies.

That might be a good book to go over in class.

I force myself to stand and walk instead of crawling to the shelf. Finding a notepad and pen, I give some thought about what to write.

Dear sexy burrito man,

I am not going to use you as a sex slave. You'll see I'm a nice girl if you wake up and get to know me. Be back in a jiffy.

~Myra. (The woman you walked with half-naked through the woods. Do you work out?)

No, that's absolutely ridiculous and will not work.

Hello, you. (I didn't get your name.)

I bet you're wondering where your clothes are, not to mention where you are. Those are great questions! I can answer them soon. Be back in a jiffy.

~Myra (Half of the dynamic duo that made sure you didn't freeze and/or bleed to death)

That note is no better. I settle on something a little more formal and to the point.

Hi.

You are in the dam's operations center. I have snuck you in here. If you wake up, please don't make yourself known. I'm coming back.

~Myra (Woman from the woods)

Good enough. Well, almost good enough. I scratch out, *I'm coming back*, and write, *be back in a jiffy*. I am who I am, and there's no point in changing now.

Making sure he doesn't miss this note, I make another copy, taping one to the door and wedging another against the blanket. His eyes are fluttering, and I want to stay and see if he'll wake up, but I'm worried I've been gone too long. Lincoln's going to come looking for me, and he isn't in the best mood after last night.

Also, I don't think that William would tell on me, but I want to make sure I fix things between them so he's not tempted. Secrets don't last long in this place, and I can't take any chances. My burrito man has already been shot. If they find him, he's at quite the disadvantage.

I step out on baby giraffe legs, doing my best to impersonate someone who can walk. The hallway looks empty, but I'm still careful not to make any noise when I shut the door. Hoping my nerves will overshadow my aching body, I stiff-walk toward the meeting room.

Before long, Bobbi's voice drifts down the hallway.

Go me! I remembered her name.

This is where my classroom should be, but some alpha males who are still teenagers took over the formal offices, demanding that they needed them for planning and strategy.

It's more likely they're playing Dungeons and Dragons in here. No shade to the game, but it's obvious after tonight that they are making decisions out of fear instead of thinking things through.

When I round the corner, I'm thrust back into the way things were only a few months ago. There are still those chairs with wheels on the bottom, old coffee pots with black and orange handles, and a white-board where someone accidentally used a permanent marker. Fragments that stir a bittersweet mix of happiness and sadness, memories from a life that feels worlds away.

"We need to set them on fire," Bobbi demands. "Who knows what could happen if their blood oozes out and gets through the walls?"

I look down, checking to see if any black ooze is covering my clothing. Luckily, I was in my underpants walking through the woods, so we are good there. Stepping through the doorway, I lean my hip against the frame. It's meant to be a power stance, but the truth is I'm likely to fall over any second.

Simon, the self-proclaimed leader of us all, sits at the head of the table. He's not a fan of being told what to do, so he made himself the decider. It's not like we are all jumping for the responsibility of keeping everyone alive, but considering he's barely twenty and makes the most asinine decisions, I should have protested.

That frontal lobe will get you every time.

"They're in the river," I say.

Bobbi turns to me, crossing her arms and squinting her eyes.

"Aaaand," she drawls.

"The river is…" I trail off. How rude is it going to be if I say this out loud? She stares at me with blank eyes while I try to be tactful. "It's water, so… The fire won't catch all that well."

She shifts her weight from foot to foot. "The top would burn."

"They would," I fib. A little white lie to save a tongue thrashing is okay. It has to be because I'm too tired to have a pointless conversation.

Lincoln clears his throat, and I do my best not to flinch. He's who I came to see, but my skin prickles as he approaches. There's a seismic shift in our casual friendship, and I wonder if he feels it too. Have I simply been blind to his personality, or was he treating me differently and could no longer mask his true self?

Bobbi watches his every step, her arms drawing tighter against her middle. She looks filled with fury the moment he reaches to tuck a stray hair behind my ear.

I'm not thrilled, either, girl.

"What do you think, Myra?" he asks. "You're the most mature one here."

"I am old," I say. I'm trying to remind him that I am not someone to flirt with, and a casual insult at myself might help Bobbi calm down. "Basically an antique."

He takes my face in his hands. "You're gorgeous."

Abort! Must redirect.

I tell myself he's trying to be nice and make up for his transgressions earlier. I'm too much of a chicken to confront him, and he knows this. What happened in the hallway will never come up again, and I'll forgive him without his asking.

"I don't think they pose an immediate threat," I say. "But if you want to burn some, it won't hurt. It's whatever you all decide."

The group in here makes up the council of this shelter. There wasn't a vote, but there wasn't a protest, either. I haven't minded until they decided to blow up the dam and murder everyone in its path. I disagree with the leadership on that, but I don't know how to get them to see it my way.

"We will discuss it," Bobbi says, emphasizing the *we*. "It's not a good time right now, Myra. And your school is canceled until we sort this out. I'm doubling the watch."

Amazing news, but I do my best to look disappointed. No school means no one finds my hidden man burrito. All these burrito thoughts have me salivating, and I wipe the side of my mouth with my thumb.

"You want twice as many people watching dead bodies explode?" someone on the council asks. "Why?"

Bobbi jerks her head toward him and raises a finger. I tune her out when she begins berating the kid and take the chance to get this over with.

"Can I have one minute?" I whisper to Lincoln and step back out to the hallway. Bobbi doesn't notice him leave, but I won't get a lot of time.

Good. Less of a chance for me to give myself away.

I'm sweating with nerves. Lying is not my strong suit, and I've already fibbed today, so I may have hit my quota.

"Hey, so, I talked to William for you."

Lincoln rests a hand on my shoulder, and I refuse to shake him off. He can't know that scene from earlier scared me, or we'll have to talk about it. His apologies won't fix anything, but I can't let him know that our friendship has shifted.

"That's good of you, Myra. Thanks," he says. "You're always just what I need."

That phrase feels off, but I need to tell this lie convincingly and leave. My focus must be undeterred.

"Yep." I shift back on my heels and eye Bobbi, who is about to make some young man cry. "Listen, he's very upset about his actions and doesn't want to disappoint you. That's important to him. He thinks he let you down."

"He did," Lincoln says. His voice is without emotion, and it sends a shiver down my spine.

"Right, well. He'd like a chance to make it up to you. If you could find it in your heart to not give him latrine duty, or some other awful mission, that would mean so much."

Lincoln's thumb runs along my cheek, and my heart thuds against my ribs. Bobbi is steps away and will slap me right in the face if she sees this.

"Who would it mean a lot to?" he asks. "William? Or you?"

This is where I'm going to mess up. My stomach rolls, the contents of a can of honey-baked beans threatening to escape all over Lincoln.

"Both of us."

I meant it as a statement, but my voice rose with the question.

"Are you okay?" he asks. "You look a little flushed."

He steps closer just as I hear Bobbi shriek his name through the doorway. "Lincoln! We need you. Now! Dammit, Myra. I told you we are busy."

"I'm sorry, Bobbi," I say, and I mean it. I am sorry I'm out here in this hallway with her boyfriend acting like this. He's off, and I can't pin exactly how or why, but something is different about Lincoln.

I think back to when we first met. It was only a month ago, but he looks so much older standing before me here today. Bright-eyed and full of mischief, I remember finding him when I walked the path here.

He'd asked me if I was coming for the fireworks, and I let him know I was coming to prevent anyone from getting hurt. He asked me who my kid was, assuming I was some parent who heard about their All Hallows' Eve party.

It was far more boring than that. I was a teacher who knew many of her students were bound to make bad choices while drinking and playing with explosives. I didn't want them to drown, so I marched out here, the oldest of the crew, and climbed to the top of the dam with Lincoln's help.

A few soldiers were there too, barely eighteen, willing to take cash to look the other way. For a moment, I thought maybe I wasn't needed, that someone else would watch over them. Then they started chugging from red Solo cups, and I settled in with the rest.

We watched the sky light up in beautiful colors, and I poured out the liquor when no one was looking. When the last firework exploded into the night sky, the screaming began. It dragged on for days while a bunch of hungover teenagers and I hid here, convincing ourselves it would all be over soon.

It was over, but not in the way we thought.

"Why do you care so much?" Lincoln's question sounds so unlike the kid I met that night. The one checking on all his friends and making new ones. He seemed like a caretaker. Like me.

I shrug. "I can't help it."

Lincoln smiles, and my gaze locks onto his, searching for the young man I once knew. Is he still somewhere behind those dark eyes?

No.

He's gone.

"You are always just so nice," he says. "It's great to have someone kind around like you."

"I'm glad I'm able to help," I reply.

"I'll back off of William, then."

"So, no latrine duty?" I ask. "Because if you do, I'll help him, and I vomit when I clean latrines, and then I have to clean them again, and it's a whole cycle of gross."

Lincoln's other hand moves to my neck, gentle this time, and I stop rambling. He doesn't turn to look at his girlfriend, who is hissing his name, but instead, inspects the skin he had in his clutches earlier.

I don't recoil when he gently presses into the tender flesh. Bruises are forming, I'm sure, not that I've had the chance to check a mirror.

"Are you listening to me, Lincoln?" Bobbi shouts.

"Get your fat ass back in that room," he snaps at her. "And be glad I let you in there."

She gasps, and I refuse to look in her direction. I know Bobbi's not the nicest, but she doesn't deserve to be spoken to that way. The secondhand embarrassment makes me flush just as Lincoln slides his fingertips across a tender spot. I suck in air between my teeth, and he releases his grip.

"For you," Lincoln says. "I'll give William leniency."

"Thank you," I say. "I should clean up before the lockdown meeting."

"Do you need to use the leader's washroom?"

"No, I can manage without it."

The conversation is over, but he's not breaking his hold. I see Bobbi in my periphery, but I can't bear to meet her eyes.

"Lincoln, I—"

His lips press against mine, cutting off my words, and I do my best to kiss him back.

It's the polite thing to do, and the only way I can think to keep that half-dead burrito man alive.

CHAPTER
EIGHT

I can feel my dick again, but I can't move my hands to make sure it's still there. Face down on a cement floor, I rock my body to roll onto my back. My arm stings and burns with every movement. That tells me two things.

I'm alive.

And the people in the woods were real.

With a loud grunt, I heave myself over for the last time, my back hitting the hard ground, and the blanket they wrapped me in flapping open on my side.

My clothes are gone, except for some ripe boxer briefs, and the crisp air hits my skin, making me shiver. I'm far from hypothermic, but I'm lightheaded due to what I gather is massive blood loss and last night's adventure through the woods. I don't think my heart has worked that hard since the last time I had sex.

Which was… a long time ago.

The rest of the blanket falls to the ground, and I stare up at a ceiling of flickering fluorescent lights. The pulse in my forearm is almost audible, thumping hard while blood moves around the broken vessels.

A rattle echoes, followed by a sharp clang of metal, and my head snaps toward the sound. Old pipes shake against a dirty cement wall, and I rub my eyes, unsure of what I was expecting to see.

"They shot me," I mumble to myself.

It's not the first time I've been shot at, but damn, I hope it's the last. People are less neighborly these days, not that they were full of kindness before the world ended. It's shocking how terrible the survivors can be here in the Bible Belt. I have a theory that the more churches per capita, the more assholes, too. There hasn't been a formal poll, but in my experience, I find it to be true.

I try and fail to stand multiple times. Despite my brain giving my legs very clear instructions, my body doesn't cooperate. On the third attempt, I manage using a bookshelf for support, cursing with every inch upward. I'm wheezing for air, but at least I'm upright, staring at office supplies and a few crumpled pieces of paper.

I reach for one and notice the silver makeshift bandage covering my forearm.

"Duct tape," I say to myself. "Work with what you've got, I guess."

Pulling that off is going to be the biggest bitch, but I'm not dead, so no complaints to the nurse. My focus shifts to the pages, one of which is partially open and reads, *"freeze and/or bleed to death."* That catches my eye.

Reaching forward, slowly so I don't topple over and take the entire shelf down, I flatten out the paper and continue to read.

Hello, you. (I didn't get your name)

I bet you're wondering where your clothes are and where you are. Those are great questions! I can answer them soon. Be back in a jiffy.

~Myra (Half of the dynamic duo that made sure you didn't freeze and/or bleed to death)

My eyes scan the words again, amused by the tone and general message. Do people say jiffy anymore?

"Is she serious?" I mumble.

I laugh and realize I may have a broken rib along with a gunshot wound. That or the exertion of frantic swimming tore my muscles apart. The latter is certainly possible because ever since my age started with a three, which was more than a few years ago, things haven't rebounded like they used to. It doesn't help that I can't remember the last time I had a full meal. The physique I worked so hard to build is shriveling.

"Myra," I sound out her name, enjoying the feeling of it on my tongue. It was her skin against mine, slick and hot, keeping me warm when we walked over. The curve of her body melted against me, trying with all her might to keep me walking.

To save me.

Yep, I can certainly feel my dick.

Metal creaks from the other side of the room, and I turn my head, white-knuckling the side of the bookshelf with one hand while holding the note in the other. A trickle of blood slides out from the duct tape on my forearm, slow and thick.

"Hiya," a small voice says. "Oh my goodness, I forgot you're still naked."

The door clicks behind her, and she jumps, startled by the noise. She's found clothes since our little adventure, but I would prefer if she were in my same manner of undress.

I blink a few times, taking her in, watching as she wrings her hands with worry.

Myra's thin, like most everyone a month into this apocalyptic nightmare. I imagine she's suffering the same fate with a lack of resources. Four weeks would fly by when everyone was busy with work and a social life. When you're hungry, time drags on forever, and it's been over thirty days of rationing food to its limit.

Her curly hair is tied at the base of her neck, but it spills out over her shoulders, long, dark, and thick. I make myself shut my jaw, which must be falling to the floor, but no matter what I do, I can't stop staring.

There's an aura to her, something I can't explain. Immediately, I can tell I like her. I'm attracted to this woman, but if she said she wasn't interested, I would still want to be friends. People can spot right away who they'll mesh with and who's bound to cause trouble. Whether we listen to that inner voice is up to us.

"Am I that forgettable?" I ask, but my voice doesn't sound like my own. It's hoarse and ragged, slicing against my throat with every word.

Her eyes flick over my body, and heat rushes to my chest. "I've had a lot going on," she admits. "I should leave and get you some clothes." She wags her finger in the air, a flush rising in her cheeks.

"Please don't go," I say, sounding a bit pathetic. "You just got here. Can we talk?"

"I need to get some medical supplies, too, and I forgot until now. I walked back here like a zombie," she says. "Well, not like a zombie because my blood is still red and I'm not the undead, last I checked, but I was sort of in a daze, you know."

I loosen my grip on the cabinet, hoping I can take a few steps toward her without plunging to the ground. "My bandage is holding fine," I insist. "Please. Stay a minute. I don't know what's going on."

"Gauze, antiseptic. Maybe a bandage that isn't duct tape," she murmurs to herself, making an invisible list. "I'll be right back. Just a jiffy."

She turns to leave, takes a forceful step forward, and slams into the closed metal door. Her head rears back, the metal sounding dull and angry against her face before she lets out a sharp cry. I lunge forward to help, momentarily forgetting that I have not regained my ability to walk.

I manage only two steps before we crash to the ground, a tangle of limbs wrapped awkwardly in each other's arms.

I'm not making a very good second impression.

Her body rests on top of mine, chest heaving with shaky breaths. I'm flat on my back where I started only moments ago, except now we're both hurt. Bright red blood smears her face, and I hate the sight, wishing I hadn't been so forceful about her staying.

"Your nose is bleeding," I say.

She tries to pull her hand to her face, but it's trapped behind my shoulder.

"Oh, no. Let me just..." She grunts, and in an effort to move, rocks her body up and down.

My dick springs to life.

"Hang on. One second, okay?" I plead.

I adjust and free her hand just as her warm blood pools onto my chest.

"Oh, no. Oh, no. Oh, no. I'm so sorry. This is a horrible rescue operation," she whines.

She's not wrong, but I appreciate the effort. I'm happy with the cavalry, even if it's a bit clumsy and bleeding on my chest.

Her eyes focus on the piece of paper in my hand.

"And that's the wrong note," she grumbles, ripping the page from me. "You should have read that one." Her head turns toward the door where a less crumpled page is taped.

Her hands slap to the ground, and she brings herself to her feet. I sit up and adjust myself to hide my attraction. It's been a month since I've seen a woman who didn't have a shotgun pointed at my head, and longer since I've seen one my age.

I can't remember the last time I saw anyone as beautiful as her.

"Does that note say something all that different?" I ask.

"Not really," she shrugs, looking deflated. She brings her fingertips to her nose, almost scared to touch her skin.

"It's bleeding a lot, right?" she asks. "How bad is it?"

Slowly, and using the wall for balance, I bring myself back to standing. I ignore my wobbly legs and usher her closer. "Let me see."

Her hands shake a little when they lower, and I hope it's not my presence making her nervous. She's in an enclosed space with a strange man dressed in stinky underpants. If I were her, I'd regret helping me.

"I'm going to touch your face, but I'll be gentle. Is that okay?"

She nods, her eyes welling with tears. It could be the blow to the face or fear, but the hurt in her expression eats at my soul.

My fingertips press gently into her skin, and I turn her head from side to side. She whacked herself hard, but I don't think this will cause more than discomfort and bruising.

"Not broken," I tell her. "But it's going to be sore for a while."

"I'm so sorry," she blurts out. "Not just for leaving you here naked. Not that you're bad to look at. I mean, you're—"

My heart flutters with her words, and I smile as her face turns a shade of red I didn't think possible.

"I'm so grateful to you," I say. "Please. There's nothing to be sorry for."

"But we shot at you."

I raise my eyebrows and rest a hand on her shoulder. She doesn't seem to mind, but I don't want to scare her away. In truth, I need her for balance, but it's wonderful to feel the warmth of her skin. "Did you personally aim a gun at me?"

She makes a face but regrets it, the pain from her nose making her let out a small gasp.

"No," she mumbles.

"I didn't think so. What can I do to help you?" I ask. "I doubt your gun-happy friends know I'm here. And from the looks of this hole in my arm, I'm not welcome."

"You can barely stand," she says, and points at my swaying frame.

"Hey!" I touch my chest and feign offense. "I thought I was doing good for someone who swam in a frozen river after they got shot." Without holding the wall, I risk sending us both to the floor again, but I'm feeling sturdier by the second. It's almost as if her presence gives me strength.

"Oh, and I will get you warm clothes and better bandages," she says. I can tell she's continuing her mental checklist, thinking of everything she wants to do for me, but this woman has done enough.

"I think my being here is putting you in danger," I say. "Leaving should be the top priority."

The words sting when I say them. I don't want to be away from this beautiful creature, but I can't put her in danger. I use every ounce of willpower not to ask her to come with me, though in truth, why would she? They have food and firepower, and all I have to offer is half a fishing net and a broken kayak.

"I don't know how to do that right now," she admits. "We're kind of on lockdown."

"Kind of?" I ask.

She nods.

"What do you mean by lockdown? I can break locks."

She rests her hand over mine, and the spark from her touch gives me life. I try not to pull her towards me, wrap her in my arms, and hold her close.

For once, I have to think things through, focus on what's right for her and my brother. This is the time to listen.

"It's more than locked doors," she explains. "They'll keep a careful count of everyone, and they'll move people off other duties to stand guard. Not a great time for an escape plan."

"Oh."

There's not much more to say. She knows this place top to bottom, and if she says it's more than a locked door we need to deal with, I trust her.

"We'll figure something out, Myra," I promise.

"How do you… Oh, yes. The note," she says with a smile. "What is your name?" Blood from her nose has trickled into her mouth, staining her white teeth a pale pink. I almost laugh at the sight, but offer my name instead.

"Cade Miller."

"Nice to meet you, Cade. I'm Myra Smirnov."

"Like the alcohol?" I ask.

She shrugs. "It's Russian, I think."

"You think?" I take a deep breath, every rib screaming with the intake of air.

"I didn't know my parents all that well."

"I'm sorry," I tell her.

I'm not sure if it's the right thing to say. Most of us with parents we loved, ones who cared for us since infancy, are faced with the horrible reality of their demise. We watched them disappear or worse.

Never having that love in your life is awful, but is having it ripped away from you tragically worse? It's a question I'm still struggling with. My parents never came back on Halloween night, and sometimes I imagine they are somewhere like this, safe and together.

But I know the truth, as does Dillon. They're one of those things wandering the city, and I have to live with the loss of the two best people in the world.

"Me too," she says.

She averts her eyes, focusing back on the door. "So listen, I have zero medical supplies here, which is terrible for a teacher. I can't believe I did that. Also, you're naked."

"Not totally," I say, and snap the waistband of my boxer briefs.

An awkward giggle escapes her lips, and she slides past me, mumbling to herself about gauze and underpants.

"You're leaving?"

"I am this time," she admits. "There's going to be a meeting later about the infected outside, and I need to get some things before I miss the window."

"Watch out for the door," I tell her.

She stops, grabs the handle dramatically, and hoists it backward. "I'll be—"

"Back in a jiffy," I finish her sentence.

"Don't make me laugh," she says. "It hurts."

The door slams shut, and I let myself crumble to the ground.

Somehow, after everything I've been through and all I've seen, I can still manage to be shocked by what a new day brings.

CHAPTER
NINE

He is hot.

No, that's not the right word.

Smoldering.

Sexy.

Someone who I want to get naked with.

"Stop it," I mutter to myself.

"Stop what?" William asks.

"Jesus Henry Christ on a cracker," I blurt out. "Where did you come from?"

William isn't exactly stealthy, so I must have been lost in my thoughts about burrito man, er, Cade.

Damn, that's a sexy name.

"Did you talk to Lincoln?"

My mind goes blank. All that I can see is the shirtless hottie in his underpants. "What?" I manage to get out.

"Did you—" William jabs a finger into my shoulder.

"—talk to—" His fingertips and thumb pat together mimicking a talker.

"Lincoln." He makes a twirl with his finger at his forehead. I take note that Lincoln is considered crazy by William. I have missed every sign of that man's psychosis.

"Yes, I talked to Lincoln." I march forward, desperate to find my sexy man-burrito some pants so I don't catch fire with lust the next time I see him. We could also both use some bandages while I'm at it. "And do you know what he did?"

William chases after me, quick on my heels. "Hit you in the face?"

"What? No!"

Although considering his hostility tonight, I wonder if it's possible. He did put his hand around my neck, twice. One time, I think it may have been foreplay, but I'm not sure.

I frown, regretting my lack of adventure in the bedroom. Why didn't I sow any wild oats before ending up in the world's worst summer camp?

"So who hit you?" William asks, perplexed.

"I hit me," I admit.

He scurries in front, stopping me in my tracks. "That doesn't make any sense."

I scoot around him and grumble. "I ran into a steel door."

"Because you were scared?"

No, because a sexy piece of man candy is locked up in my school room, half-naked, and I panicked like an inexperienced imbecile.

"No, it was an accident," I groan. "Wasn't paying attention."

Turning the corner, I practically jog toward the clinic, grateful there is no one inside. The excitement of the night has caused some good chaos, and I won't have to run into anyone and answer questions. Also, people won't see how I'm the biggest klutz who has no game with a man, even when I save his life.

"Can we stop talking about my face?" I beg. "I talked to Lincoln, and you're off the hook. No latrine duty."

"You think latrine duty is what I'm scared of?"

"No one likes cleaning poop, William. It's okay. Remember last time I helped. I vomited—"

"Everywhere," William interrupts. "Yes, we all remember. It was on the ceiling. In the air vents. The projectile force was impressive, but I'd clean that up a thousand times if it keeps me out of Lincoln's way."

"Really? You would choose poop and vomit over getting on Lincoln's bad side?" My stomach churns from all the bodily fluids talk, and I cover my mouth with my hand, flinching from the touch. I keep forgetting I smashed my face into metal.

"He has a way of thinking of some unusual punishments, is all."

"I think he's distracted by too many other things to offer up some special torture," I say.

William lets out a long sigh, his shoulders slumping forward as we enter the clinic. The stress of Lincoln's wrath must have taken a toll, and I wonder how I could have so badly misjudged him.

I have a habit of seeing the good in everyone, believing there is always kindness within, but I can't ignore the facts piling up around me.

What if spicy burrito Cade is a serial killer, and I can't see it?

I shake my head and push the thought away. My misplaced trust in Lincoln can't change the way I interact with the handful of people still alive outside these walls.

"Thanks," William sighs. "How's the guy from the woods?"

"He's perfectly safe," I say, believing the words as they leave my lips.

William narrows his eyes. "From Lincoln and the council, or for you to be around?"

"Boooooooth," I draw out, not sure if I'm giving the correct answer. William isn't convinced, but I smile as best I can with my face smashed in.

"He needs some pants. Could you grab some from your box and meet me back here? I have to get a few things for this mess." I wave my hand in front of my broken face, and he gives me a sympathetic look.

William wants to refuse or argue about how he's helped me enough tonight, but Cade will not fit into my singular spare pair of pants. I'm desperate, and I fold my hands as if in prayer and beg.

"Please, William. I'll triple-check with Lincoln that the whole situation between you both is settled. I'll make sure he's nothing but nice to you. And if I have to clean latrines…"

"No," William says. "Please don't ever do that ever again."

I have nothing else to offer except maybe a pint of blood at the rate it's running down my face.

Despite the empty clinic, William lowers his voice to a whisper as he leans in. "So, he's alive, and you think he'll stay that way?"

I'm a teacher, not a doctor, but I nod in agreement. "I think he's going to be okay."

Cade looked fit and healthy, and his color had returned, replacing the shade of blue-grey that made us think he was a goner.

"His name's Cade," I tell William.

He raises his palms and shakes his head. "I don't want any details. I only wanted to know if I needed to get a body out. That would be fairly easy."

"Ew, William."

"Well, it would be. Did you hear about the lockdown?" William backs up, heading for the door. I take it as a good sign he's going to get the clothes I need.

"Couldn't miss it."

The intercom system is spotty at best, but I heard the message Bobbi repeated into the microphone about ten times.

All citizens of the Briarland Wall. We are on lockdown until the infected are eradicated. Do not attempt to exit the building. Further instructions will be given in the cafeteria momentarily.

We are not citizens, and who is trying to leave besides me and my stowaway?

Judging by the empty hallways on my way to the clinic, everyone must have headed to the cafeteria to catch the latest news. There isn't much to do around here besides complain, have sex, and gossip. This event almost hit the trifecta, and for some exhibitionists, it might.

William stands in the doorway, tapping his hand on the frame. "It makes things tricky, is all."

"I'll take care of it," I promise.

"After you get him clothes," William reminds me.

"Yes. That tiny part I do need you to take care of, but after that, it's all me. You are off the hook."

He doesn't say anything more, turning to leave at a jogging pace, and I make a mental note to talk to Lincoln again. I can't let William get in trouble after all he's done for me.

For us.

Spinning in a circle, I scan the room for what I'll take.

There are plenty of medical supplies available, well stocked for thousands of people who may need assistance on this massive river. Food, we are a little low on, but antibiotics and Advil are in great supply.

I'm throwing everything that may prove helpful into a bag when a voice makes me almost pee my pants.

"What happened to your face?" Lincoln asks.

CHAPTER TEN

MYRA

I am not the best liar.

Terrible, in fact.

I can't even fake an orgasm, much to my ex-boyfriend's annoyance.

"I-I," I stutter and swallow hard, doing my best to calm my skyrocketing pulse. "I misjudged the space between my face and a steel door while walking incredibly fast."

Lincoln strides over, his expression laced with concern, or is that frustration? I'm scrutinizing his every move and reaction, as if the past twenty-four hours have stripped away the mask and shown me who he truly is.

He lifts my chin, inspecting the carnage before turning on the sink and waiting for the water to warm. Another benefit of this place is the unlimited water supply, made possible by the filtration system and solar panels.

Why they want to blow it up, I'll never understand.

"You're tired," he says. "You need to get some rest. I hate seeing you like this."

The heat from the rag stings my cheek, and I suck in a breath between my shut teeth. It's the best way to remove the dried blood caked there, but Lincoln's touch isn't always kind.

"We have a meeting in the cafeteria," I object. "I'll get cleaned up, go to that, and then I'll sleep. I promise."

"They're probably upping the date for the explosion," he says. "I can keep you informed."

My heart sinks, and I hold my breath, trying my best not to tear up with Lincoln so close to my face. I open my mouth to speak, but I can't think of what to say. Nothing from me will change their minds. I'm helpless.

"I see you're still not pleased about the idea," Lincoln says. Small strokes across my nose create pinpricks of pain, and I feel a hot tear slide down my cheek. "Am I hurting you?"

"Just a little sore," I reply.

This Lincoln feels so foreign to the one with his hand around my neck not long ago. The person who would chastise me for giving away food, only to sneak me some extra for dinner. But he only seems that way. Things have changed, and I have to protect myself and the man-burrito.

Everyone has a sliver of depravity inside them. A piece of our heart that hardens when it should open. In a setting like this, surrounded by death and sadness, maybe that tiny piece of him that would never normally make its way to the surface... escaped.

It's not an excuse.

"Almost done," he whispers, re-wetting the cloth. "We have good reason for thinking over the date. There's concern that all of those dead bloats are a sign of a larger army coming south."

"Then let them pass, and we can go north," I argue. "We don't need to pave a road of destruction to leave."

His jaw clenches, and my heart thuds inside my chest. Only hours before, he had me pinned in a corner, and I'm reminded to bite my tongue. There are bigger problems down the hall.

Problems that have pants arriving via William right at this moment.

My eyes flick to him before I can stop myself, and Lincoln turns.

"What are you doing here?" Lincoln seethes.

William rocks back on his heels and clutches the clothing in his hand. I make wide eyes at him and bite my lip, silently praying he's a better liar than I am.

"Bringing Myra some clothes." He steps over and hands me the items, which I crumple together and shove under my arm. "She had some blood on hers."

"How kind of you, William. Our girl, Myra, must be rubbing off on you with the generosity. Not sure why you brought her men's clothes."

"They're mine," he explains. "I looked in her stuff, and she's only got one pair of pants, and they're torn up real bad."

That part isn't a lie, and I exhale. If Lincoln gets a wild hair to go check, he'll find the truth of how I've given almost all of my things away.

"Really, Myra?" Lincoln smirks and shakes his head. "You're charity is going to make you naked."

I chuckle and shrug while Lincoln eyes me. It takes ninja focus not to hurl all over him when I see him wet his lips and then look me up and down. How have I missed this side of him for a month? Am I living under a naive rock?

"Get back to your station," Lincoln orders William. "And try not to fuck up this time."

Lincoln throws the bloody towel on the counter and motions for William to leave.

"Thank you, William," I call after him.

Lincoln faces me, and I offer a pleading look.

"Yes, very thoughtful, William," Lincoln adds. "Now get out."

William pauses, shifting his weight from side to side. I give him a quick nod, encouraging him to walk away. He does, but mouths, "Be careful," as he walks back out the door.

"Do you need help getting changed?" Lincoln asks.

"Nope," I say, emphasizing the p with a pop. "I'm okie dokey artichokee."

My level of dork doesn't deter his expression, which I'm fairly certain is full of desire. Does he have a thing for injured women? I shiver at the thought and wait for him to leave.

"Do you have what you need?" he asks, pointing toward my bag of medical supplies.

Please don't look through it.

"Yes, I think so," I say.

He steps toward the bag, and my adrenaline spikes. He's going to find things that don't make sense for a smashed face, like an arm sling. I've hit my lying quota for the day, and desperate to stop him, I blurt out the only thing that comes to mind.

"Why did you kiss me?"

It works, and he pauses, turning his head over his shoulder to glance at me.

"I'm just curious," I add. "Because ever since I met you, you've never seemed to want to kiss me, and you've had opportunities, but you never did anything, so it's weird you are today."

Thirty seconds of silence stretch on, and I picture myself melting into the floor, vanishing entirely just to escape this moment.

"I am going to stop talking now," I mumble.

He turns around, which is a relief, and leans against the counter, crossing his arms at his chest.

"Did you like it?"

Fudge. Landmine. What do I say?

"You have a lot of experience kissing."

That is not a lie. I've seen him make out with Bobbi every day. It doesn't confirm or deny my thoughts about his kissing technique, which, honestly, is a little wet and not in a good way.

"Not a lot kissing you," he says. "But maybe we can change that."

Oh, Cookie Monster, this is not good.

"Right," I say and bite my lip.

"Maybe I was trying to piss off Bobbi," he offers. "She's been getting a little too big for her britches."

I've never understood that saying, especially here, where none of us are growing out of anything since we're all literally starving. His answer makes me relax the slightest bit, but I can't help but think he's testing me, gauging what I'll say next.

Does he want me to ask for another kiss? I don't think I can do that, but if he goes for that bag again, I guess I'd better pucker up.

"Oh. Just checking," I say.

"Checking on…" he trails off.

More silence from him, a test I'm sure I'm failing as we begin a staring contest. It's awkward as heck, but he may think this is flirting. I think this is insanity, but I can't leave.

"I… I think I lost the plot," I admit, breaking the silence. "What is going on?"

He laughs, and for a moment, the light in his eyes is back. The Lincoln I remember from when we first arrived brightens the space, and I smile at the sight.

"I guess you need to get changed, girl." He frowns at the clothes under my arm.

"And then I'll meet you all in the cafeteria," I add.

"If you need to stay back, I can find you and brief you—"

"No. No. No," I interrupt him. "It's just, people think I'm already a problem with this whole plan, and if I'm not there, it may look like I'm backing out."

This satisfies Lincoln, who nods in agreement.

He passes by me without stopping or grabbing me for another kiss, and I'm left alone in the clinic, with two black eyes forming. This may be a low. The apocalypse hasn't had a lot of highs, but today feels exorbitantly horrible.

Except I can't stop myself from smiling, and I know for some stupid girly reason, it's because I'm heading back to Cade.

CHAPTER
ELEVEN

Myra

Should I knock?

No, that's ridiculous. If someone out here hears me knocking, they may get suspicious.

But what if he's naked? More naked than before.

That might be good.

The door creaks open, Cade's eyes peering through the crack, and I shove forward and burst inside.

"Don't open the door!" I hiss at him.

"Don't stand out there for ten minutes. What were you doing?"

Lusting.

"Nothing."

I shove the wad of clothes at him and walk to the other end of the room. "I got you some pants," I call out from the room's corner. I've put myself in a time-out, resting my forehead against the wall while he puts on fresh underwear.

The sound of cloth hitting the floor makes my heart race. He's behind me, completely naked, dick out and everything. I could turn around and…

"Thank you," Cade says.

"Sure thing," I reply with the most high-pitched squeaky voice that I didn't know could exit my body.

"You can turn around," he chuckles.

Doing so, I find him smirking in boxer briefs again. They are clean, and I'm grateful William thought to get underwear, but they're a little tight in certain areas. The man stands before me in all his glory.

It's a lot of glory.

He shakes out the pants before stepping a leg inside, still a bit wobbly on his feet, but much better than the crawling and falling mess he was before. "I found a few energy bars," he says. "I feel bad that I ate them, but I couldn't stop myself. My body sort of took over."

"Oh, that's my secret stash, and you're welcome to them. Honestly, I forgot that I put them there for the kids. Do you need more?"

"Kids? Your kids?"

"No, I'm a teacher. Or, I was, and I gave some lessons here to pass the time," I explain. "Anyway, sometimes they would be hungry. Everyone's hungry, really. I'm sure you know how it is."

He nods, and although the man is full of lean muscle, I see how his ribs stick out on both sides, more so when he takes a deep breath.

Stop staring. Stop staring. Stop staring.

"What do you do? Or did? Or, er, um…" I trail off. I was never good at casual conversation, and the skill has been lost for good ever since the world fell apart.

"My dad has a home renovation business. Had is more accurate. I worked with him, but now I mostly spend time with my brother and try not to die." William's shirt slides over his head, and he pulls it down his chest, stretching the cotton tight and making me drool.

"That's wonderful that your brother survived," I say. It's the oddest compliment I have ever given, but he smiles because he knows it's true. I'm sure Cade's thankful that, after maybe ninety-nine percent of the world is dead, he has someone.

He's fully dressed except for shoes, and I wait for the fluttering in my stomach to cease, for the excitement I feel from merely being in his presence to stop taking over my sensibilities, but it doesn't. I'm the epitome of hot and bothered, and no amount of clothing will fix me.

"Any family?" he dares to ask.

I shake my head. "I never had much to begin with, so it's not that bad. The people here are nice despite the shooting at you thing. They're scared, that's all. And young. I think the average age in this place is nineteen. I feel like the mother hen, except no one listens to me. Not that I speak up, but…" Stopping myself, I step over to the cabinet and rustle around for secret stash number two, which holds four sodas.

I had hoped to give them to the first four students who passed the assessment tests I created, but Cade had a rough night with us trying to murder him and all.

His eyes light up when he sees the red can full of sugar and calories.

"Here," I say, and offer the drink.

"I couldn't possibly."

"Please. It would make me happy."

There's a small ache in my stomach remembering that all this food came from Lincoln. He would sneak me special treats, but I couldn't bear to eat them all. Most made it into this classroom, and I could live with the knowledge that a deserving student would be rewarded.

Cade tilts his head and takes the can, holding it for a moment and staring in awe. "Will you split it with me?"

"You can have it," I offer again. "Really, I don't need it."

"I won't drink it if you don't have half. That's my deal."

He takes a small step forward, closing the gap between us, and I feel that flush in my cheeks return. Does he notice how I burn when I'm around him?

"Okay," I concede. "Just a little."

The sound of the pop and fizz is music to our ears. We are simple creatures, and that's something that hasn't changed throughout my life. I never needed much, not even my own bed or three meals a day.

A normal childhood for me meant something much different. What I craved growing up, and what I still need, is kindness. He has no idea what offering half a can of soda means, but I might burst into tears.

"I know it's only been about a month, but we only got soda when we went out to eat, which wasn't often," Cade explains. "So it's been a long time since I've had something like this. The fact that I can't have it, well…"

"It makes you want it more," I say.

I take the tiniest sip, and he narrows his eyes. "Big gulp," he orders. "Make it burn."

Laughing a little first, I tip my chin up and take a nice long swig, my head spinning a little once the liquid hits my stomach and sugar permeates my veins. I'll be able to run a marathon after half a can of caffeine.

"Your turn." I hand him the can, and our fingers touch. The spark is immediate and laced with everything I don't dare say. I hope my face is bruised enough to hide my embarrassment.

His Adam's apple bobs up and down as he drinks, my eyes never leaving his lips and throat as he lets out an "Ahhh" before passing the can back to me.

We are sharing our first meal together.

"I heard the announcement," he says. "The lockdown stuff and going to the cafeteria. Are you going?"

Licking my lips and nodding, I hand the drink back to him. "I sort of have to, or someone might notice."

"Hasn't someone already? Wasn't there a guy with you?"

"Oh, that's William," I tell him. "He won't say anything. Someone else."

Lincoln's face flickers in my mind, and a pit forms in my stomach. I'll be shoulder to shoulder with Lincoln and Bobbi soon.

Even if I'm just a pawn he's using to rile her up, it's a brand of drama I don't want to handle, today or any day.

"Will that be a good time to get out of here?" he asks. "I need to get back to my brother."

"Why did you leave him? I mean… Shoot, that sounded rude. I was curious, is all, about how you ended up here."

"Food," Cade says. One side of his mouth lifts in a smile, but his eyes are sad. "We haven't left our house much. It's right on the river with a few acres. I was gonna fish, but all these infected bodies started coming, and well, here I am."

"That was weird, right?" I ask. "All those bloats."

Cade nods, eyes wide.

"Bloats?" he questions. "That's fitting, actually. Not sure what else to call them. They're not zombies, and I haven't seen any brain-eating. Only infecting people and making them all bloated and bleeding that black ooze. One exploded by our house, which is odd because they don't stop when you fill them with bullets. It's like they have an expiration date."

"I know, right? We could probably just wait them out," I say. "And you know they can't swim. Just like me," I do a one-sided cheers with the soda can and chuckle at myself. "It makes this place somewhat safe. High ground by the river, but we're running out of food, too."

"I know I'm a broken record here, but I need to get back to my brother, Dillon. He'll be worried, and I can't risk him trying to look for me. There's more than the bloats to be scared of out there."

Cade insists I take the last sip of soda, and I'm so addicted to the sugar already, I don't say no.

"Right, like strangers," I agree. "You're a stranger."

"Are you afraid of me?"

I gulp and think about how I'm afraid of myself around him.

"Should I be?" I ask. "You do seem bulletproof."

Cade holds up his arm, waiving it in my line of sight.

"You lived is all I'm pointing out."

I hold the empty can in my hands, savoring the sweet flavor still leftover on my tongue, and lick my lips, hoping for one last taste.

"I am so sorry about the gunfire stuff," I apologize. "There are good people here, even if they are young and they get jumpy."

"Why do you keep apologizing for something you didn't do? This is not your fault. It's all mine. I should have listened to Dillon before diving out into the river to fish. Made a plan like he insisted. This is on me. All of it."

Staring down at my feet, I realize William didn't bring him any shoes, which poses a problem if his house is far upstream. I don't have long before Lincoln starts looking for me again, but the way Cade is talking, I'm afraid he may try to escape on his own.

Lincoln may recognize William's clothes if he's spotted, which is likely with all the doors locked and guarded. Even if Cade believes this predicament is his responsibility, he's mine now.

My responsibility, that is. The man is not mine, even though I'm drooling over his pecs and the fact that he shared a sugary substance with a woman he just met.

"You can't go to your brother right now, but I'll figure something out. It's dangerous to leave during lockdown. Actually, it's impossible. Give me some time."

"You snuck me in. I bet I could find a way to sneak out," he counters.

"Please, don't," I plead. "You don't know the layout, and if you're spotted, it could cause trouble. If I had any family or friends out there, I would want to run for the hills too, but you just can't."

Cade starts to speak, but a knock at the door cuts him off, and a knot of worry tightens.

Our time might already be up.

CHAPTER
TWELVE

Cade

She mumbles something about me becoming a man burrito. The sugar has definitely gone to her head. There's more knocking, louder and harder this time, and then a female voice.

"Myra," the woman growls from behind the door. "Are you in there? Lincoln sent me to bring you fresh clothes."

Myra's eyes widen, and she guides me to the wall beside the door. From there, I'm mostly hidden, at least until whoever's coming in shuts the door and leaves me fully exposed.

There's also the overwhelming task of remaining upright, which, despite the food, drink, and company, is growing increasingly difficult once more. My head spins, and I worry that my knees will give out and send me crashing to the concrete.

"I'm on my way to the cafeteria now, and don't worry, I have clothes," Myra calls out.

A fist slams on the door, fast and angry. "Open the fucking door, Myra."

Myra swallows hard, then twists the handle and eases the door open just a crack. I freeze, holding my breath, praying the stranger remains oblivious to my presence.

"Here," the woman says, pushing the door open wider. My warm breath, coming out in a shudder, fogs the steel. I focus on controlling every inhale and exhale. Clothing rustles to the floor, and I hear someone bend down to retrieve it.

There's a pause before Myra responds. "These are your clothes. This is your favorite top. It's Nirvana."

"Well, Captain's orders and all that bullshit." The woman sniffles, and I hear the uncomfortable shuffling of feet.

"Why would he do this?" Myra asks. She's confused. Her voice gives her away, and although I sense these women know each other, it doesn't sound like they are friends. There's a harshness in the air, and Myra speaks softly, as if she's soothing a wild animal who might bite.

"Bobbi, I can't accept these," Myra protests. "This is your Nirvana shirt. That's like… better than food. I wouldn't feel right."

"Don't be so difficult," Bobbi argues as she puts her weight on the door.

Through the narrow gap in the frame, I catch a partial glimpse of her and press my head tight against the wall, doing my best to vanish from sight.

Bobbi is young, early twenties, I would guess, and her swollen face and cracking voice give away that she's been crying.

"But it's Nirvana," Myra whispers.

"Lincoln wants you in that outfit, and we'll both be in trouble if you're not, so just stop."

"'Teen Spirit', Nirvana. 'Heart-Shaped Box', Nirvana," Myra sighs.

Bobbi grumbles. "I am aware of what they sing, Myra. Put on the damn shirt and come to the cafeteria."

"'Lithium," Myra mumbles in a voice so soft, it's barely audible.

Both women are silent again for far too long, and my lungs burn as I try to control my breathing, keeping it slow, steady, and silent. "I'll take good care of it and get it back to you after."

Bobbi sniffles, but doesn't say anything before turning on her heel and leaving. The door creaks shut, and I inhale a large gulp of oxygen and slide down the wall until my ass is back on the floor.

"Friend of yours?" I huff.

She shakes her head, holding a black oversized T-shirt and a pair of light denim jeans. Running her thumbs over the fabric, she looks to be in a trance.

"I should change," she sighs.

"Sounds like your boyfriend wants you to."

Her head whips up. "I don't have a boyfriend." It was a cheap shot to find out if this woman was single, but it worked.

Except she looks offended, her face contorting in what might be anger, but I doubt Myra ever gets all that angry.

I raise my hands in surrender and smile, but she doesn't return the gesture. She might cry, and the thought makes my insides ache.

"Do you see this?" she says, tossing the clothing to me. I lift the shirt and spot the faded print of the band name on the front.

"It's Nirvana," I say.

I've heard the word Nirvana more times in the past five minutes than I have in my entire life. Is this place a grunge music cult? I'm not understanding the significance.

"Everyone loves that shirt and most of all Bobbi," Myra explains. "And everyone knows it's Bobbi's, and worst of all—"

"You hate Nirvana," I interject, hoping for a moment of levity.

"No, Cade. Worst of all, it's her absolute favorite."

I hand her back the clothing, and she mindlessly throws it on a cabinet shelf before removing her top. Shit, this woman is beautiful. I'm staring intently, but I can't look away. She turns her back, probably because she sees me gaping slack-jawed at her exposed skin.

"It was nice of her to let you borrow it then," my voice cracks. She unbuttons her jeans, and I hear the zipper.

"She's not trying to be nice. She's been forced into public humiliation," Myra says. "And close your eyes."

I comply, not out of gentlemanly virtue or a sense of duty, but because Myra asked. After everything she's done in the last twenty-four hours, I'd do anything she wanted. A nagging feeling settles in my gut. Refusing her might be impossible, even without the debt of my life hanging over me.

It feels good to say yes to Myra.

I remember my dad explaining to me how he would love getting his honey-do list from Mom. She would make little notes on things to fix or stick a Post-It to the refrigerator. My dad treated those words like gospel and got excited when he presented her with the finished product or an item she needed.

At the time, I didn't understand. If she forgot sugar at the grocery store, that was her problem because it's her job to grocery shop. He quickly set me straight, saying that with the right person, helping them isn't a choice. You simply want to and feel that you must. Love is an action, and he showed it every day.

It's too soon to call it love, but something deep inside me pulls toward Myra, a quiet tug that urges me to do more for her, to listen when she speaks, and that tightens every time I sense she needs something.

She holds the other end.

"Are your eyes still closed?" she asks, and I assume by the squeak of the floor, she's turning around.

"Yes," I tell her.

"Okay, well, I'm dressed. Open sesame."

She's adorable in the oversized clothes and a shy half-smile while she looks at the floor.

"Is that shirt Nirvana?" I joke.

Myra grumbles and crouches down next to me. Sitting cross-legged, she places a hand on my knee, and my stomach flips from her touch. "I have to go again, but are you going to be okay for a few hours? No running off?"

"Who's Lincoln, and why is he into public humiliation?" I ask.

I watch her draw in a deep breath, her chest rising before she rests a hand against her cheek, tilts into the touch, and releases a slow sigh. She's tired. We both are, and I want nothing more than to have her in my arms. Even on this cold, hard floor, we'd sleep like the dead.

"He's one of the troop leaders around here. They call themselves the council."

"Fancy," I retort.

"They make the decisions around here. They divided everyone into groups like lookouts, food, and other jobs. I thought Lincoln and I were friends because, well, I'm friendly with everyone," she explains. "I'm even nice to Bobbi, who is Lincoln's girlfriend, but he kissed me this morning, and now I don't know what's going on, especially after he shoved me against a wall earlier."

"What?" I growl and startle Myra.

She scoots back, and I realize I've lunged forward and grabbed her wrists. Blood oozes out from underneath the duct tape, dripping onto the floor.

My reaction doesn't make sense, but I'm full of fire and rage, my heart pounding in my chest, and all I see is red.

Backing away, I release her, but she reaches back out to hold my hand. Her kindness soothes me, slowing my heartbeat and letting the fury in my veins fade until only a steady undercurrent of agitation remains.

"I tend to ramble," she says. "That was a bit much."

"I'm sorry. It's not my business. But, Myra. What the fuck?"

"I know," she says, eyes wide. "I was surprised, too. He's always been so nice."

Lincoln has not been nice. He's been manipulating her, and the mask is beginning to crack. I know men like that, ones who will pretend to be a friend only to take what they want later. It's a tactic, and she doesn't see it, because she's the nice one.

"He's not a friend," I grit out.

She frowns, her hold on me tensing. "I'm getting that feeling. Let me fix your bandage before I head out. It shouldn't take long, but it's going to hurt a little."

I want the pain. It will distract me from my feeling of helplessness. This Lincoln character can't be trusted, and he's got his eyes on Myra. He's branded her with his girlfriend's clothing and forced her to kiss him. I know where this leads.

We both need to get out of here.

She scoots backwards and reaches for the bag she brought with her, her stomach showing when she leans back. I'm staring again, wanting to hold her and touch the soft skin.

"I have had a total of two first aid classes," she announces. "Both of them involved not touching the kid unless they were almost dead because people tend to sue, but I feel confident that anything is better than duct tape."

"Hey, duct tape isn't so bad," I tell her. "You know they use super glue on the battlefield."

"I know!" she exclaims, picking at the edge of the silver tape. "That's exactly what I was thinking, too."

She carefully unwinds the makeshift bandage, but due to all the bleeding, there isn't a dramatic rip from the wound. It slides off my arm, and we both let out a sigh of relief.

I'm quiet as she works to clean the wound with some antiseptic, even when liquid fire sears deep into my arm.

"Are you allergic to penicillin?" she asks.

"No, but are you sure you want to use that?" I ask.

"It's got an expiration that's coming up. Better used on you than wasted, but I don't know how much."

We can't search the internet, and I don't want her going back to that clinic for a guide and possibly getting caught.

"Just guess," I say. "Pull a syringe. It's an antibiotic, not heroin."

She giggles, and I smile even when she plunges the needle into my sore arm. There's gauze and a strong bandage wrapped around the bullet hole in no time, and although I can feel my pulse in my fingers, it's better. A pulse means there's circulation, and after a few minutes, there's still no red showing through the beige covering.

Myra cleans up around her, plunging the used packaging into the bottom of a random box to hide any evidence before she turns back to me, hands on her hips.

"I think you're set, and I have to go," she says. "He'll cause problems if I'm not there."

I reach for her hands and hold them in mine. "Could we leave while everyone is in the cafeteria? I'm not going to let you be in danger because of me. You've risked your life already."

"We?" she asks.

"Well… you need to lead me out."

We both fall silent, the unspoken thought circling between us. She's probably wondering about getting out of here. I've heard nothing good so far, though the outside world isn't exactly promising either, but this place feels like a sinking ship.

"The doors will still be locked, and he may have them guarded," she explains. "Also, I don't think I'll be in any danger in the cafeteria. He's showing off, is all. Nothing bad will happen before I get back."

"The bullet hole in my arm would disagree. You could have been shot bringing me in here, and now you're telling me that some guy who has assaulted you wants to keep an eye on you, or he'll freak out."

"He's twenty. Everyone freaks out about everything when they're twenty."

When she lets go of my hands, I do my best not to draw her back to me. There's that string pulling at my heart, telling me to keep her safe. She's in more danger than she realizes, but I've known this woman for less than a day. She doesn't trust me yet.

"He has assaulted you with his mouth and his hands."

"Most of my bruises are self-induced, but when you put it that way," she admits, scratching her head. "Yeah, it's um, not great. Still, we're dag-nabbed if we do and dag-nabbed if we don't."

I can't help but smile at her phrasing. "Dag-nabbed?"

"Definitely. Maybe this cafeteria time is dangerous, but I'm in just as much trouble if he finds you here."

"Right, well…" I trail off. "Dag-nabbit, I guess." I wonder if she's ever cursed and if my constant trail of bad words causes her discomfort. I'll stop, or at least start a swear jar. There's no money to put in it, but the thought may count enough.

She gives me a little smile, and I concede that the safest bet is for her to go and for us to take some time to think and make a plan. As much as I'm worried about Dillon, I'm no good to him dead.

He'd want me to consider every option, to think it through. I can almost hear his lecturing voice now, scolding me for trying to bolt without weighing it all out first.

"But I'll come back," she promises. "I won't leave you here. We'll figure something out."

I'm silent as she leaves the room, the heavy door clicking closed behind her, and as the seconds turn into minutes, my eyes grow heavy. There's nothing to do but wait, and I've never felt more useless.

I won't keep repeating the same mistakes.

This time, I'll be patient.

We'll make a plan to get out.

And we'll do it together.

CHAPTER
THIRTEEN

Myra

Why is he so gosh darn good looking?

No one injured should look that good. It's criminal, even though crime isn't really a thing anymore. There are a few rules to this little habitat. I didn't make any of them, but most I agree with.

1. **Food is guarded at all times. You get your share and no more. If you're sick, you can't stock up, but you can donate your portion with council approval.**

Pressing my palm to my stomach that swirls with sugary soda, I think about all the rations I've given away. Lincoln approved almost all of them, trying to talk me out of it every time. He's also broken this rule many times himself, but he's council, and I somehow thought it was okay.

2. **The council assigns duties, and they are non-negotiable. There is no switching of assignments, but you may help others.**

It didn't take them long to figure out the no-switching rule when they realized the meek or frail kept volunteering to clean toilets instead of preparing food. There are still bullies after the world ends. I've cleaned my fair share of bathrooms without being forced because sometimes the assignments seemed like a punishment. I understand it's meant to keep order, but who can be on their best behavior when things are so darn hard here?

3. **Lights out is for everyone who is not on lookout duty. You cannot loiter or sneak off to other areas.**

This one will be a problem to get around. People break it all the time, usually to have sex somewhere, but they come back to their bed. I guarantee someone here is pregnant. A few someones. I've never broken this, but I do make excuses for others sometimes. Everyone stretches the boundaries of freedom when they are trapped in a cage. Birds need to spread their wings and all that. I just wish they could do it with condoms.

4. **Insubordination will result in removal.**

That's the one keeping all of us in line because, yes, it's happened. We didn't make it seventy-two hours before someone got booted. I didn't know his name, but I remember his face. The regret, unforgettable and so avoidable. He stood his ground on something as silly as mopping, and when they made an example out of him, they did it in a flamboyant fashion. There was a march reminiscent of walking the plank.

I sigh at the memory, and a shiver runs through me.

We're led by the lost boys of Neverland, where chaos thrives and violence calls the shots.

The self-appointed council rules with an iron fist, but they bend those rules when it's someone they like. I'm still one of those someones unless Lincoln has caught onto me.

"No," I say to myself and shake my head. He still looks at me like I'm a snack and was salivating over me in the clinic. I think I was a good enough actress.

Turning down another familiar hallway, lights flickering from the low ceiling, I hear one of the council members shouting for everyone to quiet down. I quicken my steps, skidding to the door and throwing it open, only for the room to fall silent as every head swivels in my direction.

At least he'll know I'm here.

I wave and try to smile, but it hurts. A girl in the crowd mouths,

"What happened to your face?" and I try to act out running into a door without speaking.

Everyone is still staring.

"Someone hit you with a door?" a young man asks, and before I can continue the worst charades game imaginable, William grabs me by the elbow and drags me to the back of the crowd. There are some chuckles, but the group silences when one of the council members clears his throat, signaling we've begun.

It's Lincoln's best buddy, Simon, standing on a makeshift podium. He's probably my least favorite, but none of them are in the running for saint status. I don't make it a habit to dislike people. That energy is better used elsewhere, and there's no point wasting it on hate. Still, he makes me uneasy. Every time Simon speaks, I feel his words slither over my skin.

"Now that I have everyone's attention," he says, and I lower my head, hiding behind a group of teens who attend my classes. One of the girls smiles at me and puts her arm around my shoulders.

Simon motions for us all to sit because if he's not domineering over his crowd of constituents, then what's the point?

Heat creeps into my cheeks, a sudden fear gripping me that everyone around can somehow hear the thoughts rattling through my head.

"As some of you have seen, and many of you have heard, we have a swarm of infected at our doors," Simon bellows.

Chatter erupts amongst the group, many of them presumably heard the story about the bloat mountain, but assumed it was a rumor.

"Quiet down," Lincoln yells.

He steps up next to Simon, and we all notice the gun in his hand. That's a new accessory, but considering how the past day has gone, I'm not surprised. The gloves are off with Lincoln.

If Cade were to ask me how a group of four men... make that boys, were able to come into power over the rest of us, I would explain in one word.

Guns.

Lincoln, Simon, and the twins, as we call them, found the security room first. When they got inside, they made a discovery that put them one step ahead of everyone else.

It didn't bother me much in the beginning. People on lookout were given guns, so it wasn't like they never let the weapons out of their sight. Their rules never hurt anyone, and I was allowed to have my school, and everyone got enough food.

Then the idea of blowing up the dam popped into someone's head, or heads. I predict the twins made that decision. They love fire and firepower. Both of them are the kind of men who look at something majestic or grand and want to figure out how to gut it.

That explosive little idea turned into a plan, and Lincoln's going to make sure it happens because he's the one holding a weapon while we're all sitting on the cement floor listening.

"We have hundreds of infected along the wall of the dam," Simon continues. "We are in lockdown to protect everyone, because if one gets in, we're all dead."

"But aren't they all dead?" a young woman calls out. "They can't swim."

There's a shift in Simon, his face hardening and eyes narrowing. It's subtle but terrifying, and I feel my heart pound against my ribs as my breath catches in my throat.

The girl opens her mouth to speak again, raising her hand this time, but she notices his expression and stops herself. She stares at the floor, and the room grows so silent, I can hear everyone breathing.

We are waiting for the bubble to burst with this group, and the gun in Lincoln's hand tells us it's happening any moment.

"How many fucking times do I have to tell you all to shut up?" Simon grits out. He's not yelling, but he doesn't have to, and my skin tingles from adrenaline and fear. "How are you not dead yet if you are this fucking stupid, Lydia?"

Lincoln steps down from the podium while Simon keeps his eyes glued on the teen. He moves toward her, a feeble girl barely sixteen, and before I realize it, I'm on my feet, heading in her direction.

A few hands reach out attempting to stop me, but I'm zoned in on the tiny redhead with eyes as big as saucers. Lincoln sees me in his peripheral vision and freezes, shocked at my apparent defiance.

I'm shocked, too. What in the world am I doing?

There's a voice in my head telling me that they will make an example of Lydia, a normally shy girl who was speaking out in hopes that she could ease the fears of herself and others. I wish I had chosen to take a stance when they brought up blowing this place to bits, but better to find my voice late than never.

Simon continues talking to the crowd, his voice sounding far away. Lincoln reaches for Lydia, jerking her towards him, and she trips over her feet and falls to her knees.

"What?" he hisses in my direction.

"I, um. You w-wanted—" I'm stuttering over my own words, realizing all too late I have zero plan, and Lincoln looks pissed.

"I'm here, and I know you wanted me here," I say.

"Everyone knows you're fucking here after that display with the door, Myra," he seethes. "What the fuck?"

Lydia trembles on the floor, curling in on herself as if she could vanish entirely.

"I told her you were looking for her," Bobbi chimes in behind me.

Her voice makes me jolt, and I feel my neck turning red while I force a smile on my strained face.

"Hi," I mutter. "I'm here."

"I just got in from checking on the guards and told her," Bobbi says.

She's lying. I saw her before Simon started talking. She was standing in the opposite doorway, out of sight from the podium.

Lincoln's expression softens, but his grip on Lydia's wrist does not. Simon bangs on the microphone, making my spine straighten, and everyone goes silent. The only sound is Lydia's soft sniffles, her bright red hair falling like a curtain over her face as she stays crouched down.

"There has to be a smaller explosion," Simon continues. Those words catch my attention. "Controlled. We cannot leave after the dam's destruction with a thousand bloats right outside."

But they are dead.

I don't dare speak up, knowing this might be the only thing that delays their inevitable plan. There's also wanting to keep my head on my shoulders and my man-burrito, Cade, safe and alive.

"After breakfast tomorrow, I want the following individuals to meet with the council," Simon continues.

He lists the names of the smartest and brightest, ones that by some miracle may be able to ensure we don't all die during this mini bomb, but there are no guarantees. No one's an engineer, but it's one problem at a time these days.

"Porter Harris. You too, you fucking imbecile," Simon fumes.

Porter belches in response, and all heads turn in his direction.

Porter is the smartest kid in here. He's the most intelligent student who isn't a student because he's never come to my class, but if he did… he'd be the brightest bulb lighting up the place.

Downright offensive, and a little off-putting, but Porter can read a five-hundred-page book in a couple of hours and then recite everything he learned. There are several manuals down here about the dam's construction and plans for the next repair. I imagine they want him to read them and use his photographic memory to help with their mission. I would bet he could read a book about building a skyscraper and then pass every inspection.

There are, however, a few unique problems when it comes to Porter.

Firstly, Porter is seventeen, so since the day he taught himself how to make moonshine, he's remained perpetually drunk. Despite the ridiculousness of wasting corn or whatever he uses to create the alcohol, the immature council approved this. Maybe they understand how his intelligence can help us, but my bet is they, too, enjoy staying tipsy.

Secondly, and I cannot stress how this seemingly insignificant choice has permeated every day of our lives, he is still dressed in his Halloween outfit. He wore it the night the infected took hold of our world, and I have never seen him in anything else.

The tattered T-Rex inflatable costume, covered in bits of duct tape and perhaps some vomit, makes a loud buzzing sound in the cafeteria. Porter's second belch echoes in its green head, and I bite my lip so I don't laugh.

"Sure thing, boss," he says, his third burp sounding a little wet.

Porter stands, the tail of the costume inflating to a full four feet before it smacks a few people close to him. He bows, almost falling flat on his fake dinosaur teeth.

Whoever gave that man an unlimited supply of batteries is either evil or a genius. It's hard to decide when he drunkenly inflates himself at three in the morning and walks around the beds looking for a snack, but in this moment, his distraction has given poor Lydia a reprieve.

Punishing her when Porter openly mocks the council is a step too far, and Lincoln releases the girl, allowing Lydia to scoot back to her group of girlfriends.

Simon may dislike Porter's apparent rebellious nature, but he knows we all need him. His brain, although it is inside a vinyl dinosaur head, has saved us more than once.

I turn to look at Bobbi, who is giving Porter an annoyed gaze as he waves his tiny T-Rex hand at Simon. Painfully aware that I am wearing her favorite shirt, I cross my arms at my chest and watch Porter's movements.

He clasps the miniature clawed hands together in prayer, which is a sign that he will say something serious, ask someone to dance, or recite the Pledge of Allegiance.

All scenarios happen regularly.

I have danced once.

"It's going to be more like five or six explosions," Porter's voice echoes through the plastic. "Unless you want to die. In which case, let's all have an orgy first. I'll even take off Mr. Rex for the event."

"No, Porter," Simon grits out. "We'd like to live. I'll speak with you after breakfast."

Porter nods and wags his tail, scooting back to his former spot.

"That's all, everyone," Simon closes. "And rations are getting cut again. Can't be helped."

He hops down and turns on his heel while a few groans are let out amongst the crowd. When I go to leave, Bobbi grabs my arm, her lips close to my ear. "Don't be so stupid next time."

I hang my head and wait for her to release me, knowing she saved me from the council's wrath. It might have been for Lydia's benefit, but I'm grateful all the same.

Lincoln waits by the door, and though I try to melt into the exiting crowd, I catch him curling a finger, signaling me to come closer.

My face aches as I tense, and I do my best to act like nothing is wrong and I'm not rushing to get back to my spicy burrito.

He's not mine. Stop it.

"Are you feeling alright?" Lincoln asks. Every word is laced with frustration.

I freeze, my mind searching for a way to avoid lying while not giving away every secret I've had since birth. Not that I had many secrets until last night. I'm a very boring open book.

"I. Hit. My. Head," I tell him. Every word comes out slow and precise, doing my best to keep my voice from shaking.

His lips thin, and he looks over my face, which is undoubtedly purple. "Yes," he agrees.

"So, no," I continue. "Things aren't alright, but I'll rest. Like you said."

"So you listen to me now."

I nod and bite my lip. This interaction needs to end before I screw it up.

There's a swooshing sound and the steady buzz of a tiny motor as Porter walks in our direction. He steps to Lincoln's side, pressing the green vinyl against him when he places his tiny arm on his shoulder.

Lincoln rolls his eyes, and he leans away, shaking Porter's arm loose. The smell of alcohol permeates from the flapping plastic, one piece of duct tape coming loose while a steady rush of air flattens one side.

I reach forward and secure the tape, pinching it in place for ten seconds before releasing it to see if it holds. It does, and I give Porter a little nod. We all have a love-hate relationship with Mr. Rex, but today I adore the ensemble.

"Thanks, M," Porter says before belching once more. How he can stand the stench inside that thing is beyond me, but he is and will always be, kind of drunk.

"Simon wants you," he tells Lincoln.

A pair of young women wait a few feet from Porter, one of them unbuttoning her blouse enough to show off her cleavage. They want alcohol, and considering that we just got the news that hundreds of infected are banging on the door, and we're going to try and explode them into orbit, I can't blame them.

"Sure. Be right there," Lincoln says. "I need you to take care of Myra. She hit her head, smashed up her face a bit."

"Damn, I can see that. Thought you took a swing at another one of your lady friends."

My breathing stops, and the buzzing in my head rushes into my ears and drowns out all the noise.

Lincoln goes to grab Porter, but he misses. With the giant dinosaur suit, it's hard to tell where the plastic ends and he begins.

"Hands off the merchandise," Porter snips. "Who do you think you are?"

"I'll tell you, motherfucker. Come here."

"Lincoln!" Simon bellows. The twins are at his sides, encasing him in a jerk sandwich.

Porter's two women friends take the opportunity to swarm him and see about those drinks.

"I'm coming," Lincoln yells back.

The place has all but cleared out, and I want to leave. If that means I need to be walked to my door by a trick-or-treater, fine.

I wedge myself between the two women who grimace when they see my face. "Let's go, Porter," I say.

"You make sure she gets to bed alright," Lincoln demands, his closed fists shaking at his side.

"Will do, boss," Porter says, giving a miniature salute with his tiny arms.

Lincoln storms off, the twins following. Simon stares for a moment, but I can't keep his gaze. He's never had a soft spot for me, so there is no love lost there. Bobbi grabs his attention, showing him something on a clipboard, and I exhale when they both head for the door.

"You good, Myra?" Porter asks.

"Yes, I'm fine. Thank you for asking. Really, I can get back on my own. My face doesn't feel as bad as it looks."

Porter studies me for a moment, weighing his options. The less time he spends with me, the more time he gets to drink and have sex. His choice is obvious.

"Awesome," he concludes. "Gonna go fuck these two dino style. You, uh, don't want to join, do ya?"

"No, thank you, Porter. Have fun."

He gives me a hand gesture, which I surmise is a thumbs up, and tells me to "Stay sweet."

The three shuffle off, and I'm alone in the room. There aren't any guards in here, and all the footsteps fade away until it's completely silent. This is an opportunity I didn't think would arise, but now that it's happened, I'd be a fool to turn my back.

Hopping onto the counter, I grab one of the meat skewers and a small knife.

I am not one who breaks the rules in this place, and I feel bad, but not bad enough to stop.

Sometimes, the line between right and wrong is blurry. Other times, the line is drawn by people with guns.

I feel in my heart that what I'm doing is right.

It's time to get to work.

CHAPTER FOURTEEN

The little I know about my parents didn't take me very long to discover.

Edna and Maurice were not desperate to get me back. No, they never cried to a judge about how they needed one more chance to save their baby girl.

That was the song and dance for many of my foster siblings, and even though many stopped believing the theatrics over time, I envied the performance. A crying mother telling her fourteen-year-old that she'll get a job, while knowing damn well her boyfriend is outside ready to take her to their next fix, tends to lose its luster after the tenth time.

It would have been nice, at least once, for someone to care enough to lie to me.

My parents never once showed up in court.

I told myself that was the kinder approach. Never get my hopes up, so they won't be crushed over time and leave me in a puddle of tears. I knew where they stood, and I made the best of my situation.

I knew my parents' names and many other details from a court file

I swiped from one of the attorneys. They didn't look like me, with flat expressions and swollen faces. For a few years, I thought the hospital had made some horrible mistake.

The older I got, the more I understood how that was only a fantasy. My mother and I have the same curly, thick hair and wide-set eyes. I'm freckled like my father. Tall like him, too.

The foster system spits out kids with different stories every day, and even if you're placed with your biological family, you are at the mercy of luck. In my case, some homes were good, and some not so much, but in all of them, I learned something.

I've stayed in places with libraries and spent weekends reading from sunup to sundown. There was a farm once where I got kicked by a horse, but I also learned how to milk a cow and butcher rabbits. I can make bread from scratch, tell you which plants you can eat and which can kill, and when times are dire, pick a lock.

It's not something I thought I would use, but when one of my foster brothers insisted I learn, I couldn't tell him, "No thanks." He was so adamant, and it didn't take me long to figure out why.

Foster parents tend to lock up food and medicine. I had one who refused to let us use feminine hygiene products and told us to just grab a rag and wash it.

Sometimes, when a house was asleep, and someone desperately needed something, I'd find the tools necessary and take action. I never took anything extra, and never for myself. Just enough to get by, and not too much to be noticed.

Today, I'll dust off my skills and do it again.

Something clangs to the floor, a sharp vibration echoing throughout the empty space, and I crane my neck to look around the room. A small rodent scurries along the wall, and I gag from the sight. Rats and roaches are unavoidable, but we've never become good roommates.

I turn to focus on the task at hand. Lockdown has happened twice before, and both times, it made things a little haywire. Our organization is spotty at best, but throw in a mountain of infected, and something gets forgotten.

With everyone either meeting with the council, off to gossip, or having sex, the food is not guarded. In the rush of everyone leaving and Lincoln's little outburst, no one thought about this station. Simon requested some of his goons to go with him now and didn't think about pulling them from this post.

With their youth comes a lack of patience and planning. Everything they do is reactionary instead of thinking ahead, but I may not have long. Who knows when someone realizes our most precious asset is left unattended?

My hands tremble, the nervous energy coursing through my limbs and shooting out from my fingers. I shake my hands a few times and will myself to calm down.

Breathe, Myra.

Pressing the thin metal into the keyhole, I close my eyes and feel for the gears. This thing barely qualifies for a locker room padlock, and it clicks open after a few tries. I exhale, my shoulders lowering from my ears while I listen. The scurrying rat is my only companion, and I turn the doorknob, sliding it open before pocketing my tools.

I can't take much time in here knowing Simon will yell at his underlings for maybe fifteen minutes before sending them back to work. Porter embarrassed him, but no one did anything to stop the drunk. He'll need to retaliate in some way and release his anger.

They need Porter to help with the infected issue and whatever comes up next, but they want Simon and others like him to feel like they're in power.

Dagg-nabbed if you do and dag-nabbed if you don't.

The door clicks behind me, and I zero in on the meal bars sealed in plastic tubs toward the back. Each one is almost three hundred calories, and they have the shelf life of a millennium.

Everything stored here was for emergency purposes in case there were tornadoes or floods, food to keep hundreds fed until federal aid came to help.

Well, someone did come, and we should help him.

We being me in this situation and help meaning theft.

I push down the pit of guilt in my stomach and carry on.

Counting in my head, I think about how much we would need to get through the next month. Hopefully, Cade will let me go with him, but I'm making a big assumption that we're leaving here as some dynamic duo.

He said "we" earlier, so I don't think it's unreasonable to ask if I can go.

With or without me, I pry open the containers and count the maximum amount I'm comfortable taking until I remember.

Dillon.

Cade's brother will need to eat, too. He went out on the river because they were running out of food.

Shame washes over me, but I do my best to ignore the nagging voice in my head telling me not to steal. It's against the rules, and I don't want anyone here going hungry, but if I leave, they never have to feed me again. That's bound to even out somehow, right?

Oh, fudge it.

I take another dozen bars. No one will notice for three or four days, and even then, they'll be rushing to pack everything before the big boom. Eyeing a cloth tote hanging on the wall, I consider how I'll get this out of here. A bag won't do. Anyone seeing me carrying it will ask what I've got. It's not like anyone can go shopping down here, and we're all so nosy and a little bored.

I'll need to improvise.

A few fit inside my bra, and the thighs of my pants are snug enough once they're shoved down there. Bobbi's oversized shirt covers my waistband and further down my legs, where I line up our food and make myself a walking snack cart.

When I'm back in the cafeteria, the padlock secured behind me and still not a person in sight, I finally breathe. Stars form in my eyes, and I have to feel along the wall before exiting. The stress I've put upon myself for raiding the pantry almost takes me out.

"Are you alright?" Bobbi asks.

"Cheese and crackers, woman!" I shriek.

She's only a few steps away and came out of nowhere. I run a mental inventory of where I've stuffed forty protein bars, some of which are probably melting against my backside.

Can she hear the crinkling sounds of betrayal?

"Yessss," I drag out the word so it's more of a question. "I hit my head."

"So I've heard."

Her eyes cast over her stolen Nirvana shirt that hides my deceit.

"I'll return the shirt," I promise. "I didn't want to—"

She raises a hand to stop me, and I'm grateful because if I keep rambling, I'll mention how there is a peanut butter whey bar tucked between my cleavage.

"You look weird today. Weirder than normal."

"Well, I, um. I hit my head," I repeat.

"Running into a door, I heard," she says.

"Yep. That is what happened."

I'm not lying, but she looks at me like I am. Bobbi still doesn't like me, and although I've never seen her with a gun, I wouldn't be surprised if they gave her a weapon. She is, or was, Lincoln's girlfriend.

"I'm sorry about Lincoln, too," I say, unable to help myself from apologizing all over this girl. "That was not okay."

She stiffens, clenching and unclenching her fists at her sides.

"Which part?" she asks.

"All… all the parts. The kissing part and clothing part."

"No. It wasn't okay, but," she stops herself, and I can only hope the end of that statement would have been to forgive me for the transgression. She must know I didn't kiss him or order her to declothe, but women can lose sight of the real villain, especially when we have feelings for him.

"What are you assigned to do anyway? Everyone has a job here, you know. We can't all frolic around as we like."

I can't frolic at all because there is a bar that may become a tampon if I clench too hard.

"I will get to it," I answer. "Sorry."

Bobbi turns to leave, and when I exhale, I feel a bar slide down my thigh. I lean against the wall to stop it from hitting the ground. She pauses, looks over her shoulder at me, and narrows her eyes.

"I hope you're done taking from me, Myra."

My stomach turns, and I hang my head, knowing I've taken more from her than she realizes.

"I am sorry," I mumble, but she doesn't stick around to listen.

Once she's out of my sight, I shuffle back to the classroom, doing my best to keep the sound of crinkling plastic at bay.

CHAPTER
FIFTEEN

"Are you hurt?"

Myra's walking with a limp, one foot dragging behind her as she enters our small space.

I jump up, pain slicing through my ribs, but I ignore it and reach for her. She closes the door behind her and rests her forehead on the metal while I look her over. When I graze my fingertips along her back and press onto her spine, she doesn't pull away.

I don't know if I'll be able to take my hands off of her.

"Does this hurt?" I ask as I make my way down to her hips.

I feel something hard, but before I can ask, it falls through her pant leg and down to the ground. I reach for the rectangular object when something else escapes her pants and slides across the floor.

Her clothes are raining treasures.

"Are those protein bars?" I ask, holding back a chuckle.

Her body relaxes, and a half dozen more slide onto the floor from unknown origins.

"Yes," she sighs.

She shakes her hips while I'm lucky enough to have my hands on them, and more appear.

My laugh escapes, relief that her awkward walk was nothing more than poorly-placed contraband. "Where all do you have those?"

I lift the back of her shirt as I joke, shaking it a few times to pry a few more loose. The sight of her bare skin sends a jolt of longing straight to my groin.

"You don't want to know," she answers.

I do want to know, and the thought of searching her body only makes the arousal I feel around her more difficult to ignore.

Bending over, she picks up the fallen food, tossing it on top of a desk one by one. More falls from her shirt, and I help collect the bounty.

She's got dozens of bars here, and my confusion grows as we stack them in a pile. What's the purpose of this? Am I some prisoner with rations? Do I get conjugal visits?

That might be okay.

A knot tightens in my stomach as my thoughts drift to Dillon. He's alone and scared, and I need to focus on getting back to my brother, not into Myra's pants.

"How long are you going to keep me in this room?" I ask.

"Not long," she answers.

"But the food?" I point to the tower of protein bars and raise an eyebrow.

"That's for us when we leave, which needs to be before they start burning the bloats," she explains. "Everyone is distracted and sloppy. I take back what I said earlier. Now's the time."

My heart thuds inside my chest. "We?"

"We need to get—"

She pauses, the realization of what she just said out loud stopping her mid-sentence. "I-I'll need to help you escape."

"Am I escaping, or are we escaping?" I press.

More silence, and I question if I assumed something that was never there. Maybe she means we are leaving this room, not this building. Or it could be just her and me until she kicks me out the back door and shoves me into a river teeming with bloats.

Could I be lucky enough for her to come with me?

"That's a lot of food for just me," I say. "It's maybe a day's walk back to our house."

"But you said you are out of food," she reminds me. "And there's Dillon. So you need enough to get there and feed him for a while."

I look over at the mountain of rations, and I can't imagine she took them only for me and Dillon. She's nice, but she's not irresponsible. "I don't think I can accept this. It's too much food from your people."

She hangs her head and fiddles with her hands. "Right," she says. "It's just that…" she trails off.

What have I got to lose? I try to think about what Dillon would do. He'd weigh the pros and cons, deciding what's best not just for him but for us. I tick through the facts of her life here, and what she's facing with this guy Lincoln.

The choice is clear.

"It would be wonderful if you could come with me," I say. "I think you would be safer in the long run. You don't know me, but I hope you can learn to trust me."

I always jump first and think later, but this time, I know the benefits outweigh the risks. That, and I can't let this opportunity pass me by. There's something about her kindness and the way she makes me feel that I'm not ready to give up.

Myra feels like home, and not the shitty place where Dillan and I are surviving right now.

The home of my memories.

She's frozen, the words weighing on her and keeping her still.

"If you have the time to get away for a few weeks. Maybe years if we live that long," I joke. "Check your schedule and let me know."

She raises her head and smiles. "That is a lot of food. I didn't realize how much I was shoving down my pantaloons."

"It would be wrong to give it all to me," I tell her. "And with your help, I have a better chance of getting back to Dillon."

"I don't know how true that is," she shrugs. "But I agree the right thing to do is to go with you so we don't waste. Food is a precious commodity."

I take a step toward her and lean down until our faces are only inches apart. "So it's decided, then."

She nods, and I know I should back away, but I like being this close to her, especially when she's smiling.

"Cade?"

"Yes, Myra."

"I sort of assumed I would go with you and didn't ask."

"There's no need. I'd love to have you with me anywhere," I blurt out. "And you know, when they discover all this is gone, it could get traced back to you. You don't strike me as a savvy thief."

"Oh, you'd be surprised. I've been stealing for quite some time."

My back straightens from surprise. "Naughty girl."

"It's not like that," she explains, her cheeks flushing.

I wait, giving her some time to respond. She grabs a chair from a desk and slides it over, ushering me to sit down. I'm stronger, but I'm not one hundred percent yet, so I ease myself into sitting and watch her do the same.

Her face is beginning to show shades of purple and green beneath the skin, and she must be sore from carrying me across the forest. I feel terrible about that, but my home will be more comfortable than the accommodations here. She will rest and recuperate once we make it out of this place.

"I would only take when it was life or death," she says. "Which, come to think of it, happened a lot."

"The past few months have been a little rough," I agree.

She waves her hand and shakes her head. "Oh, no. I mean, when I was growing up. I'm a foster kid, and I bounced around a lot. Some places were really great, but others didn't give us what we needed sometimes."

"Like food?" I ask.

"Like everything. Food, medicine, tampons. Anything that costs money. Some families spent every penny they got from the state on the kids and more, buying clothes and doing little outings around town. Others were more… frugal." She swallows hard, and I clench my fists, anticipating what's coming. "They may have had some bad apples and got burned. They would assume a kid was lying if they said they were hungry or sick, and in response, they would lock everything up."

"The food?" I ask. "They would padlock the fridge?" I'm joking, but when I see her face doesn't move, her eyes staring blankly into mine, I realize my dark humor was right.

"Oh, wow. I'm so sorry. That's terrible."

She shrugs. "It wasn't all bad, but there was a kid whose name I can't remember. Goodness, I'm bad with names." She squints, looking up at the ceiling, but nothing comes to her. "Anyway, he taught me how to pick locks, and a few months later, when my foster sister needed Tylenol for a fever, it came in handy. Then I just sort of…" She trails off, rubbing the back of her neck, her eyes avoiding mine. "I mean, if someone needs something, who am I to say no? Especially when I can do math and tell the foster parents are pocketing some of the check."

"So you would pick locks and get the kids what they needed."

"I know it wasn't right."

"Oh, I disagree," I argue. "I think you were most certainly in the right. You should have put some eye drops in their coffee creamer and Miralax in their drinks while you were looting."

Myra nods and giggles, wincing a little from the pain in her face. "One house wouldn't give us pads. She told us to use our shirts and wash them in the tub. But another house gave me a gift card for five hundred dollars when I left, just in case I ever needed anything. It wasn't ever consistent, but I promise, they weren't all bad."

I silently hope that the generous family made it through this apocalyptic nightmare. We need good people like that in what's left of the world.

"I made the best of it wherever I went," she sighs. "But yes, I stole what other kids needed if I felt it was the right thing to do. I have a lot of mixed feelings about that."

"You are kind of a badass," I tell her, meaning every word. "And then you became a teacher. Myra, I'm so glad I met you."

"I'm not special," she argues. "I may do a few things behind the scenes, help where I can, but I haven't done anything about them blowing up this place."

"I'm sorry, what?"

She's mentioned setting fire to things, but never a full-scale bombing. My head spins, the implications of what she's suggesting not computing in my mind. "What's getting blown up?"

"All of it," she answers. "That's another reason we should leave. They are kinda sorta blowing up the dam after they take care of the little infected problem, which honestly is not a problem because they are dead. But anyway, there's a plan to blow this place to bits."

"W-why?" I stutter. The science of the thing boggles the mind, and I try to think what this would do to the state. Ten years ago, they had to do repairs here, and the news said that if the dam burst, it would flood all the way to Nashville. Would our house be safe? We're upstream, but I'm not as smart as Dillon and can't be sure.

"It will flood everything for hundreds of miles, taking out the bloats along the way," she answers. "Everyone's hungry, but too scared to go out and find food. Their idea clearly takes care of the bloat problem."

"Is it that bad out there?" I ask.

I imagine that view high in the sky shows them how dangerous the world has become, and dammit, Dillon had better be holed up in that basement when I return. I swear, if he's out searching for me, there'll be hell to pay.

"I think some worries were created in their mind, but they're right that bloats don't float," she says. "I guess they do a little from what we saw yesterday, but they can't swim. Releasing the river water will kill everything in its path."

"Everyone," I correct her.

She bites her lips and raises her hands to her hips.

"There are people alive out there," I say. "It won't only kill bloats."

Her face falls, and I watch as tears fill her eyes. "I tried…" she trails off. "I did try to tell them that. When we saw you, I thought they would understand."

I understand that the world isn't full of bleeding hearts when starving people are trying not to become zombies, but the level of destruction from this would be immeasurable. The devastation would far outweigh the benefit.

"How do we stop it?" I ask.

I don't know why I say that, but there's a sick feeling in my gut with this news. A gnawing eats at me that we can't let them do this. I can't fathom how to blow up a dam, but I know people will get hurt in the process. They won't stand a chance, and after everything they've been through, it's cruel for them to lose their lives that way.

What I expect to be an argument becomes the opposite.

"Really?" she says. "You think we could stop them?"

The truth is, I have no idea what we could or couldn't do, but the world is hard enough these days. Anyone surviving out there doesn't deserve to be hit with a catastrophic flood amid the everyday, impending threat of death.

Maybe I'm making another snap decision, but this one feels right.

I shrug, offering a smile. "We can try."

"Succeed or fail, we'll need to run afterward," she explains. "I'm the only one here against the bomb squad. They'll know any counterattack is me."

"We've already established you're coming with me," I tell her.

She smiles, and it's infectious, my lips curving up and beaming back at her. "Just giving you the opportunity to change your mind," she says.

"Not a chance, Myra." I reach for her, and her hand finds mine, trembling fingers slipping into my grasp. "You're with me now."

CHAPTER
SIXTEEN

Myra

We are definitely flirting.

It's been a while since I was all doe-eyed over a man, and longer since I knew one felt the same way. Maybe he isn't falling head over heels like me, but I've seen him in his underwear, and I can't help it.

We both tear open a protein bar and talk over some ideas. The best way to figure things out is if I give him a visual, and luckily, we're in a school room. It's like a craft store in here, and I've covered the floor with a large sheet of packing paper to draw out the layout of this place.

"Am I the shoe?" Cade asks.

I've thrown some old Monopoly pieces on the board to represent critical characters in the escape plan.

"No, Lincoln's the shoe. He stomps on people," I explain. "You don't even have shoes. You're the thimble."

We need to find him shoes before we leave.

"Doesn't the shoe represent travel? We're the ones leaving."

"Do you want to be the shoe, Cade? Is it that important?"

He sits cross-legged on the floor on the other side of the paper, his eyes fixed on the shoe. "No," he fibs. "Not at all."

"Were you the shoe growing up?" I ask.

"Maybe," he admits.

"Do you want to be—"

"It doesn't matter," he interrupts me. "What piece did you always play?"

"The iron," I sigh.

"And on this map, what piece are you?"

I clear my throat. "The iron."

He has a point.

"Okay, you should be the shoe. That makes sense."

Cade laughs, and I can't tell if he's attempting levity or truly has an obsession with the shoe. Either way, I switch the pieces.

"William is the thimble," I continue. "Porter is the T-Rex." I chuckle to myself with that, and Cade gives me a quizzical look.

"Who's Porter?" he asks.

"You'll know him when you see him. Just remember he's the T-Rex."

Cade gives me a quizzical look, but shrugs and accepts my answer.

"This place is not that big, which is good and bad," I continue. "We aren't far from the exits, but the chances of them being guarded are high. The chances that we will run into someone are higher."

There are only two levels to the building where we live and sleep. There's the walkway on top of the dam and exits near the base, but it's a lot of stairs to get to either spot. I shudder remembering us carrying Cade up all those flights, and I had William do most of the grunt work.

"There are two exits to get to the lower stairwells, here." I point to the doors that are an equal distance from us.

"What about this?" Cade asks.

"Those are stairwells to the roof. They may not be guarded, but the lookouts are always there. And given the bloat problem, I can guarantee some looky-loos will be joining them. That's no dice."

"And this?" Cade points to an exit on the second-floor hallway. I've marked it in red, which I thought clearly signified danger, but I suppose we are in dangerous territory already.

"This is an exit to the river, but it poses multiple problems."

Cade raises his eyebrows. "The river?"

I nod.

"You mean you open that door and jump like a high dive?" he asks.

"It's a little more complex than that. The door leads to a hallway that leads to a more giant and waterproof door that then leads to an opening that you could then, hypothetically, jump out of and into the water."

"The water full of bloats."

I roll a monopoly piece in my hand. It's a top hat, and I ponder who would fit that bill. "Come to think of it, that hallway may be full of bloats. I'm not sure how high they're stacked out there."

"No one would be at that exit, I bet."

"Because it's suicide," I say. "They may not have it guarded, but what are you gonna do? Go dive into a bloat hill and slide down the black sludge until you hit water."

"Hypothetically…"

"You're nuts."

Cade moves a few pieces around, and I watch as he uses a marker to complete the drawing I've described. There are people in the cafeteria and on the lookout wall. The meeting rooms are on a separate floor, but he fills them with green Monopoly houses representing people.

"What other areas would people be stationed at or loiter around?"

"Hallways, the bunk area, and these big storage closets."

Cade puts a few houses in those spots and places his palms flat on the paper, looking over the layout.

"Why would people be in the closets?" he asks with a smile because he already knows the answer.

"For sex." It's difficult to manage the words straight-faced. Visions of Cade and me half-naked and ravenous in a closet fill my mind.

"I'll add a few more houses then. People get horny when they think they're about to die."

I let out a slow, even breath and stare at the plans, hoping I can focus on what we need to accomplish, which unfortunately is not an orgasm.

I miss sex.

"Do you see any other options?" he asks. "Even if we get to these lower doors with no one seeing us, which looks unlikely, they'll have guards."

Shaking my head, I acknowledge that he's right.

"Would you be able to tell if that hallway is bloat-filled from above?"

The lookout gives a good view if you're on the far right or left side, and the opening would either be a dark rectangle in the wall or covered up.

"Yes," I concede. "But there's one major problem."

"I was in the water with these things, Myra. I'm not infected. Once they're dead, they can't transfer whatever this virus is to you."

"That's not it."

He sits back, his eyes moving from the map to me, and waits.

"I can't swim," I admit. "Like, at all. Stone level sinking. I cannot express to you how I can't even doggy paddle to keep myself above water."

There's silence, Cade bringing his hand to his mouth to think over the problem I've posed. This is where he should admit to himself that I'm a liability, and what's best is that he runs back to his brother, and leaves me here to rot or explode.

The idea makes my heart ache. I didn't realize until recently how desperately I've wanted to leave this place. We make the best of things, especially when there is no other choice, but these walls are a prison. Cade is freedom.

It took this stranger to jolt me awake and realize the truth, and now I'm about to tell him to leave me locked in here.

"Maybe you should go out that way," I offer. "I could help you, and then you get to your brother, and I come back here."

"No way," he argues.

"You could rescue me later," I offer. "What if I grow my hair really long and hang it over the side. I've heard of a chick that did that once."

I'm talking nonsense, and we both know it, but I'm grasping at straws, forcing him to realize I can't go with him.

"There must be life jackets in this place somewhere," Cade offers.

He's right, and I picture the dusty red cushions with black ties hanging along the walls of the sex closets.

"You're nodding," he goes on. "So there's our solution."

"You want me to strap some plastic cushions around my chest and jump onto a trampoline of bloats until I hit the murky waters below, when I cannot swim. I'll then hopefully bob to the shoreline."

"I'll be there to help you. We'll get to land together."

I look down at the drawing, waiting for another option to pop out at me, but there's nothing. Little houses and hotels scatter everywhere, and I place the T-Rex in the hallway right outside the exit door.

"Why did you move Porter?" Cade asks.

"He makes his alcohol in that hall, so he might be there checking on it."

"It's one guy. Not much of a threat."

"Right, especially if we slice his costume or something. He'd go bananas and go look for more duct tape."

"What?"

Cade's again giving me that confused look, and I raise my palm and shake my head. "Don't worry about it. The point is, I'm not worried about him much."

Cade slaps his thighs and nods. "So we have a plan?"

I clasp my waist and hold myself, my fingers digging into my sides. "Do we?"

"We do, Myra. We're getting out of here. We're going home."

His words carry a kindness he doesn't know, and I swallow the lump in my throat and smile.

I've had places to stay, apartments I rented, but I don't think I've ever truly had a home.

I can't wait to go.

CHAPTER
SEVENTEEN

Myra looks like she's on the verge of either crying or laughing. Her lip wobbles as she tries to smile.

"It's going to be okay," I tell her. It's a promise I have no right to make, but I want to reassure her and give her the confidence she needs to do this.

She rests her head in her hands, rubbing her temples. "Right. I'm just a little nervous. I don't do things like this."

"No one will get hurt," I promise. "You're leaving to help yourself."

"That's the thing," she says. She raises her head, tears forming in her eyes. "I've spent my entire life leaving, but never by choice. I'm not someone who gives up on people. I don't throw them away like trash."

"That's not what you're doing."

"I care about the people in here," she insists. "I don't want to just cut them loose. What will happen to everyone without me here?"

She's crying between ragged breaths, steady streams of tears falling down her slightly bruised cheeks.

I pull her into my arms, not hesitating to think, but this isn't something I need to analyze. Even Dillon would agree that when a beautiful woman is crying, you don't gawk at her without moving. Comforting her is the least I can do.

"If you don't want to leave, you don't have to, but I don't think anyone would be angry at you for it."

She continues to cry, her tears wetting my shirt while her shoulders shake. Standing this way, she steadies me somehow. Her body folded into mine, grounding me and making me stronger, feels right.

"I could stay here like a pet," I offer. "You've provided enough energy bars for a month. Would you visit?"

Her tears have slowed, and I feel her pull her head up to look at me. I meet her gaze and smile.

"You can't leave Dillon," she says.

"I won't ever be able to leave you like this. Your face all busted up and crying."

The truth is, I can't leave her in any condition. She's a part of me somehow, and going on without her isn't an option anymore.

"I've decided," she says. "And the truth is, I'm so happy, but also sad. Does that make sense?"

She reaches up to cover her face, and I hold her wrists in place. Her watery eyes stare into mine, and I lean forward until my lips scarcely touch hers. It's a soft kiss, too gentle to count for some, but it's everything to me.

She moves her mouth against mine for a second more before pulling away, and I resist the urge to keep kissing her, fearful the bruising on her face would cause pain instead of pleasure.

"I know exactly what that's like," I say. "But for once, do what's best for you. We can do this."

"I'm sorry." Her eyes search mine, and I'm unsure why she's sorry. My heart thuds with worry that she regrets kissing me. Did I misread the signs?

"I just want everyone to be okay," she answers my silent question. "I don't feel deserving somehow."

"You are," I choke out. "They have to find their own way, but we'll do what we can to help."

She's silent, her eyes drifting past me while she thinks. "No. You're right. I'm not safe here, so it's not a choice anyway."

"Is there someone you want to come with us?"

"No. I guess not," she says. "I don't have a best friend or anything, but I'm the elder here. They're a mess of teens, and I guarantee some of those girls are pregnant."

Her cheek presses against my chest, and I wrap my arms around her. She must hear the rapid thudding of my heart, but she doesn't pull away.

"They're not your responsibility, and neither am I. But I'll take care of you."

"Dillon's your responsibility," she says. "And I got him all those protein bars. We can't waste them."

I reach up and run my hand down her braided hair. "Yes, you and Dillon are what matters." My voice is almost a whisper, but I know she heard me.

"So the plan is still a go for launch?" I ask.

"Yes, but tomorrow. I have to go to the bunk room tonight. They'll notice if I'm gone."

My jaw tightens. "Lincoln will notice."

She pulls back, and when her warmth escapes, I feel a piece of me leave with her. I'm unsteady on my feet again, and I have to put my hand against the wall to stay upright.

"It's a rule here," she says and takes another step back. "I'm really sorry about all the crying. I promise I'm not always like this."

"Don't ever apologize for tears," I tell her. "They're always safe with me."

"I've never left a place," she says. "I sort of grow where I'm planted before I'm plucked from the ground, so making this choice, it's new to me."

The words fall like weights from her lips, each one crashing to the ground. Something in the air lightens when she says them, and everything clicks into place. A foster kid yanked from house to house, never getting a say in where she lives.

"Well, starting now, you're not staying anywhere if it's not what's best for you," I tell her.

"Tomorrow," she corrects me. "We can't do anything until tomorrow."

I give her a little salute, and she turns around in a circle, examining the room. There's a blanket I've been sleeping on, and she finds a tattered sweatshirt and folds it so it resembles a pillow.

The announcement for lockdown reverberates from the hallway outside, and I know she needs to leave.

"You better make yourself seen." It's obvious how deflated my words sound, but I can't feel good about her leaving again, especially with this Lincoln guy out there.

We hug once more, and I kiss the top of her head. She doesn't look up and offer her lips again, and I wonder if I imagined the kiss. I'm sleep-deprived and down a few liters of blood, so a vivid fantasy isn't out of the question.

She tears herself away and heads toward the door with me at her heels. Her hand reaches back, and I grab it, pulling her back against my chest. We stay there for a moment, my arms wrapped around her, while her other hand reaches for the exit.

"I'll come back to you," she says.

I release her, believing that the sadness in her voice means I didn't imagine our kiss. It was real, and so is the fact that I'm alone with a dirty blanket and a stranger's clothes once the door clicks closed.

I make my way to the floor, bunching the blanket as best I can to get some sleep. Shoving the hoodie under my head, I let my eyes drift closed, but my mind won't relax. I should be thinking about the plan to stop the explosion, leave here, and find Dillon.

He's got to be scared, and with every passing minute, chances increase that he might come looking for me.

Except all my thoughts are about Myra.

The way she felt in my arms, her soft lips against mine, and how, when I held her, everything else went away. A part of me wonders if I died on the river and all of this is some sort of afterlife. The steady pulse of pain coming from my arm tells me this is real.

After the infected took over, I didn't think much could surprise me. No one can imagine the end of the world. Not truly. We turn it into movies and books, think about the possibility as entertainment, but never believe it's possible.

Halloween took us all by surprise. All trick and no treat.

That was until I met Myra.

She's the last thing on my mind when my eyes grow heavy and my body stills. Her face is all I see when I drift off to sleep, and a part of me knows that won't change until I take my last breath.

CHAPTER
EIGHTEEN

"Myra, wake up."

A whisper grazes my ear, snapping me awake, and before I can react, a hand seals over my mouth, pressing me into silence. I claw at someone's wrist, my eyes darting around the pitch black room.

Someone pulls me from my mattress, and it takes me a moment to realize I'm in the bunk room, and not with Cade. People form lumps beneath their blankets, silent and still, broken only by soft snores and heavy breathing. I put up a small fight, kicking a few times before I realize it's William who is hissing in my ear for me to stop.

Once he senses I've settled, and I manage to signal in awkward mime that I won't scream, his grip loosens. He catches my hand, hauls me to my feet, and tugs me toward the exit.

We don't make it far.

Footsteps echo, accompanied by the low buzz of Porter's costume. We dart to the far wall, sinking into the shadows behind a cabinet. I'm fairly sure we haven't been spotted, but William's hand clamps over my mouth again, a firm reminder to keep quiet.

Hushed voices carry over the costume's fan as Porter leads a group of people further inside. I can't understand what they're saying, but

Bobbi is with them. I catch the edge of her sharp tone, and she sounds less cheerful than usual. Probably because I'm sleeping in her favorite T-shirt and made out with her boyfriend. She isn't having a great week.

"That one," she says, uncrossing her arms and pointing to a bed. She stomps around them as dark figures go to awaken the person. With the sound of Porter's motor revving occasionally, I can't hear who is talking, but William and I both hear the word "explosion," clear as a bell.

I tug at William's hand, silently pleading for a breath of air. When the group turns to leave, he lets go, and I fight the urge to gulp in oxygen too loudly.

They depart with another person added to the fold, and if others heard the exchange, they aren't acting like it.

I'm disoriented, my heart pounding rapidly after being asleep minutes earlier, and I grab onto the cabinet to steady myself. It makes a clang, and I freeze. William's eyes meet mine, and even in the dark, I see they're as large as saucers.

Porter's the last to go, amused by something and laughing to himself, seemingly unaffected by the noise. I assume he's drunk as always, and this time I'm grateful for his constant inebriation.

A few people dare to sit up in their bunks, disturbed by the interruption. They tilt their head in the direction of Porter's shuffling, the sway of his green tail waving until he's out of sight. After a minute, everyone settles back down, knowing there's no point in curiosity.

The door closest to us is locked, and it takes William what feels like years to get the deadbolt and chain unlocked. We slide out and ease it closed until both of us collapse in the empty hallway, heaving breaths and prickling with nervous sweat.

I sit on the ground and gesture to William to explain. "What?" I press a hand to my chest, each heavy thud of my heart pounding against my palm. "The heck, sir?"

"I'm sorry," William says. His eyes are wild, searching the hallway for anything or anyone.

"Oh, I think I peed my pants," I admit. "Oh, dagnabbit, these are Bobbi's pants, and she's already mad."

"How do you not know if you peed your pants?" William asks.

"Because sometimes just a little…" I trail off, not knowing how to explain this to a man. "You know what, it doesn't matter. What's going on?"

William runs his hands through his hair, the vein in his neck protruding and throbbing. He's more stressed than when Lincoln was up his tailpipe.

"You're not okay," I tell him.

"None of us is. I got you because they're doing the whole shebang in the morning, evacuating everyone at dawn," he explains.

"What!" There goes my slowing heart rate, along with the plan to stop this explosion. "That's not enough time. I have to get my man-burrito outta here."

He doesn't question my odd nickname but nods and lets me know that's only partly why he woke me up.

"They're going to sweep all the rooms in a few hours, pack up, and then tell everyone to go."

My heart jumps into my throat. "Oh shishkabob."

"Not great, I know," William says. "Especially because the rumor around is that I snuck out the other night."

"Why is that a rumor? Did someone see us, or you, when we left?"

"No, but I may have turned down Penny yesterday," William admits. "She's not taking it well."

Although it's William's decision who he wants to be with, his discernment couldn't have worse timing. Seems like Penny took her shot, hoping our secret would mean a guaranteed yes.

"Penny is very smart and pretty. I think she's nice too," I say.

"It's too late, M," William argues. "We've had the conversation. She's pissed, and she's talking. You gotta go and get rid of the evidence or I'll be tied to this mess."

By evidence, he means Cade, and I shudder. How am I going to get two hundred pounds of man meat out of here unnoticed?

Worse than that, I've failed. We were never sure we could stop them from blowing up the dam, but if it's going to happen within hours, we're out of time and out of a plan.

"You couldn't just spend some time with her?" I beg.

"I don't like girls, Myra," William hisses at me.

My mouth opens, but I don't say anything at first, taking far too long to understand what he means. "Oh, I get it." I rest my head on the wall and stare up at the ceiling. "That poses an issue for her love affair plans. Did you tell her that?"

"She didn't believe me," he says. "Thought it was an elaborate rejection."

I jerk my head toward him. "Well, that's sad. She shouldn't think so poorly of herself."

William's eyes widen. "Could you focus, M?"

"Yes. You're right. Mission one. Get Cade out of here."

I stand up and begin the journey to the school room with William on my heels.

"Do you know what they'll have unguarded?" I ask. "How did you find all this out?"

"I don't know all the details. I was spending time with Brian, and they needed him to get the explosions going. They're going around and grabbing everyone that's a part of it."

My curiosity piqued, I can't help but ask. "Spending what kind of time with Brian? Lovey-dovey time."

William groans and turns me around by the shoulder. "You need to be careful. Not everyone here is your friend."

"I know," I admit. "I'm realizing that."

"I'm assigned to lookout again," he explains. "I gotta go before they notice I'm gone. Please. Get that guy out of here."

I yank my shoulder back. "But about Brian. Is it serious? Is he the redhead who's always polite and well put-together? Very clean, considering we're not on a regular bathing schedule."

Without further explanation, William raises one hand in a goodbye, turns, and jogs away. I go my way, hoping I'll make my way back to Cade without incident. It's so silent that something ominous chokes at my throat. The vibration of the dam is almost palpable, reverberating through the thick walls and closing in on me with every step.

It's happened.

I've gone nutty in this place.

I'll pass the clinic on my way to Cade, so I decide to grab more supplies before we make our escape. It was always part of the plan, but now the clock is ticking faster than ever.

Summoning the strength to push through a few more dark hallways, pausing every five steps to listen for movement, I finally reach the clinic door. The overhead emergency lights hum, inviting me inside, and the clock reads just after two in the morning. Dawn isn't far away.

The place doesn't look boxed up, which I take as a good sign. Tiptoeing around, I grab anything I think we might need but that won't weigh us down. Some lidocaine cream, a suture kit, and an antibiotic I recognize but can't pronounce. It's a prescription bottle for a former employee, but in a pinch, it'll do the job.

My pockets are bursting when I hear the footsteps, my hand clutching the fridge's handle. For a moment, I consider diving inside, but at twenty-ten, I'm pretty sure my body doesn't bend like that anymore.

Two men side-step through, and I don't get a look at them before I crawl into a cabinet. I remember from my last visit that it was empty, and just big enough for me to squeeze into. Barely.

This poses an issue when they start packing, but one problem at a time is my motto.

I hear them jump up on the beds, the old springs creaking and moaning from the pressure. They're talking and laughing without a care in the world, droning on about nothing, and I wait, my cramped hiding space growing warm. It's dark, and I think I can taste the recirculated air while minutes creep by, feeling like hours.

I don't think I can take it anymore.

It's a miracle I've survived this long after the apocalypse. Twenty minutes stuck in a hutch and I'm about to lose my mind.

I crack open one of the doors, just enough to see them through the space. A rush of cool air hits my face, and it's heavenly.

The two haven't moved from the beds, both of them holding cups of what I guess is Porter's hooch by the volume of their laughter and slurring speech. This does not look like packing.

Neither of them notices me, and I open the door wider, checking to see if anything in the room has moved. It's the exact way I left it, but with two semi-drunk guys. They sound familiar, but I can't tell who they are without seeing their faces.

I have to get out before someone finds Cade, but there's no way to do it without being seen. Stuck in the middle of the clinic, I'd have to crawl out of this cabinet on all fours, completely exposed.

I'll have to wait them out.

Another fifteen minutes pass, and the only thing they do is drink more. Apparently, they brought a makeshift keg with them. I watch as they get a refill and pee in the sink. Why couldn't they use the bathroom so I could escape? Their actions are gross and inconvenient.

More waiting, my patience running thin, while my butt is falling asleep and my legs are covered in pins and needles. My thoughts drift to Cade. There's no way to know if someone's made it into the school area, and I'm too far away to hear if there's been a struggle.

All he wants to do is help his brother, and we shoot at him before we blow him up or worse. This is not how I wanted to start a relationship.

I close my eyes and think about that kiss. The soft and sweet way he tried not to hurt me, but still, those lips met mine with such angst, and butterflies fluttered in my stomach for an hour.

A thunderous belch interrupts my memory, and I cover my mouth trying not to breathe in the putrid air.

"Still waiting on Simon," one of them says. "Could be waiting a while."

"Smart to get everyone when they're exhausted," the other agrees. "But it won't be long now."

Adjusting myself so I don't lose a leg, I turn onto my side and crack the door open a little more.

"Do you feel bad?" one asks. He's leaning back on one arm, stretching out on the bed. It's Tyler, one of the older kids at twenty-one. I'm getting so much better at remembering names, but it's no time to celebrate.

Tyler brought alcohol to the party on Halloween night, and lots of the kids found him to be a likable guy. I've never had a problem with him, but when have I had a problem with anybody? He shouldn't have served alcohol to minors, but that frontal lobe still needs to form, so I forgave him.

"No, because I get to keep Lydia," the other one says. He turns to speak to Tyler, and I see that it's Pete or Paul or Patrick.

Definitely a P name.

He's not a fan favorite and touts himself as a tell-it-like-it-is person when, in actuality, he's just rude and usually wrong. Most people in here have a lot of opinions and not a lot of life experience to back them up, but Pete/Paul/Patrick can take it to another level.

"Keep?" Tyler asks. "Damn, Pete. You make her sound like an animal you brought home from the outside."

I knew it! Pete.

"She's lucky I'm picking her," Pete says.

"You want her because you can't have her. She's turned you down too many times. What happens when she gives up the pussy and you're bored?"

What in the H-E-double-hockey sticks are these two talking about? I lean forward, daring to be seen, but I need to hear. Something isn't right. Why aren't they packing up yet, and who sets off massive explosions drunk?

"I'll pass her around," Pete shrugs. "Let you all have a turn. You'd better keep someone. Who we gonna have, anyway? Bobbi? Shit, that's not doing anything for me."

Tyler slips off the bed and shuffles to the counter, filling his cup to the brim. He nods toward Pete in a silent offer, and Pete extends his cup for a refill.

"Bobbi's not staying," Tyler says.

Pete slaps his hand on his thigh and lets out a whoop. "No fucking way. Does she know that?"

Tyler hands him the cup, and he takes a few long swallows. They need to slow down, but maybe I'll get lucky and they'll pass out. "Fuck no," Tyler tells him. "She'd shoot Lincoln's ass if she knew."

"Why?" Pete asks. "Bobbi and Lincoln have been fuckin' and suckin' since we got here. I heard she does three-ways."

"Lincoln's fed up with her. He's got his eyes on Myra."

I nearly spill out of the cabinet, catching myself just in time to stay concealed.

"The old chick?"

Ouch.

I am not old by conventional standards, but I guess to them I'm ancient.

"I don't get to pick anyone," Tyler says. "Simon says I'm lucky I get to stay."

"You don't get a chick because Porter's getting two." Pete laughs at his revelation, but Tyler doesn't find it funny.

"Porter's not staying, either," Tyler deadpans.

Pete jumps off the bed, his drink splashing onto the floor. "Now you're just making shit up!"

Tyler nods. "He's getting loose lips. Told one of the chicks he's banging about the plan, and now she has to stay, which wasn't approved."

"That still doesn't make sense why you don't get a woman," Pete remarks. "Damn, poor Porter. He has no clue, or he'd blow this shit wide open."

Tyler shakes his head and almost slips on the spilled drink. "He's too drunk to know what's going on." He grabs a towel and throws it on the ground, using his foot to sop up the liquid.

"Do you think it's just an act to like… get girls? I heard he doesn't have enough food to make all that booze, but he offers what he's got to chicks he wants to sleep with. He just pretends to be all drunk and shit so he gets away with everything."

"Who cares," Tyler says. "He'll be dead in a week."

Pete cocks his head. "No one's killing anybody, right?"

"Nah, but you think they'll make it out there very long? Especially with all the noise from the explosion."

Tyler makes quotation marks with his fingers when he says, "Explosion."

I'm riddled with confusion, but catching on that something isn't right about tonight. They aren't going to blow this place up by the sound of it, but then what's going on with the early wake-up calls and the packing? I scan the room once more.

They aren't packing.

Leaning forward to hear, my foot hits a pipe under the cabinet, and it thrums louder than I thought possible. I ease the door shut, the latch giving a soft tap against the wood.

"What was that?" Tyler asks.

Pete shrugs him off. "Probably just a rat. They're everywhere. More hooch?"

My hands shake, and I think my heart stops for a solid thirty seconds.

"Dude, we can't drink all the reserves. Simon's gonna get so mad."

"No, he won't," Pete reassures him. "Once everyone's gone, we'll have more than we know what to do with. We haven't even touched those wine bottles back there. And we're celebrating, man."

I can't decide if I'm more furious about their scheming or the fact that there's wine and no one bothered to tell me. Where have they been hiding it? My mouth salivates thinking about a dark red cabernet.

"I don't feel much like celebrating," Tyler says. "Hey, I gotta go take a shit. Be back."

Tyler skips out of the room, and I sit in my dark cabinet, their words repeating over and over again in my mind.

What did they mean by keeping Lydia and by surviving out there? Then there's the explosion that isn't an explosion.

I gasp, throwing my hand over my mouth, and it all clicks into place.

They're deceiving everyone, staging a fake explosion to drive people out, leaving them to die outside while they barricade themselves in here with enough food for the chosen few.

Not me because I'm the new, but somehow the very old, plaything for Lincoln. This is their pitiful reasoning for solving the food problem.

Not to mention the rejection problem.

Despite the council being mostly men, the rest of this little civilization is two-to-one female. Whoever arranged the All Hallows' Eve festivities wanted lots of ladies, but that made the guys outnumbered. It also makes it easier for a girl to reject a boy, and they do it frequently.

They're changing the rules of the game by getting rid of all the players.

This is my moment to escape. If I know anything about all men, it's that they will take thirty minutes in the bathroom to poop. That gives me some time.

Pete's peeing in the sink again when I crawl out of my hiding space.

I'm upright, standing eye-to-eye with him before he has a chance to zip up.

CHAPTER
NINETEEN

Myra

Whap.

"I don't condone violence, sir, but you need to back up, or I'll do it again."

"Did you just hit me with a stethoscope?" Pete asks.

He holds one hand over his cheek where I've smacked him with the medical device, but I don't think it left a scratch.

"Back up!" I order.

"Whoa, Myra. I'm not going to hurt you. What's wrong? And where did you come from?"

"The cabinet," I answer.

Pete's eyes search the room, his face perplexed, until I tilt my head toward the open cabinet door.

His eyebrows lift. "Wow, you're bendy for an old bitch."

"Hey!" I retort and fling the stethoscope again.

He backs up, but it clips him on the ear.

"So you heard us talking?" he asks. "About what's happening this morning."

That's an impossible question to answer correctly, and I realize I should have spent a few more minutes coming up with a plan.

I step aside to block the exit, my knuckles still white around the stethoscope. Pete isn't afraid of me, and he doesn't view me as a threat. He's got one side of his mouth curved up in a smile, more curious than fearful about where this conversation leads.

"I heard some things," I admit, taking another step. Pete rocks back on his heels, and I find myself between the doorway and some storage. I could bolt, or work with what I've got. "Care to expand on this explosion business?" I do air quotes while still holding the stethoscope, my other hand furiously searching for a handle.

"How about we talk about how you're safe, and everything will be okay," Pete offers. "Lincoln's taking care of you. Did you hear that part?"

I'm trembling, my nerves getting the better of me, but I manage to crack open a drawer, fingertips diving inside, hoping for something better than plastic tubing.

"And what about everyone else?" I retort. "What about all the people that don't deserve this?"

"They'll have the same shot at life the rest of the world gets," Pete says. "And they got a head start staying here for a month. I thought you'd be happy. We aren't killing other survivors in a flood."

"No, just your friends, Pete. That's really mean." I frown, realizing I have not appropriately conveyed the cruelty. "That makes you a monster."

"I don't have friends here," he says. Something shifts in his eyes, a flicker that darkens his gaze as he looks me over. Threat or not, I'm in the way, and we are not friends.

My fingers graze over what feels like syringes, and I try my best to release a cap with one hand.

"Are you going to hurt me if I put this stethoscope down? Because Lincoln wouldn't want that!" I warn.

"Seriously, Myra," Pete smirks. "Do you think that would stop me if I wanted to hurt you?"

"Good point."

I lower the stethoscope and move both hands behind my back, popping the needle and plunger free. All I have between myself and a man twice my size is a small-gauge syringe.

"Why say you're going to blow this place up?" I ask. "It makes no sense."

"We were going to, but it can't work. When Porter had a lucid moment, which is rare, he ran the numbers. They can only make so many bombs, and even when they chain them up."

"Chain them up?" I ask, and take a step toward the door. Pete's inching closer to me, and I'll be in the hallway soon at this rate. "Why would they chain the bombs up?"

"So they blow each other up."

"A chain reaction, Pete. Is that what you mean?"

"Whatever," he groans. "Whatever Porter did with his fancy numbers and big brain, it doesn't work. They can't nuke the place, but everyone already thought they would, so..." He shrugs without finishing his thought.

"So, what?"

"Listen, don't worry. You're going to be safe and sound in here with everyone else."

I work the needle in my hand, positioning my thumb over the plunger.

"And Bobbi?" I ask.

"Bobbi hates you."

That's true.

"And you don't give a shit about her," Pete adds.

That is not true.

As mean as she can be sometimes, I don't hate Bobbi. No one comes to mind that I've ever hated. Even in the worst houses with people I thought were selfish, I never felt hate. People aren't born evil, and everyone has a story.

That empathy is why I'm struggling with plunging this needle into Pete's neck. My two weeks of nursing school before I discovered my inability to deal with vomit tell me this won't stop him, only slow him down if I'm lucky.

"Why can't we just stay here and send out some scouts for food?" I ask. "People will die out there. Maybe not everyone, but a lot of them. You've seen the McFyre sisters. They are barely surviving in here. They've asked to leave."

"They won't come back with anything. Not enough to feed us all," Pete argues. "And they're too stupid to survive out there."

"Pete! I can't believe you."

He glides forward, too fast for me to react, his face inches from mine. I hold the needle in my shaking hand, waiting until just the right moment.

"We need to go tell Lincoln that you know," he says. "Come on."

When he clasps my elbow, I don't jerk back, instead, I switch the needle to my other hand.

"Could we do it later?" I ask. "Please."

"Come on, M. Don't make me do this the hard way."

"You should wait for Tyler."

He shakes his head. "I'll holler through the door on the way out. Let's go."

"Pete."

"What, Myra. Stop being difficult. Ouch. What the Fuck?"

The needle sticks out from his side, and I'm pushing the plunger hard and fast.

"Bitch," he moans and jerks away from me. The needle falls to the floor, and he stares at it in disbelief.

"Pete, did you call me a bitch? That is not nice."

He leans to one side, his body swaying as his jaw goes slack. His feet stumble before he tumbles to the ground. I do my best to soften the fall, but his head bounces on the cement once.

"What in the world?" I say to myself. He's passed out cold, body limp and listless at my feet.

I stare at him, curious what was in that needle to cause such a fuss. He's still breathing, his brow covered in sweat beads while he lies in a tangle. Although my very limited medical knowledge can't diagnose this, it looks like he passed out.

There's not a lot of time to problem-solve. He's alive enough, and I'm guessing I don't have more than ten minutes before Tyler gets back from his poop.

Grabbing Pete by the ankles, I tug with all my might. Nothing happens, and my grip slips on his pant leg, sending me backwards.

"I need leverage," I mumble.

After wiping my hands down the front of my pants, I grab his ankles again, leaning back as if I'm sitting in a chair, and arch my back. By some miracle, he moves. The smooth cement floor helps as I drag him toward the closet. I'll have to stow him away, hoping Tyler thinks he walked off somewhere.

There's some grunting and sweating combined with loads of adrenaline, but I get him jammed in there and lock it from the outside. I know one thing for sure by the time it's finished.

I need to work out.

My lack of strength training over the years was always pitiful, but we are in an apocalypse. I need to get some muscles if I'm going to make it outside these walls.

I make my way over to the needle rolling on the floor and pick it up. There's a small part of me that worries I've injected him with zombie juice, and when I read the label, I'm more confused than ever.

Fluzone Quadrivalent.

The man passed out from a flu vaccine. I suppose we all have our Achilles heel. There's no more time to waste, and I throw the needle in the sink and rush out the door.

Tyler never appears, and I've never been so grateful that men can be gross.

CHAPTER TWENTY

Myra

"You gave him what?"

"A Quadrivalent Influenza shot," I say.

I'm back in the school room and wrapped in Cade's arms after telling him everything that's happened. All the while, Pete may have awoken and alerted Tyler or someone else about being whipped with a stethoscope and locked in the closet.

We need to get a new plan and fast.

"I have no idea what that is," Cade admits.

"I'm not completely sure, but I think it means it vaccinates you from more than one strain of the virus."

Cade chuckles, his chest vibrating against me.

"You gave him a flu shot?" he asks.

I nod, my cheek rubbing against his shirt. Cade's thumb runs along my cheek, and I examine his bandage, pulling away to get a better look at his arm. There's no more blood, and he's moving it well, so that's another win for the day.

"And the guy hit the deck?" Cade asks.

"Yes," I confirm. "Do you think he's okay? The internet would be so helpful right now. I think people can have bad reactions."

"He's probably just a sissy when it comes to needles," Cade assures me. "Let's go."

He heads for the door and turns the handle.

"Wait, stop! You can't just go barging out there."

Cade moves away from the door like it's on fire, stepping back and placing his hands on his hips. "You're right," he says. "Shit, I can't believe I almost went barreling out of here. We have to think and make a new plan."

Bouncing on my toes, I wring my hands and bite my lip. I've left us with no good options, but then again, neither did the council. That band of unruly teens is about to kill everybody.

"What's your plan?" I ask. "To get Pete or leave?"

Cade's eyebrows bunch together before he changes course and starts shoving protein bars into a bag.

"So leaving, then," I murmur. "I'd like to make sure Pete isn't dead before we run out of here."

He moves to the shelves, shoving things aside to look for supplies. We might need another satchel to carry our loot.

"Pete's fine, but we probably should talk to him," he says. "Go over it again. What were they talking about?"

I repeat the conversation I overheard almost verbatim, cringing when I get to the part about the chosen concubine and how I'm part of the plan. It's clear to both of us that it's a cowardly act to risk the lives of many so a few can survive.

"I can't believe they are doing this," I say. "Don't they have any loyalty?"

Cade secures our food on his back, shoving a few extra items into pockets. I worry about how he's feeling and whether he'll make it sprinting through this place, but adrenaline is on his side, keeping the pain at bay.

"It's every man for himself, Myra. They kick out ninety percent of the people, and they have food for months. It's math. And as far as women, well, we both know why they want to keep some of you around."

My brain won't stop serving up the cursed mental image of Leia in that infamous gold bikini, prisoner to Jabba the giant space slug. That alien does resemble a bloat, but I'm no Princess Leia.

"Ew," is my only response.

"As far as explosions," he says with a shrug. "It's smart to do that instead of just locking people out."

"But people will know the dam didn't burst," I counter.

"Not at first," he says. "You draw bloats here while people are outside. That will be chaotic. If they can get everyone far from the area, they'll assume some of your council died, or they'll die running away. There's a risk people could band together and try to break back in. They're minimizing those chances."

"The council is such a pack of jerks."

Cade offers me a consolatory glance. It doesn't compute in my brain that people would abandon friends like that. What's the point of thriving alone?

"I have a stronger word for them, but you may not like it," he says.

I may not like it, but I agree. Huffing to myself in frustration, I realize there's only one thing to do. The council may only think of themselves, but that doesn't change who I am. Just because inhuman beings outnumber us doesn't mean we have to lose our humanity.

"I really hope I didn't accidentally kill Pete," I worry.

"Even though he was about to kill everyone else?" Cade jokes.

"It's not that," I sigh. "It's because I'm pretty sure he has a key to the control room."

Cade tilts his head, confused.

"Where the intercom system is," I explain.

The smile on his lips gives me the go-ahead I need. Maybe we don't need to stop an explosion, but there's still work to be done.

Cade knows without asking what I'm thinking, and if it works, I leave with a clean conscience.

When we enter the clinic, Pete is banging on the closet door, and we're lucky the sound didn't carry through to the hallway. He's up and mad about it, but I need to get that key from him.

"I don't want to hurt him," I tell Cade. "There are more Flu shots. We could knock him out again."

"He'll be expecting a needle," Cade argues. "A needle that could easily break. We need to batter up."

Bang! Bang! Bang!

"Get me the fuck outta here, Myra," Pete screams. "I can hear you, bitch."

Cade bristles at Pete's words, but I understand where he's coming from. I'd be none too happy waking up from that nap if I were him.

"How sure are you that he has this key?" Cade asks.

"Ninety-nine percent," I say. "Maybe ninety-five."

"Is the intercom behind a steel door or wood?"

I grimace and then flinch from the pain of my bruised face. "Steel."

"Okay," Cade sighs. "Let's do this."

"Ninety at least," I mumble.

"Good enough for me," Cade says.

"You want to whack him?" I ask. "That's the plan?"

"Yes, and preferably with something stronger than a stethoscope."

"Hey! It worked."

Bang! Bang! Bang!

I'm guessing by the way the door shakes that Pete has resorted to plowing his body against the wood. It's good that he can't get a running start because he might get the thing down if he keeps up this pace.

"You'll be outta here like the rest of them," Pete warns. "After Lincoln finds out about this, you're gone."

Cade sighs and looks back at the clinic doorway. Lincoln's name reminds us both that there are foes not locked in closets. We need to be quick about this.

Pete doesn't know that I have zero intention of staying, so threatening to kick me out doesn't rattle me. If all goes well, no one is leaving this place except for Simon and his goons.

"Whatever we do, we need to hurry," I say with one eye on the hallway.

It's still the middle of the night, and most everyone to worry about is planning out mass murders, but time is running out.

Cade stands next to one of the medical beds and gives it a hard shake. He tugs at the hardware a few times until a metal bar pops free.

It's embarrassing how much his strength turns me on. I mean all that grunting and flexing – he's yanking the bed apart like Thor or some equally muscled Marvel superhero. This form of vandalism is hot.

After fiddling with the screws, the bar fully releases, and he twirls it a few times before taking a practice swing.

"Myra, open the door," he demands.

"Just… open the door and let out the beast like he's some gladiator running into the arena?"

Cade nods. "He's not a beast. Just a man."

"He's more like a boy. I think he's eighteen."

"Myra," Cade groans. "Open. The. Door."

I freeze, my mind telling me to let him out, but nerves take over, and before I know it, the hiccups start.

Cade lowers the bar, tapping it on the floor a few times and smacking his lips.

"Darling, Myra."

I swoon a little when he says darling. It's pathetic, but I can't help the butterflies collecting in my stomach.

Why is he so hot right now?

"Yes," I chirp, followed by a hiccup.

"You get hiccups when you're nervous?"

"Sometimes," I admit. "Hasn't happened in a while."

"I'm a little nervous, too, but do you have a better plan? If not, we need to get moving."

I shake my head, no, conceding, but stand frozen, hiccuping before him.

"Someone could come in here. They could announce that the explosion is happening," Cade continues. "There are a number of threats only seconds away, so if you don't mind."

He points the bar toward the door, and I nod and hiccup. Nothing since he washed up on my shore has been ideal, but for some unknown reason, I trust him.

"Should I count, *hiccup*, down?" I whisper.

"Myra, just open the door."

Cade assumes a batter position, shifting his weight from foot to foot and holding the bar high.

I turn the lock and swing it open just as Pete plows forward to try and break it down. He tumbles through the open doorframe, falling onto his right shoulder and skidding across the slick floor.

Cade holds the bar over Pete, who, upon seeing my backup, doesn't try to stand or fight back.

"Anti, *hiccup*, climactic," I mutter.

"Who the fuck are you?" Pete spits, hands held up in surrender.

"A lost kayaker," Cade responds. "Thank you for your hospitality."

CHAPTER
TWENTY-ONE

My hiccups are unfortunate, but they stop once Pete assumes the fetal position. He is just a kid, and a grown man is standing over him with a bar-bat.

I crouch down and dare to rest a hand on his shoulder. "Hey, Pete. Nobody has to get hurt, but I'm gonna need the key to the intercom room."

He shakes me off, muttering something about me being a bitch. Cade swings, whacking him in the kneecap and causing Pete to howl out in pain.

"Come on, Cade," I plead.

"Myra. He is part of a conspiracy to murder dozens of people." He raises the bat back up to position. "He has it coming."

"He's got a point, Pete," I say. "I'm disappointed in you."

"Is this some mom speech?" Pete grumbles. "This hurts me more than it hurts you, bullshit?"

Cade takes a fake swing for that comment, and Pete flinches, raising his hands to protect his face.

"As a matter of fact, it does hurt me, and as you can see by my face,

I've already been through it today," I snip. "Now, where is the key to the intercom system?"

"Why?"

"It doesn't matter why, asshole," Cade chimes in. "Give her the fucking key or I'll break your other kneecap."

"It's not broken, you kayaking dick."

Whap!

Cade's swing is so fast, I fall back on my bottom, startled. Pete screams out in agony, and I turn my attention to the door, sure someone can hear his cries.

"It's broken now."

Pete claws at the cement floor, drooling and wailing until Cade's boot is on his back.

"We don't have time for this," he says. "Check his pockets and get the key."

I stand, rushing over to the cabinet to find some lidocaine and one of the diabetic needles.

"What are you doing, Myra?" Cade grumbles.

I scurry back with the meds and a needle. "Just getting a little something for the pain," I sing-song.

"I'm gonna be sick," Pete whines.

"Myra, you have got to be kidding me," Cade argues. "He's a murderer. He's cruel."

"But I'm not," I say. "You made your point. We are getting the key, and he's in a lot of pain."

Maybe I'm not built for cold-blooded choices, but leaving someone to suffer feels wrong, no matter what they've done or plan to do. Pete pales and slumps, going limp before the needle even brushes his skin.

"You really can't handle needles, man," Cade huffs.

Pete's on the verge of passing out again, sweat slicking his skin as his head lolls from side to side while I search his clothes.

"See, the needle thing worked," I say.

"The bat worked. It's stronger than a stethoscope."

"Got it!" I say, ignoring his remark.

Securing the gold key in my pocket, I stare down at poor Pete.

"What do we do with him?" I ask. "He doesn't look good."

Pete turns his head to the side and vomits, which causes me to wretch in my mouth.

"Oh, I can't. I can't do puke," I gag and turn away, fanning my hands in my face. "Oh, gee, I need air."

There's a loud clang when Cade drops the bar-bat before he grabs Pete by his good leg and drags him back to the closet. He stops for a moment to remove his shoes, a wise choice since they look to be about the same size. This is our only option, I suppose.

"Why do I feel bad?" I ask as he locks him inside.

"Because you can't handle throw up," Cade answers.

"No, I mean, why do I feel guilty. We just broke his knee and injected him with medicine. Twice. We're like the mob."

Cade wraps an arm around my shoulders. "I don't think there's a post-apocalyptic mob."

I shrug. "Oh, well, that's a positive. Are you okay to get around? You did an awful lot of swinging with a bad arm."

He pulls back, his warmth slipping from my shoulders, and reality rushes in. We need to get out of here. It's a miracle the guerrilla warfare hasn't drawn attention.

"Things hurt," he admits. "But I'm too hyped up to let it stop me."

"It's going to get harder from here," I admit. "This might have been the easy part."

I don't realize my hand is reaching for his until his fingers lace into mine. If he didn't know I liked him when I invited myself to his house, it has to be obvious now.

Deciding not to leave it to chance, and considering the high probability that we'll die soon, I go for it.

"I'm into you," I blurt out. "And not just your body because you've been half-naked a lot."

Cade steps closer, his lips curving into a smile.

"I can't pinpoint why, exactly," I admit. "I've been secluded with teenagers for a while, and the male population has decreased quite a bit, but even if that wasn't a factor, I would still really... like you." I gulp, swallowing the lump in my throat.

"So, you think I have a nice body?" he jokes.

I bite my bottom lip and take a deep breath.

"I like you, too," Cade says. "And I can't explain why yet because I don't know you all that well. It's just a feeling."

"That's good," I exhale. "It's just, if we die."

"We won't."

"In case things go a little sideways," I say. My face has to be the oddest mix of black, blue, and bright red. "I just wanted to tell you."

He takes my other hand, holding it tight, and stares into my eyes. My instinct is to run away humiliated, but I keep my feet on the ground.

"I'm glad you did. I have a habit of not thinking things through, and I've been trying to do better."

My stomach sinks. The world's ending, and he wants to take it slow?

"But maybe trusting my gut is what's kept me alive, even before those bloats came around. I went out for food, and I'm leaving with fifty protein bars and a beautiful woman."

Sweet relief washes over me.

"What's your gut say about our plan to help everyone here?" I ask.

"That it's the right thing to do."

"Not a lot of people doing that these days," I sigh.

"But you do, and I'm not going to say no to you. Not about this. Maybe not about anything. I don't know. Something about you feels right."

His lips are on mine, soft and yearning, like before, but so much better. I press my mouth against his, ignoring the twinge of pain from my bruised face, letting the fluttering of my heart override any discomfort.

This could be our last kiss, and I'm going to make it count.

His hands snake around my waist, one finding its way underneath the Nirvana shirt I intend to return. The sensation of his skin against mine sends a rush of heat between my legs, and like the hussy I am, I wrap them both around his middle.

I climb this man like a tree without a single regret.

When his tongue massages mine, and I groan into his mouth, I decide the second we get out of here, I'm having wild woods sex with him. We're going to get naked outside and get dirt in places one should never have dirt. He's worth the inconvenient pine needles and tiny rocks digging into my back.

"We should stop," he rasps.

"Uh-huh," I agree and kiss him again. It's fierce and desperate, but I catch a glimpse of the clock hanging above our heads. It's after four in the morning, and dawn will be here soon.

"Okay, let's come back to this later," I say and place my feet back on the ground.

"I'll hold you to that," he grits out, adjusting himself before he turns.

Grabbing my hand, he pulls me along after him, but he doesn't know where he's going. I hurry ahead, still floating sky-high from that kiss. If we die, at least I had that phenomenal moment with a man who has his full frontal lobe.

We poke our heads into the hallway, finding nothing but emergency lights and the smell of mildew and dust. The intercom blares to life, and I almost jump out of my skin.

Everyone. Wake up. Emergency meeting in the mess hall. Bring your things.

"Well, shit," Cade says.

They could spin any number of lies to herd everyone into one spot in this building, and I guess it doesn't matter which they use. No one will question the council. They're hungry and trusting, and it's been too long since they've felt the grass beneath their feet.

"Someone's in the intercom room," I gasp. "They always repeat announcements a dozen times."

"Are you saying we could have just knocked on the door instead of breaking kneecaps?"

I shoot him a look and plaster myself against the wall as we scoot down the hallway. This one should remain clear if everyone is heading to the mess hall.

"There are only two people who are allowed in there," I tell Cade. "We had a fifty percent chance it would be locked up or empty."

"You can still knock and tell whoever is in there that Lincoln needs them," Cade says. "Then, when they leave, we can use the key to get back inside and make the announcement."

I nod, and so does Cade, and then we both stand there, still nodding.

I rock back on my heels, hyping myself up for the tasks ahead.

"Myra," Cade says.

"Yes. Don't worry. I'm ready."

"Myra, you have to lead the way. I don't know where we're going."

"Oh, right. This way." I almost trip over my feet rushing toward the offices. Doing my best game of charades, I signal that the door is around the next corner.

"We should be prepared if they ask questions," Cade says.

"I think it will be fine," I tell Cade. "It's not like we have cell phones around here. I really miss cell phones. Not that they were always good for me with social media, but it was so handy, and—"

"Myra," Cade cuts me off. "I need you to focus."

"Yes. I am focused and not delaying because I'm terrified."

Cade places his hands on my shoulders, and I feel his grip is weaker on one side. No matter what he says, I still feel guilty that he got shot.

"I'll be here the whole time," Cade says. "I won't leave you."

"That's not the part I'm most worried about," I admit. "It's when we leave together. It's the getting out bit."

There are three exits, but the closest one leads straight out to the river, or rather, down into the river. If we get cornered and forced to go out through the wall, I'll bounce off a mountain of bloats before I drown. It's awful, followed by tragic.

"We'll figure it out," he promises. "One step at a time."

"I know. Thank you for doing this." I turn to leave, but before I go, I have to ask. "You miss cell phones, too, right? It sounds vain, but I dream of them. Cell phones were great."

"That loss was tough," Cade agrees. "But there were harder ones."

His parents and possibly his brother. I feel like a selfish idiot.

"Sorry," I say.

"No, I didn't mean it like that. Everyone misses cell phones, and soda, and the internet. Now go get 'em. I'll be right here."

I march toward the office door where the intercom is held. It's more like a fancy closet with breakers and electrical equipment that I don't understand, but I need to get in there.

Rapping on the door a few times, I hear movement coming from the inside while my pulse skyrockets.

"What?" someone hollers through the door.

"Hey, um," I stutter.

I realize if Lincoln sent me to get this person, I should know their name. It's okay. I can think on my feet. Sure, I couldn't remember the name of every student in my class even after an entire school year, and I was sometimes surprised by who was walking at graduation because I'd been using the wrong name for close to a year, but I've got this.

"So, hello. Lincoln sent me. You need to go to the cafeteria."

"Now?"

"No, in three business days."

There's silence, and I may have missed the mark with that one. Not everyone understands sarcasm, especially if they are under the age of twenty.

"That was a joke," I say.

"Simon told me to stay here."

"Well, there's been a change, and you need to go." I count to ten, bouncing on my toes and hoping he's buying this story. "He'll get upset."

The door flies open, an angry-looking teenager a foot taller than me on the other side.

"Myra?"

"Yes, it's me. And you need to go. Lincoln needs you."

"I need to know why. I'm supposed to stay here," he reiterates. "All night."

He raises his eyebrows, his eyes casting over my body. I have to stretch my neck to speak to him, his frame looming over mine.

I feel the shadow of Cade around the corner, and I can't let him come out here and risk himself. He's been hurt enough by this group, and this guy, whose name I cannot for the life of me remember, is enormous.

There's no other option, so I take the risk.

"Some people found out about the plan," I say. "They are

demanding Simon let them stay here, and he needs your help because you're so..." I point to him, wagging my finger at his enormous height. "Sturdy."

"Shit," he says. In a swift motion, he grabs his bag and slams the door, locking it behind him and grabbing my arm to run with him.

Not a part of the plan!

Doing my best to fight against his hold, I beg him to wait. "I have to get things from the clinic."

He slows but doesn't stop. "Why?"

"Someone got hurt. I need to get them some lidocaine," I lie.

"Damn, this is bad. Fine. Be careful."

No-name giant man sprints down the hallway, and when I whip around, Cade is already fitting the key into the lock.

"Did you see how great I lied back there?" I whisper.

"You were fantastic," Cade agrees, and the door flies open.

We bolt inside, hoping we have enough time before they catch onto the rouse. For a large man, he sure ran fast.

"Do you know how to work this?" Cade asks.

"Yes!" One benefit of working at a school built in the seventies is that the equipment was never updated. This is the same wood panel, off-white system we used every day for morning announcements, and I flick it on, watching the buttons come to life.

I switch it off.

"Myra?"

"When we make a run for it, don't let me slow you down. You need to get to your brother."

"Not a chance."

"He's your brother. And I'm nobody to you. Think through this."

"No," Cade argues. "I will not think through this one. My gut is right. We're here, together, for a reason. You came and got me, and I'm not letting you go. Make the damn announcement."

The receiver feels cold in my hand, and I twist the wire around my finger.

"You're nodding," Cade says. "I take that as a yes."

He reaches over and presses the button, turning the intercom on, and moves it toward my lips.

I open my mouth to speak a few times before words escape.

"Do you want me to?" he whispers.

I lift one hand and push him back. This is something I have to do. No one will believe a stranger's voice. They'll think we've been infiltrated, but me, they'll trust me.

It's not only that. I've always focused on being polite and sort of invisible, and it's never mattered much. This time, it's taking lives, and I need to make that right.

"Hey, everyone. It's me, Myra."

Cade steps over to the door and cracks it open.

"I think most everyone here knows me," I continue. Cade gives me a thumbs-up. The message is getting through, which means we have only a minute or two before that lumberjack and the rest of the council get back here.

"The thing is, when the bloats, um, er, the infected killed everyone, I went into this protective mode with you all, trying to keep you alive. I'm a little older. Well, a decade older, and I've learned that a person can survive almost anything, but when you're young, it doesn't seem that way."

Cade signals I need to get on with it, and he's right, but if I just scream for them to run, they may not do it.

"I love to help people, and I'm not going to stop today even if it gets me killed. It doesn't seem like it now, but you have your whole lives ahead of you. It may be full of running from these creatures, but you can endure hard things. I promise."

Cade's smile fades as the sound of footsteps thunders from somewhere down the hall. We don't have a lot of time.

"Simon, Lincoln, and the rest of the council aren't blowing up the dam. They're getting you all to evacuate and then faking some explosions so you run. The council is staying here. It's being faked so that they can lock you out."

Cade is pulling me out of my chair, but I'm still clutching the intercom receiver.

"They got the message. We have to go," he pleads. "Now."

"You have to fight back," I beg them. "Do not believe the lies. I know they have guns, but you can fight. Try to stay alive together."

"Now, Myra. You told them, and we have to go."

"Oh, and Bobbi," I say into the intercom. "I know I'm wearing your Nirvana shirt, and I'll try to get it back to you."

The cord stretches as Cade drags me to the doorway until the microphone springs from my hand.

"Do you think they'll listen?"

"Somebody did," Cade says as he points to the three boys sprinting toward us.

"Oh, Nelly," I scream as I run alongside him.

"You have to lead us to the closest exit," Cade says. "Wherever that is."

I groan, knowing the one less than a minute away might kill us even if we make it there. We turn a corner, and I don't dare look back, sure the group is right on our heels.

The sound of my heartbeat thuds in my ears, my blood rushing and making my head fill with a steady buzz. Pure panic pushes me forward, my legs numb while my arms pump back and forth. Every limb feels disjointed, as if it's not me running but some Olympian version of myself.

"Hey bitch," someone yells from behind us. "Who's that asshole?"

Not very original insults, and I don't have the lung capacity to respond.

They're close, and I'm guessing they don't recognize Cade, thinking he's someone who lives here.

We skid around the last corner, and the first door to the outside is within sight.

"There," I gasp, breathless. Cade picks up his pace, seizing me with his good arm and dragging me along. We slam into the steel door, yanking on the handle, but it doesn't budge.

"The alarm," I get out. "Emergency." I cough and catch my breath. "Exit. Emergency Exit."

Cade pulls on the red lever, the hallway brightening with red light and a blaring siren.

My head yanks back, someone pulling my hair and flinging me to the ground just as the door whooshes open. Cade swings around and throws a punch. Even with a bullet hole in that arm, there's a crack, and the kid's face slams into the wall.

He pushes off the brick and comes out swinging just as I scramble to my feet and jump on the kid's back. Someone else enters the fight, punching Cade in the stomach. He hits his knees, and I'm sandwiched against the wall. The boy I'm piggybacking, Billy, I think, suffocates me with his body weight.

"You fucking cunt," he says. "You've ruined everything."

My lungs won't expand with air, and I claw at his neck, trying everything I can to get him to let me go. Cade's getting beaten next to our exit, but he's still fighting.

From the looks of things, he's losing.

We both are.

I fall to the ground, Billy releasing me, but I can't get to my feet. Gasping for air, I crawl toward Cade, who's gotten himself to standing.

Billy's large body falls to the ground between me and Cade, and I try to scream, but my throat is dry. A fire extinguisher slams onto his head, and he turns toward me, spitting out a tooth and groaning.

I'm yanked up by my elbow, unsteady on my feet, and using the wall for balance. White smoke shoots out, the fire extinguisher in Cade's hands, spraying over his assailant.

"Thanks, William," Cade says.

"William!" I cry out, or I think I do. It's more a gargle of coughs and half-words. "Thank you. You saved us."

"When I saw Simon's crew running from the mess hall, I knew what they were after," William says. "You need to go. Some are getting weapons."

"What about you?"

"I need to help the people here," William says.

"I can't just leave you," I argue.

Cade wraps an arm around my middle, pulling me toward the exit. "Dammit, Myra. If William has a girl he wants to fight for, let him."

In unison, both William and I announce, "I/He doesn't like girls."

"Whatever. Tell her she has to leave, William."

"They'll target you," William explains. "And they'll have guns. You don't stand a chance. Now, go."

Cade doesn't need to be told again as he pulls open the door to the outside, using his body weight to move the thick metal outward. William pushes me through, the rush of cold air slicing into my skin.

"Oh, one thing," I say. I rip off the Nirvana shirt and hand it to William. Standing there in my bra is odd, but not the weirdest thing to happen in the last twenty-four hours. "That's Bobbi's. Can you get it to her?"

William balls the shirt in one hand and shoves me all the way through the exit.

"Now I'm naked," I sigh.

"I'm not complaining," Cade says with a smirk. The weight of the door creates a loud thud as we're closed off from the danger inside.

"It's a little cold."

"It's going to get colder," Cade tells me, and the enormity of what we have to do hits me like a brick.

This hallway leads to a hole in the wall of the dam. When we reach the end, there's nothing but a drop to the river.

A river piled high with bloats in freezing water.

This might be a good time to remind Cade that I can't swim.

CHAPTER
TWENTY-TWO

Cade

"It's too far to jump," I say, unsure if that's good or bad news.

My voice echoes throughout the long hallway. River water might reach this high, but the surface is far too low today, a steep drop to death if we jump from here.

"Thank goodness," Myra sighs. "Because I don't think you understand how much I can't swim. I can't even doggie paddle."

I peer over the border of the rectangular opening in the dam wall, leaning through the open door so I can dangle outside.

"You're really getting over the edge there," she yells from behind me. "Might want to back up a bit."

"This is not good, Myra," I say. "We can't go back inside. We'll have to climb down the ladder system."

"System?" she yells back, her eyebrows raising.

She's staying away from the edge, and I wave my arm, urging her to come over.

"Get over here. Someone could come through the door and grab you."

She makes her way toward me, almost stepping toe-heel, slow and fearful.

"Are you afraid of heights?" I ask.

"Does that make a difference at this point?"

"Shit," I murmur to myself, and turn back toward the opening. Leaning past the rim, I reach out to the steel ladder and give it a shake. The good news is it doesn't snap loose and launch off the dam's wall, but it's rusty and poorly maintained.

I reach my hand out to Myra, who's resorted to clinging to the wall, pulling herself along with her palms. Wind whips her hair, and she's squinting her eyes closed, refusing to look at the water below.

"Just breathe," I tell her. "You can do this."

"How far up are we?" she asks.

"Does that make a difference at this point?" I ask, repeating her words back to her.

She makes it to the edge, clutching the wall with one hand as I hold her other wrist.

Bang. Bang. Bang.

We both cringe at the sound we knew would come. They're at the door. We don't have time to think about heights or drowning anymore.

"That didn't take long," Myra says. She cranes her neck down the hallway, and I turn her chin back toward me.

"Look at me. Don't worry about them. I want you to keep your eyes on me. I'll guide you to the ladder."

"You don't want me to look down?" she asks. "I guess that's smart."

"I'm not just a pretty face, you know," I joke.

She smiles, but it doesn't reach her eyes.

"We might die," she says. Before I can object, she places her palm over my lips and keeps talking. "But we saved a lot of people today."

I pull her hand down, kissing her lips and feeling her body relax. The banging continues, and we separate, but I refuse to look at the door. We have to keep going forward.

"You've done all you can to save them," I tell her. "Maybe one day we can come back. If they overthrow the council, it will be safer."

She shakes her head and dares to look through the door to nowhere.

"It doesn't matter anymore. I already decided I'm going with you," she affirms, pushing her shoulders back. She lets go of the wall and me, trembling a little but feigning strength. "So how do we get down this Chutes and Ladders nightmare?"

"You'll need to reach out and over to the right." I point to the ladder running vertically to the opening. "Grab a bar of the ladder with one hand and then place one foot on a rung. Once you feel secure, swing over with the other."

"I'll need to go first," she says.

"Whatever you need," I tell her. "You'll be safe."

"Right, but I would like you above me in case I plummet to my death. What if I took you down with me? I'll never forgive myself. I'd be dead, so I might not care, but still."

She doesn't move, and the banging on the door gets louder. They're breaking through the lock, and I'm thinking the coup isn't going well.

"But what if I'm too slow, and you die because I can't move fast enough?" she asks.

"Okay. Okay," I say, interrupting her. "I'm going."

Stepping in front of her, I whip myself onto the ladder and start to climb down. It's still dark, but the sunrise isn't far away. There's a haze on the dam's wall, lighter than the night, but there's no sun peeking through the trees yet.

I pause, waiting and hoping she gets the courage to follow me out. A fall from this high would kill us, even with the tower of bloats below. My stomach churns at the thought of them popping from our fall. I'm not sure how we'll get around the monsters, but one problem at a time.

"Please, Myra," I call out. My arm reaches out for her in case she loses her footing. "You can do it."

One small hand creeps out of the opening, sliding against the wall until it finds a rung of the ladder. She feels without looking and touches the bar, her fingers lacing around the metal. A foot follows, and then her face, looking upward toward the clouds.

"That's right, baby. Don't look down."

I hope that calling her baby doesn't throw her off and send her plummeting to the river, but she doesn't falter. She swings around, her other hand and foot making it to the ladder, and I exhale.

"I did it," she says, her voice shaking.

"Climb down," I order. "One rung at a time. You got this."

I keep my eyes on her, making sure I don't create too much distance between us. There are a few landings as we make our way down, and I'm hoping we get to one soon. Once she has her confidence, it should be smooth sailing toward the water.

Moving from rung to rung, her limbs shake, but she keeps going, one foot after the other.

"Hey, Myra," I say. "You're doing great, babe. Almost to the first landing."

She takes three more steps. "Are we almost there?" she asks.

We are very far from there, but telling her that won't help. I look down and eyeball the distance from the landing. "Twenty rungs until we get a break."

"That's a troubling answer," she replies. "Maybe if you call me babe some more, it will help."

"You noticed that, huh?" I ask.

"I'm into it. I've been calling you a man-burrito, so I'll need to come up with something better."

"Whatever you want, babe."

Damn, a burrito sounds so good right now.

I make it to the first landing, and I look upward, expecting to see some goons looking out from the opening or worse, making their way toward the ladder. There's no one, and I'm feeling lucky.

Then I look down.

There are two options, both horrible.

We'll need to continue scaling two more stretches of ladder before we get to the final landing. Then we have a choice to make.

Reaching for Myra, I take her by the hips and tell her to let go before placing her on the landing. She follows my gaze and sees it, too.

If we jump to the right, we plunge into cold water that's likely over a hundred feet deep. To the left are bloats, their expanded bodies oozing black slime and occasionally popping.

She puts her hands on her hips and groans. "This doesn't look good, burrito-boy."

"Don't worry, babe. I'll figure something out."

CHAPTER
TWENTY-THREE

Myra

I think we should kiss again.

The chances of dying are high. I'm not a mathematician, but it's grim by the looks of things. I don't want to die without being kissed by Cade once more.

We're both standing on a metal landing, the grates below our feet showing us the water below covered in bloats. The flow of water has pushed them away from one section, which would be a great place to jump when we make it down there.

Except I can't swim.

"Next ladder," Cade says. "Let's go."

My nerves have eased the tiniest bit, and by tiny, I mean minuscule. I open and close my fists, trying to stop my shaking hands, but when I grip onto the rungs, I tremble down to my bones. The cold isn't helping as the wind whips up and around our bodies and cuts into my skin.

This is not a great time to be topless.

I'm somewhat covered by a bra that is doing a poor job of hiding my hard nipples. I bet anyone within a hundred miles can spot these headlights, but I'm still glad Bobbi's getting her shirt back.

Cade's eyes never leave my body, and although I'm out of practice with seduction, I think he's okay with the apocalypse wardrobe. He might be into a Red Sonja bikini warrior thing. What man wouldn't enjoy that?

Except instead of red flowing hair, mine is dark, curly, and in a pile of knots. My bra is old, slightly too small, and missing an underwire on one side. Instead of a sword, I have protein bars and some expired antibiotics.

We make it down another stretch of the ladder and closer to the bloats. I wonder if Red Sonja can swim, but I remember she wears bikini armor. That chick would sink straight to the bottom.

Cade removes his shirt and hands it to me.

"I'm sorry," he says. "I should have given this to you back there."

"Oh, so you're *not* into the she devil with a sword?" I mumble to myself.

"Huh?"

I shake my head and wave him off. "No, we had a lot going on. Keep your shirt. It's cold."

"Myra, please," he insists. He pulls me by my wrists, my body pressing into his, and I sink into the warmth. The shirt slides over my head, and the fabric feels like it just came out of the dryer.

It doesn't smell like it, but it's not like we have a washing machine on hand, so I'll take the warmth.

I slide through one arm and then the other, the trembling of my body slowing, and then I'm face to face with his shirtless chest. That sends a rush of heat through every vein, pulsing and throbbing.

We should definitely kiss again.

"They certainly look dead. For undead, I mean," Cade says.

That's not an interlude to kissing, so I make my way to the next and final stretch of the ladder. It's a slow crawl down toward the dark water and bobbing bloats.

The sun has crested, and when I look up, the opening to the dam wall is a black box. No one looks out from the exit, which also means there aren't guns pointing down on us. I hope they overthrew the council, or at least came to their senses and refused to leave.

It's silent except for my heavy breathing and Cade asking me how I'm doing every sixty seconds. I'm not great, but that's because I've spent the past month doing zero cardio, which was not much different from my life before. If we survive, I'm training until I can do ten push-ups. It's my solemn vow.

We make it to the last landing, the ladder below dipping into the river, which is streaked with bloat blood. The rising sun reveals the dark lines cutting through the murky water. It's zombie soup down there, but the shore is too far to jump, and I'd do anything for something that floats.

Cade's kayak!

I point, my eyes wide. "You see it out there?" I ask. "Your boat."

"Technically not mine, but yes."

"But how do we?" My voice trails off.

He removes his shoes and climbs over the railing, his feet wedged between the bars as he faces me. "I'll be right back."

"But, wait," I object. "That's not fair. You swan diving into the abyss of the infected while I wait for a ride."

"You can't swim, and there might be a bloat over there packin'."

"Packing?" I ask. "Like a gun?"

"Like the virus that makes you a bloat," Cade says. He's not far off with the metaphor. Both can kill when pointed in your direction.

"It doesn't feel right," I say. "Making you swim out into the freezing water by yourself and then coming back to get me. Your arm has a bullet hole in it."

What I don't say, the words lodged like a stone in my throat, is how I can't bear being away from him. All my life, I've been surrounded by people, yet felt alone. With Cade, it's different. Even though he isn't going far, to someone who can't swim, he's an ocean away.

"It won't slow me down, and I'll be right back," Cade says. "You always came back for me. Trust that I'll come back for you."

I nod, my hands holding the railing until my knuckles turn white, accepting how we don't have any other choice.

"We should kiss," I say.

I expect him to ask if I hit my head today or why I waited until he was balancing off of a ledge to bring this up, but instead, all he says is, "Yes."

His lips are on mine, hot and harsh, full of desire and a promise of what's to come. It's so frantic I worry that he thinks he's diving to his death, and I wrap my arms around his shoulders and pull him against me.

The metal railing between us poses some discomfort, but I ignore how it digs into my stomach, hoping I can make this moment last a bit longer. My nails dig into his back, keeping him close, refusing to admit that in a few minutes, he's jumping into that infected cesspool to get me to safety.

The way he kisses me makes me wonder if this is what home is supposed to feel like. Warmth spreads through my limbs and into my heart, comfort wrapping around me like a memory I didn't know I missed.

We separate, both gasping for air, unable to keep kissing without taking a breath.

"I'll come back," he promises. Before I can register what's happening, he turns and dives into the water.

All I can do is look over the railing and hope he doesn't turn into a bloated monster.

Would I still be into him?

Nah.

I have boundaries, even if he is the last eligible man on earth.

One arm reaches above the water's surface, followed by his face, which turns to the side as he takes in a breath. Streaks of black slide down his skin, and it makes a shiver run down my spine.

He was in that water before. They have to be alive to turn you.

I remind myself of these facts, which have not been scientifically proven, but I believe them to be true. I've seen someone turn from the lookout, how the infected will hold a person, spreading some invisible energy inside them to cause the change. It takes action to spread, and I'm certain it can't pass on without a bloat making it happen.

Cade glides through the water, stroke after stroke, until the water over his shoulders runs clear. He's through the goop that's collected by the wall, and in a few minutes, he'll make it to the kayak, safe and healthy.

"He's going to be fine," I whisper to myself.

There's a low groan from my left, a steady gurgle and moan that I know all too well.

My stomach sinks when I realize I'm right.

They have to be alive to turn you, and one of them still is.

CHAPTER
TWENTY-FOUR

CADE

This water is foul beyond belief. I'm banking that my earlier theory, the one that believes just being soaked in their blood won't harm me, still holds true. We'll find out soon enough. Infection never takes long, at least from what I've seen.

The image of our neighbor Bill turning is still vivid in my mind. It's not something one forgets, even though I want that more than anything. I want to remember him rocking on his front porch with his Labradors, one black and one blonde, a can of cheap beer in his hand.

He would grow too many vegetables and bring them over, which my parents loved. As a kid, I hated his weekly delivery of peppers and okra because that meant I had to eat them, but the older I got, I realized it wasn't about overgrown gardens.

Bill wanted company. His wife died shortly after his boys went off to college, and dogs are great, but they don't talk back. After a hundred Sunday afternoons with Bill, fried okra, which isn't bad as far as vegetables go, and his dogs, I got used to our routine.

Halloween night, it all fell apart.

I watched bloats sprint toward Bill's house, dogs barking and sounding the alarm. I was halfway down the drive when I saw Dillon coming from the other side of ours. He tripped, and once he went down, it was like he couldn't find his footing again. The kid couldn't get a proper stride, and when I realized I couldn't save them both, I did what Bill would have wanted.

"Take care of your brother, always," he once told me. "Your siblings are the longest relationship you'll have in your life. You may spend more time with a wife, and your parents raise ya' and all, but brothers and sisters are there from beginning to end."

Watching Bill transform into something inhuman, black veins snaking under his skin, gray eyes staring at nothing, left me both thankful and afraid of the bond I shared with my brother. What if one day I found him suffering the same fate?

When my parents never came home that night, after the grief and sadness of realizing they were never coming home, I found myself grateful. I'll never see them that way, scared and suffering through some unimaginable terror. In my memory, they're the same as when they left that evening. My mom smiles with the bright red lipstick she wore only on date nights, and my dad, sitting behind the wheel of his giant truck, waves us goodbye.

It's as if that chapter of our life slammed shut, and I pulled a new book from the shelf. I can picture who we used to be, a family eating okra around the kitchen table, daring each other to leap into a cold river, but we'll never live that way again.

That's why falling for Myra comes so easily. I've seen how quickly everything can change because, in one heartbeat, the future I thought was solid vanished.

One reckless choice to go fishing altered everything again, and I should be more surprised, but nothing really shocks me anymore.

The kayak bobs in the water, hung up near the shoreline by some driftwood. It's a challenge to climb onto with only one good arm and sheer exhaustion weighing me down, but I manage it. The sun is up over the horizon, blinding my sight toward the east. It's beautiful out here, the water glittering in the dawn's light, that is, if you can ignore the heap of bloats stacked along the dam wall.

The mound of undead looks like they're swaying together, breathing in some way, but it's just the steady waves of the river pulling forward and back against their bodies. When one pops, a few fall down, and they roll and shift, readjusting the pile.

Standing on the kayak, I let out a sigh of relief, finding the oar bobbing in the water still attached by a rope. It's a stroke of luck, and I pull in the paddle, ready to get back to Myra.

A few more bloats burst, sending others slipping and tumbling into the water with splashes up ahead. Myra moves to the other side of the landing, her body as far away from the mountain of monsters as possible.

I can't blame her. The horde of infected is terrifying, whether they're undead or dead-dead.

The way she talks about things makes me chuckle, and there's a sudden ache to get to her and take her away from that place and all the dangers here.

She's staring at the mountain of bloats, her focus solely on them. Her feet press against the bars of the landing as she pushes herself up onto the ledge of the railing. It's foolish, knowing she can't swim, and I call out to her to get down, but she can't hear me.

I paddle, steady, deep strokes to move the kayak faster, all the while hoping she'll turn and look my way to see me coming. Waving doesn't work, and I lift the oar and swing it a few times in the air. It must be the position of the sun, blinding her view of me.

I let out a whistle, long and sharp, like my dad used to do when he would call Dillon and me to come inside. It works, her body jerking around. She frantically waves back at me, still awkwardly dangling over the railing.

Her response doesn't ease my worry, and I frantically paddle, the kayak rocking but holding steady. I look up toward the rectangular opening of the dam, and there's nothing. No one climbs down the ladders, and there's no one else on the water.

She points to the tower of bloats, but she's not saying anything.

"On my way," I yell. "Get down from the railing. You could fall."

She raises her finger to her lips, telling me to be silent. It makes no sense, and I scan the woods and the sides of the dam again, looking for someone or something rushing from the exit.

Still nothing.

I'm close, maybe a few minutes away if I don't fall out of this thing, but panic rises in my chest.

"What's wrong?" I call out. "Talk to me."

She climbs down, her feet hitting the landing, arms wildly directing me to look at the bloats.

A few of them tumble into the water, popping and sending a splash so high it hits the rungs by her legs.

I examine the decaying bodies, and it's unnerving how a few shift and slide. There's something off about the movement, too frequent to discount.

"Don't come over here!" Myra yells. "Run!"

CHAPTER
TWENTY-FIVE

Myra

Cade needs to turn around.

I hear them, groaning and moaning, their grotesque bodies sliding against each other and coming my way. My best shot is to get far enough ahead that they go under before they can reach me. I might drown in the process, but I'm a sitting duck on this landing.

I decide I'd rather die looking like a woman than the Michelin Man, that is, if he died and came back full of sewer water.

"Don't come over here!" I scream out. "Run!" Is it stupid to yell when I'm sure some living bloats are cascading in my direction?

Yes.

Do I care about that right now?

A little.

The mountain of infected heaves upward, almost taking a large breath in and out. I watch as a few of them crawl through the rubble, rising to the surface of bloat mountain.

"Oh, fuddruckers, they're in hyperdrive," I mumble to myself.

Were they hibernating? That's cheating!

"Stop right there and turn around!" I scream out to Cade, but he keeps paddling, and he's moving faster. "They are not dead-dead, do you hear me. They are un-dead. Kind of, sort of alive!"

Still, he continues to push forward, and from the look on his face, he knows what's happening.

A bloat climbs free from the pile, his body jerking around like a haunted marionette being operated by a drunk puppeteer. Its pudgy limbs, unlike the others, are less pronounced, as if it had been recently turned. The thing heaves itself from the pack, getting enough air to land past the base of bodies, and splats into the water. It's a little too close to the landing for my comfort, and I find myself climbing up on the railing, hoisting one leg over the side.

Time to go.

"Stay put, Myra," Cade calls out. "Almost there."

That's not comforting as another makes its way through the pile, this time hoisting itself toward Cade. It's larger and stronger, splashing so hard in the water, the kayak bobs, and Cade almost loses his footing.

"I'm coming," Cade repeats. "You're going to be okay."

A third one has its grey orbs that used to be eyes fixed on me, and it flings itself toward the landing, and by some horror, hooks a bloated limb to the edge of the railing.

I don't have a lot of regrets in life, not even coming here to keep a bunch of teenagers safe that fateful Halloween night or even stealing when my foster siblings needed something.

But if I could do one thing over, I would learn to swim.

Or at least checked if we could've snagged a life jacket before our grand escape.

There isn't time to think. Bloats drown, but I don't think it's instantaneous. They likely need time for water to enter what might be lungs, but who really knows, and suffocate them.

My best-case scenario is sinking at a more leisurely pace. Into the water I go, backwards no less, my body crashing into the river and taking my breath with it.

It's dark, the sun hidden behind streaks of dark bloat blood, and I'm instantly turned around. My arms and legs thrash, doing their best imitation of swimming in the icy depths. I imagine how Cade looked sliding across the water, his face cresting the surface for an easy breath as he pushed forward.

While my mind tells me to do a beautiful backstroke toward Cade's kayak, in reality, I'm a tornado underwater, spinning and flailing. The only direction I'm heading is down.

This is how I'll end after a month of living in that psycho nightmare dorm. All the nights sleeping in a room with dozens of smelly teens, eating cold food from a can, and putting up with drunk dinosaurs, and I drown steps away from the shore and a hottie.

It's not right.

I continue to sink, but instead of the frantic flailing of my arms, I still myself. What would an Olympic swimmer do? They would shoot their arms straight up, then kick as they sweep their arms wide, pressing down through the water. My lungs burn, desperate for air, but I ignore the panic and do as my brain tells me.

This is physics, not skill, I tell myself. I force myself to focus, and after a few tries, I see rays of light cut through the water. It's just enough to give me hope.

Again, I straighten my arms and, in sync with my legs, kick upward. It's less graceful with my body trembling from the oxygen running out, and the impending doom from bloats falling into the water isn't helping, but I try again.

This time, when my arms straighten above me, something touches my skin. I thrash, losing all my newfound swimming skills, but I'm too weak to fight.

A body dives into the water, and I go limp, an arm circling my waist and yanking me upward. The instinct to breathe takes over, and I feel liquid enter my lungs before we crest the surface.

Cade brushes the water from my face, and I force a smile between coughs, sputtering as I fight for air.

"You okay, babe?" Cade asks.

"N-no," I cough. River water laced with sludge has made its way into my lungs.

There is splashing not far from us, a clear sign we aren't out of the woods yet. Looking up, two more bloats stand on the mountain of bodies, and they hurl themselves from the top.

"The kayak!" I yell. "It's floating away and toward the monsters."

"We have to swim!" Cade shouts.

As if it's that easy. Has he forgotten who he's screaming at?

Without thinking, I attempt my frantic doggie paddle that keeps threatening to push me underwater. Black ooze pours over my face, blocking my vision. Cade's grip on me slips, and the crash of a bloat too close sends a wave that causes him to lose his grip. Back down I go, and while under the water, my eyes open.

I stare straight at a being that used to be a person. Its swollen body can't operate while submerged, but to be fair, neither can mine. Turning like a starfish, it looks at me with an open mouth, a small river of sludge pouring from its lips as it dies.

There's a humble effort to reach me, over-stuffed limbs trying but failing to touch my skin. Water is Kryptonite to the bloats, but the horrid truth is, it's mine as well.

Once more, Cade grabs me by my arm. I'm startled at first, but then I cling to him, both of us trying to keep hold in the slime-filled river. We surface, and when I look toward the infected, expecting to find more bombardiers heading our direction, there's nothing. A few float around us, their bodies motionless, rocking with the ripples of the river.

I'm dragged backward, Cade's ragged breaths and splashing strokes filling my ears as he hauls me toward the small boat. I try to swim, but I think I'm making it harder on him, and I let myself go limp until we bump against the kayak's side.

A wave of relief washes over me as he tells me to "Just hang on" until we reach the shore, and I feel dirt and rocks beneath my feet.

"It's okay. We're okay," he says.

He's covered in ooze, and I gag knowing I suffer the same fate. "We're going to turn," I panic. "There's no way we can't. Look at us. Walking viruses."

"No, we're not," he assures me. "That's not how it works."

We crawl, dirt sinking under my palms until I reach grass and tree roots, using them to hurl me forward until no part of me touches the water.

"How does it work exactly?" I ask.

His body rests next to mine, chest down, heavy breaths lifting and lowering his back. "Not like that," he repeats.

Neither of us knows, but I wipe my face in the grass, watching the black slime cover the green and gag.

I roll onto my back, watching my breath billow into the cold air. All the exertion has left me warm enough, but it's quickly fading. Cade has to be freezing, topless, and soaking wet.

"You still don't have shoes," I groan.

"Can't swim in shoes," he says. "You can't swim at all. Like, at all, Myra."

I'd smack him if I had the strength, but he's right and just saved my life, so I let him have that one.

"We need…" I pause, taking in a few more breaths, waiting for my pulse to slow. "A fire. Warmth."

Cade turns his head to look at me and reaches out, resting a palm on my stomach.

"We need…" He stops, and I look at him, curious if he disagrees. "To get the fucking kayak."

We both groan, but all our supplies are right there, drifting from the shoreline and bobbing back out to the river.

He rises, shakes his hands out a few times, and takes a few steps toward the shore.

"I could try," I offer.

He laughs, and I shrug.

"I will be right back," he says. "I mean it."

I lay back down, staring at the hazy sky. "How sure are we that the last of them are dead-dead-dead?"

"Ninety percent," he says, and I hear the sound of him walking back into the water, followed by the clunkiness of him throwing the kayak back ashore.

"We made it," I croak in disbelief.

The moment the words leave my mouth, the reality of our situation settles in. We're still miles from Cade's house, shivering in the cold, exposed and open.

This is far from over.

CHAPTER
TWENTY-SIX

Myra

Tips for surviving the apocalypse.

Learn survivalist skills.

Build an underground bunker and fill it with canned goods.

Become an expert at jujitsu.

Take swimming lessons.

Be nice?

I'm daydreaming, wondering how I got here. Not only physically here, sitting on a patch of dirt amongst pine trees and a million creepy crawly bugs, but alive in general.

Cade's definitely got a knack for this. He's collecting kindling, using the position of the sun to determine direction, and doesn't appear cold or hungry. He can swim. Huge plus for that man.

It's been a minute since my feet touched grass, and I'm trying to make the best of it, but my brain can't fathom how I got here. I'm not special or strong, and I'm not a master manipulator like some residents of my former home.

Running my fingers through my hair, I do my best to detangle the mess. It hurts because not only am I unable to start a fire, fight bloats, or float, but I am also tender-headed.

"What's with the frown?" Cade asks.

"I want to contribute," I reply.

"To the fire?"

"To the living stuff."

His eyebrows knit together as a spark ignites inside the tiny pieces of wood. "You seem very alive to me."

"What can I do to help us stay that way?"

I get up, wipe my hands on my equally dirty pants, groan, and then collect a few pieces of wood around me. They look dry, and Cade takes them, arranging them around our fresh flame. Its warmth radiates over my limbs, and I smile, closing my eyes and enjoying the feeling.

"We're both just going to take things day by day," he says. "I plan to eat and rest a bit. Gather our strength and take it slow back to the house. If we're too tired, we won't be alert enough to know what's around us."

I'm relieved to hear a plan, but scared of being out here for a night. If a group of bloats spots us, we're done. The council is another uncertainty. We aren't sure what happened back there, and they have all the guns.

"What if a group of bloats comes through?" I ask. "I don't know jujitsu."

Cade laughs and shakes his head. "Sometimes I don't know what you're talking about, and I kind of like it."

I shrug and take a seat by the fire, pulling my knees to my chest and listening to the sounds of the night. We've made camp just past the tree line, hidden enough from the dam but not too close to some of the houses.

"What was it really like in there?" he asks. "In the research facility. You seem a bit anxious about surviving outside of it."

It's true, the building gave a false sense of security. Like a shut door, it's easier to pretend that the lock keeps the bad guys at bay.

"I stood out," I admit. "The only adult over twenty-five. The only one not thinking about who to have sex with every five minutes."

Why did I bring up sex?

"Did anyone try to have sex with you?"

"If you mean Lincoln, that didn't get weird until the end. Maybe he had run through all the other girls in there."

I feel flushed from the fire, or my comment, which wasn't kind, and I don't want to paint them all that way. Most of the girls were doing their best, and if they found themselves naked in a closet, it was because they wanted comfort and love. Who doesn't need that from time to time?

"It's not like they were slutty or he was forceful," I correct myself. "That place was this strange environment where you wanted to live every day because it could be your last, so all inhibitions went to the wind."

Cade admires the blazing fire, adding a few more pieces of wood before he sits cross-legged next to me.

"And you didn't feel like letting all your inhibitions fly out the window?" he asks.

"Not with nineteen-year-olds," I groan.

"There are some cougars who would disagree with you."

I sigh and hold my palms up to the flames. This is the most comfortable I've been in a long time, warm all over, breathing fresh air, and conversing with an adult. If I'm losing my inhibitions, it's tonight.

"Young men need a lot of... training," I say. "If you know what I mean."

"I do." Cade chuckles, breaking a twig and throwing the pieces on the fire. "I learned a lot in my youth. Feel kind of bad for my first girlfriend."

Jealousy slices into my gut, angry and irrational. My jaw tenses, and I close my eyes and take a deep breath. Cade is not mine, and everyone my age has a life story.

"I was focused on taking care of everyone. Kind of a mother hen," I explain. "I was exhausted, and everyone was always hangry. Myself, included."

Because I gave all my food away.

"And I always had so much work to do," I go on.

Because I volunteered to help everyone with their job assignments.

"And sex was the last thing on my mind."

Until I met you.

"I understand," Cade says. "Will you miss them?"

"Oh, yes," I admit. "But I never belonged there. I shouldn't have even been at the party on Halloween. It's just that some of my students were on that edge of making life choices that could screw up everything, and I didn't want them to take the wrong path."

"You don't have to explain yourself," he says. "From where I sit, you're a good person, and I'm glad you're here with me instead of back there."

"How has it been with your brother?" I ask. "Since, you know, things went a little south."

He cocks one eyebrow. "A little south?"

I drop my head against my knees, eyelids heavy as the weight of everything we've endured finally starts to settle.

"Our house has a great basement for the apocalypse," Cade says with a chuckle. "It's kept us alive, and I'm lucky to have him."

He frowns, and I reach my hand out and rest it on his shoulder.

"He'll be okay," I tell him. "You haven't been gone that long, and you're the one who's been hurt." I look down at the dirty bandage on his arm, questioning if we're going to need to use some expired antibiotics for that wound.

"I'm fine, but Dillon… I get that he's an adult, but he's not good alone. He needs someone to bounce ideas off of. Someone to talk him through things," he goes on. "When we were younger, my parents' favorite phrase was, *Go with your brother.* We have never been apart for long, and I left him. I've got to get back."

"Help is on the way," I say in my best Mrs. Doubtfire voice. I'm not sure if Cade gets the reference, but he smiles and places his hand over mine.

"You know, I always thought Dillon and I would part ways right after high school, but we never did," he muses.

"You lived at home with your mommy?" I joke.

Cade nods. "I did. A real winner, I am."

"Hey, I'm not judging," I tell him. "If I had parents that loved me, a house with a view of the water, and a brother, I'd never leave."

"I moved out a couple of times, but I swear, things kept pulling me back," Cade continues. "My grandmother moved in, and they needed help with her. She was immobile for a while, and my mom couldn't lift her. It was supposed to be six months and turned into two years. When I moved back out, we had a house fire."

"Oh, my goodness," I gasp. "That's terrible."

"It was stupid. I got a house with a few of my friends, but we had a catastrophe with some fireworks. User error, and we were all to blame."

"Well, at least you can swim," I remind him.

"Win some and lose some," he says with a smile. "Anyway, I just kept coming back home. I was building a house when this all happened."

"With your own two hands?" I ask.

He nods. "With an occasional contractor, but mostly my own two hands. Also, a giant bank loan, but that's all forgiven now, I suppose."

"And Dillon?" I ask.

"He was too much of a thinker to move out. He would weigh every pro and con for so long that the apartment would no longer be available, or the house would be sold. I always thought he'd end up living with me."

"He sounds like a scholar," I point out. "That can be good."

"He sounds like someone with high-functioning anxiety," Cade remarks. "Not helpful in an apocalypse, but I'm glad we were both living at home when it happened."

The way Cade speaks about Dillon, I'm confident I'll like him. There's an inflection to his voice, and I can tell he's smiling when he talks about his brother, even if I'm not looking at him.

Cade yawns, and it's contagious. "Let's have a short rest," he offers. "It's early by the look of things. We can get walking before noon and make it to the house before nightfall."

Nodding with my eyes closed, I allow myself to drift. I may fall asleep like this, curled into myself and using Cade for balance.

When I feel his arms around my back, positioning me onto the ground, I sink into his warmth. It's not intentional, falling asleep in his arms like that, but it's the happiest I've been in years.

He holds me, and I drift off to sleep.

It's peaceful.
It's perfect.
It's short-lived.

CHAPTER
TWENTY-SEVEN

Cade

My eyes flutter open, and I pull Myra closer against my chest. The fire is nothing but embers now, flickers of orange under a smoking mound of burnt wood.

The sound of her slow and steady breathing, the feel of her heartbeat against my chest, it does something to me I never thought possible.

It gives me hope.

But there's another sound that's whispering through the woods. I'm a light sleeper, especially these past few weeks, and I can recognize the familiar noises of the night. A scurrying squirrel or the splash of a fish on the river doesn't startle me awake anymore, but this is different.

I raise my head from the dirt, ears straining for any sound. With my eyes shut, I channel every ounce of focus into the disturbance, pouring all my energy into listening.

It's steady and slow.

Rhythmic.

I know it, but I don't want to admit the truth.

My pulse quickens, my eyes opening and scanning the area.

Branches don't crack, leaves don't rustle, but they're out there. They wander in packs, seemingly unaware of their existence unless stimuli get in their way.

We need to move.

Covering Myra's mouth with my hand, I whisper in her ear. "You need to wake up. Myra. Do you hear me?"

She cuddles into my hold, her eyebrows furrowing, and I feel her let out an exasperated breath.

My lips press against her ear, and I try again. "Myra. Wake up."

Her eyes open, and when she realizes that I've covered her mouth, she squirms and fights against me.

"Please calm down," I beg. "We have to move. I can hear them."

A series of inaudible words leaves her lips before our eyes lock, and she stills herself, her mind waking up and understanding where she is and who is holding her.

"When I remove my hand, don't scream," I order.

She nods, and I let her go, the sound of their movements getting clearer, closer, but still unseen.

"What's happening?" she asks.

"We need to go," I whisper.

Getting to my knees, I grab our bag and strap it to my back. Myra's looking around, confused and growing uneasy. I motion for her to stay down while I collect the few things we need to take with us.

She sits up and brings her knees to her chest, burying her face in her hands. I know she's calming herself down, but by the crunch of wood I hear coming from up ahead, it's time to run.

I take her by the elbow, and she shoots her head up, large eyes staring at mine under bright moonlight. She's vulnerable out in the open, and I question if we've done the right thing. There were dangers inside the research facility, but outside isn't a picnic either. If something happens to her, if I can't protect her, I'll never forgive myself.

"Now," I mouth to her.

She stands, and I take her hand, guiding her through a break in the trees.

The sloshing of feet on the dirt and their groaning is clear now. It penetrates our ears, pumps blood through our veins, and sends fear into our hearts. We didn't go through all of that just to die on the first night. This can't stop us.

I don't know if they hear us, but they're close, too close, and we won't make it far without knowing how large the horde spans.

A trail comes into view, wood chips spread out on a gravel path, and the scribbled writing on a rock up ahead. I know what it reads because I've been here before. This is the Whispered Pine Trail, and if we're fast enough without them in our way, we can make it to the community. It's dozens of little cottages, all built the same, sitting on stilts to see the river from their bedroom windows and front porches.

Dillon and I used to have a buddy here, and we would play under the house during thunderstorms, enjoying the rain from the protection of a four-bedroom roof.

We couldn't wait to grow up and build matching houses of our own. Now all I do is dream about when things were simpler, when my biggest worry was getting home before dark so mom didn't get nervous.

Myra and I are jogging on the path, and I spot the roofs not far ahead.

"Where are we going?" she asks, out of breath.

"Higher ground," I answer.

She tugs at my arm a few times, and I turn to find her pointing toward our left.

If I didn't know what I was looking for, I wouldn't know it was them. The haze of grey through the trees seems to vibrate towards us, and the sight of them causes me to squeeze her hand harder and pump my legs faster.

We pick up the pace, Myra keeping up, stride by stride. The neighborhood opens up before us, dozens of houses in perfect lines with matching driveways and mailboxes. We come to a halt, both of us staring out at the possible danger up ahead when there's certain death at our heels.

People fiercely protect their homes, and I can't blame them. Anyone who takes one step on our property is met with a shotgun, and I wouldn't waste a bullet on a warning shot. It's fair to assume this place is no different.

"Cade." Myra's voice quivers, and I nod. Both of us are saying without words that we have to try our luck and find shelter in one of the houses.

I see my old buddy's home down the street, and I take a chance. If they are still there, maybe he won't shoot first.

Their moans and grunts echo, their sound making my skin prickle and forcing my feet to move. Both of us jog in silence, and Myra doesn't know where to, but she trusts me, and I want that to be enough to keep her safe.

We make it to the stairs and I take them two at a time, but Myra stumbles. Cursing myself, I turn and pick her up. She settles easily in my arms, and in a few strides, I'm face to face with a familiar front door.

It's open.

Nudging through with my shoulder, we creep inside, and I set Myra down. Her footsteps are soft and careful when she turns to shut and deadbolt the door.

It's cold in the house, but warmer than the outside. A smell permeates my nostrils. Stale air and rotten food mixed with something damp. Those are good signs considering we want this place to be abandoned.

"Stay here," I tell Myra.

"Please be careful," she whispers.

Room by room, I go through the house. There's dirty laundry in baskets, some open cat food on the counter, and empty plates with a half-eaten dinner. What used to be spaghetti and a basket of Halloween candy, ready to pass out, sits atop the dining room table.

They went out that night and never came home.

Finding my buddy's room, I open a drawer and yank out a shirt that will fit. Pulling it over my head, I recognize the vacation emblem on the pocket. It's a bar near the beach, one that lots of people in the neighborhood would visit over the summer.

I grab a few more clothes for us, satisfied that there is no one here, and head back to Myra. She's peeking through a window next to the door, the small shade pulled back while she crouches down to look.

"Are they coming this way?" I ask, my voice barely audible.

"Yes and no," she says. I follow her finger, which points to the edge of the neighborhood. They're walking between houses, flaring out toward a center street but not turning in our direction. That's their path, and unless something gets their attention, they won't deviate.

"Let's rest," I offer and take her hand from the curtain, wanting her to look away. There's nothing to do but be still and wait.

We finish changing clothes before making our way to the couch, too exhausted to bathe or scavenge. There's a thin layer of dust over the top of the deep blue fabric. It's new, or newer than when we were kids, and I unfold a blanket to cover the indented cushions.

Myra scoots next to me, both of us keeping our ears open for any noise. They don't have extraordinary hearing from what I could tell, but we aren't taking chances.

"Why did you bring us here? To this house?" she whispers. "It seems like you know this place."

"I did," I say with a nod. "Feels like a lifetime ago, but what doesn't?"

She smiles and leans against me. I take the opportunity to wrap an arm around her shoulders, allowing her to curl into my chest while I nuzzle her head beneath my chin.

"Tell me about that lifetime. Does it involve this?" She taps on the T-shirt emblem and cuddles close.

"This is an old friend's place. We went to school together," I explain. "Didn't go to the beach with him, though."

"Were you two close?" she asks.

I shrug, my eyes feeling heavy while I lean back into the cushions. There's a shift in the wind outside, and we both hear it, growing silent for a full minute before I answer. It's not them, and I force myself to relax.

"No. Not really. I was only really close to my brother. We're um, Irish twins. Barely eleven months apart."

"Your poor mother," Myra jokes.

"You have no idea." I frown at the words she meant to be a joke, but they ring too true to ignore. My poor mother, dead and gone all too soon.

"I didn't mean—"

"I know," I interrupt. "I hope whatever happened to her. It was quick."

"Dillon will be okay," she says.

Sometimes I think this woman reads my thoughts. She anticipates me somehow, always attuned to what I'm thinking and feeling.

"He's got the smarts to survive, but I don't know about the heart," I say, thinking of Dillon.

She tilts her chin, her eyes looking up at me, dark lashes blinking a few slow times.

"Dad would call us yin and yang," I answer the question she doesn't have to ask. "I don't stop to think enough, and he overanalyzes everything. I'm worried that alone, he won't make quick decisions. He never wants to go with his gut. Those bloats don't give you a lot of time, you know."

"You have shelter, and you've hidden this long. Hopefully, he won't have to make a last-minute choice."

"If he stays put," I say.

My eyelids grow heavy from exhaustion, and Myra's warmth is like a blanket lulling me to sleep. My muscles relax and I sink deeper into the couch.

"Did you have a best friend?" I ask. "Any foster siblings you stayed in touch with?"

"I stay in touch with most everyone. At least I did before the apocalypse thing."

I let out a small laugh. "Of course you did. You're that nice."

She smiles against my chest, and I can feel her breathing slowing, sleep taking over for her as well.

"Nothing that qualified as best," she admits. "Just people I knew. People I sort of grew up with. Most of them wanted to forget about the time we spent together."

"Not because of you, though," I tell her.

She sighs and adjusts herself in my arms. Despite running for our lives only moments ago, I'm not mad about the accommodations. We're on a comfortable couch, and I didn't get shot again. I consider this a win.

"Do you think we're friends?" she asks.

"Friends and?" I ask with a smile.

"And?" she coos.

I wrap another arm around her back, holding her tight.

"I want you to trust me, to be friends with me, but we both want more," I say. "That doesn't change because we left the dam."

She doesn't say anything right away, her slow, even breaths making me wonder if I've lost her to sleep. I wouldn't blame her, not after the past few days. This is the most comfortable she's slept in a month, based on what she told me about her previous arrangements.

"I'm a little scared to want sometimes," she whispers.

"I'm not going anywhere," I tell her.

I kiss the top of her head, struggling to listen to the world outside. All the sounds are far away, their steady march leaving us step by step. Her soft snores start, and they lull me to sleep.

It's the most restful night I've had since the world ended, and the happiest I've felt since before I can remember.

Light shines through the split in the curtains, bright and angry, piercing through my eyelids.

I reach for Myra, relaxing when I find her resting against me, blissfully asleep.

My back is stiff, but it's not unbearable. Stretching a little, she rolls to the inside of the couch, and I adjust her on the cushions, crawling out from our makeshift bed.

This place might have supplies, which would help us get back home and be great for Dillon when we arrive. It doesn't appear that anyone looted the neighborhood, and if the snack drawer is anything like when we were kids, we're in for a treat.

Looking outside, I see the bloat's pathway clear in the daylight. They've worn a shallow valley in the grass and dirt, leaving dark sludge along the street. Either everyone in this small neighborhood is gone, or they hide well.

The kitchen smells of decaying food, and I cover the plates with some tablecloths from the pantry. More than anything, I can't look at the half-eaten dishes. I knew the family that sat here together, enjoying this meal with laughter and good company.

We all ate here together, and it's painful to look at the emptiness of the world, to see a visual representation of a person's last meal.

There's Halloween candy littered everywhere, and I find the sour chews and allow myself some. It offers no nutritional value, but the sugar wakes me up. On the floor next to the refrigerator, I find two twenty-four packs of water. That's common here, where you're on a boil water advisory more often than not.

I grab a large bowl and pour in a few bottles before I make my way to the bathroom. Myra's still sleeping peacefully, and it doesn't take long to find a washcloth and a fresh bar of soap. I strip, ready to clean up. My arm bandage has held up well, but the rest of me still carries the residue of the river, and I can smell it. Considering my stench, it's a miracle Myra was able to sleep through the night.

I'm caught up in the idea of feeling human again, the need to get clean and wash the past few days away.

It's a peaceful few moments before I throw the washcloth to the floor and sprint from the bathroom, running towards Myra's scream.

CHAPTER
TWENTY-EIGHT

Myra

I don't know what woke me, only that something's off. I stumble off the couch, legs tangled in blankets, running my hands over myself as if to make sure nothing is amiss.

I'm lightheaded from moving so quickly, still exhausted from the middle-of-the-night sprint through the woods, and completely disgusted by my bedmate.

A scream rips out of me before I can stop it. I slap both hands over my mouth, furious at myself for being so loud. Great. Hello, neighbors. Please don't come knocking… with bullets.

"What happened?" Cade yells.

He bursts into the room, his feet vibrating the floor as he rushes towards me and spins me around.

"I'm sorry," I gasp. "I know I should be quiet. I got startled and forgot myself."

At the dam, screaming and talking didn't matter. We were behind several feet of concrete and surrounded by water. I frown, hoping they're alright. All that protection doesn't save them from themselves.

"What's going on?" Cade asks. His hands run down my arms while his eyes search throughout the room.

The moment my eyes find him, I go still, stunned by the sight before me.

"You're n-naked," I stutter.

The shift from boxer briefs to nude has had quite the impact, and I freeze, my jaw slack. I'm staring at this man's impressive penis, and I can't disguise the way my eyes drink in every inch of him.

There are a lot of inches.

"I was bathing," he says. The words are as casual as if he were describing walking or breathing. He has a perfectly reasonable explanation for standing here as bare as the day he was born, with no shame.

And why should he be bothered? The man is a perfect specimen of lean muscle and what's possibly the most perfect dick I've ever seen.

"Tell me what's going on?" he demands.

I think I might be drooling. What is wrong with me? This is just a penis, and I've seen a hundred. There were always a bunch of kids around growing up, and boys aren't shy about peeing in the yard or bathing with a water hose, so it's not like I'm a prude.

"Well, you're just so very naked," I repeat.

"You screamed, Myra." He lifts my chin, forcing my eyes to meet his. The fact that I have to be corrected to look this man in the face fills me with horror and embarrassment.

"I am so so so sorry," I blurt out. "I just didn't expect naked, and now that you are, it's just impressive. I mean, that's wrong to say, right? I shouldn't be talking about how impressive your nakedness is, especially after I just woke up to roaches crawling over me. That's not sexy. No one naked wants to be naked with someone packing roaches."

"So it was roaches?" Cade asks.

I tilt my head, forcing my gaze to remain focused on his eyeballs. "What?"

"You screamed because of roaches?"

"Oh, you bet your bottom dollar," I confirm. "Those buggers are disgusting with their little whiskers all swishing around. Yuck." I fake vomit, but there's a small chance it might happen after the visual of cockroaches crawling over my skin, and I cover my mouth with my hand and shake my head.

Cade lets out a sigh of relief. "Okay, that's good."

"I disagree," I mumble through my palm.

"I thought bloats were coming or someone broke in," Cade says. He runs his hand through his hair, stretching out his chest, and my eyes dart back to his dick.

"You have to get clothes on," I demand.

"Right." Cade snaps his fingers and smirks. "You know, bloats won't be around for a few more days if that group is like the others. We could rest today and then head out at night or in the morning."

"Are we resting with clothes?"

He laughs, turns, and walks away.

I watch.

I'm beyond help at this point.

"I'd like to wash up, too," I call out as he turns the corner, his perfect booty disappearing down a dim hallway.

His head pokes out from the doorframe. "You wanna get naked."

A roach crawls over the floor, and I yelp. "I want to get clean and maybe see about some bug spray."

"I'll finish up in here and get you some fresh water," Cade says. "And then I have an idea that will keep away some creepy crawlers."

If I didn't just admit my body was a roach motel, I would get naked right here and now, barge into that room after Cade, and have bathroom sex.

Instead, I simply tell him, "Okay," and plop down on the couch, waiting for my turn at a sink bath. A roach crawls in the corner, disappearing into a crack inside the wall.

"Thanks a lot," I bark at it, and sit back in a huff.

The water is lukewarm, but compared to the cold temperatures outside, it's not terrible. There are still clean towels here, protected in the cabinet and folded tightly by a careful housekeeper.

It saddens me a little to mess up the tidy bathroom, knowing that this towel will never be washed and folded again. This place is a pit stop, but it once was a family home with kids in this bathtub and a teenage Cade playing cards with his friends.

Washing my hair proves to be difficult, and it pains me to cut a few knotted curls free, but even with the best products and hours of time, those strands weren't coming loose. I still have mounds of it atop my head, and once I've scrubbed it three times and gotten a comb from root to tip, I tie it in two tight French braids, hopeful they will stay until my next chance to clean up.

There's a crackle from the living room, and the sound of a few soft thuds. Curious, but wanting to make sure I'm halfway presentable after the black blood river and roach disaster, I step back and stare at myself in the dusty mirror.

Bruises form under my eyes, a pale green color that doesn't look too terrible. There are some blueish marks on my neck as well, thanks to Lincoln's grip. I graze them with my fingertips, seeing clearly even in the dirty mirror how much I ignored who he truly is. Who so many of them are back at the dam.

It may have been funny watching Porter waddle around in a dinosaur costume, but he used valuable food for alcohol, which he then traded for sex. The self-appointed council was nothing more than some power-hungry teenagers with guns and an ego, and I should have stood up to them instead of going along to get along.

It wasn't even about staying alive for me. Keeping the peace felt more important, but when I look at my neck, I see the chaos.

I roll my shoulders back, blinking a few times to stop the tears that threaten to fall.

There's another thud, and I reach for the lotion in the medicine cabinet, spreading a liberal amount on my limbs before I put on the sweat pants and T-shirt of the woman who once lived here. The clothes smell like fabric softener, and my face is clean. It's energizing, and I skip into the living room, curious what's making all the noise.

"What's the ruckus?" I ask.

My eyes scan the room, and I smile wide.

"Wow, Cade," I gasp. "This looks…"

"Perfect," he finishes my thought.

I nod and bounce on my toes, ready for the most romantic night of my life.

Hopefully cockroach-free.

CHAPTER
TWENTY-NINE

Myra

"It's like we're glamping," I say.

I smile at Cade, who stacks some fresh wood and sticks into the fireplace. The flame comes to life with the fresh kindling, trickling light across the room.

"What's glamping, and is that good?" he asks.

"Glamping is when you're camping, but not really because you have shelter and usually a bathroom," I explain. I tap my finger on my bottom lip. "We don't have running water, though."

"We have a bucket," he says and stands, wiping his hands clean with a kitchen towel. "Sorry, not romantic."

I giggle and nod in agreement.

"But this—" I wave my hand around the room, "—counteracts the bucket situation."

I look around the living room, admiring how he's created quite the atmosphere with a little rearranging and some ambiance.

He's pulled a mattress from one of the bedrooms, situating it close to the fire and covering it with blankets and pillows. A sheet is tacked up blocking the walkway to the kitchen, and several candles are lit, probably to help with the smell of decaying food, but it's the apocalypse. Decay is part of the game.

"Should we be worried about the fire?" I ask. "I know bloats won't be around, but what about someone else?"

Cade takes a few cautious steps over to the coffee table he's pushed against the wall, and retrieves a handgun. He outstretches his hand, holding it carefully in one palm. "I found this in the master bedroom. Remembered they always had one by the bed."

"Right, well, just because you've been shot doesn't mean shooting is okay," I tell him. "And speaking of, did you clean that wound?"

Cade checks the safety and puts the gun back. "You're right, Myra. Shooting is wrong."

He checks his bandage, turning his arm over, and from the looks of the stained fabric and frayed edges, we both know it needs to be changed.

"Is the fire keeping you warm enough?" Cade asks.

"I'm very comfortable and warm," I tell him. "But about that wound…"

"And the fire and smoke will keep roaches away," he adds.

"Bonus," I squeak and clap my hands together. "But, first, your bandage. This will hurt, but sepsis hurts worse." No matter how many times he tries to change the subject, I'm not relaxing under a dozen blankets by the fire until I feel better about his arm.

"Okay," Cade agrees. "As long as you aren't avoiding being in this bed with me. If it's too much, I get it. I just thought—"

"It's exactly where I want to be," I rush out.

My skin flushes, and I know I'm anxious. When I decided to leave with him, I did it willingly, knowing and hoping this is where it would lead. That doesn't change how nervous I am about all the things I want to do with this practical stranger.

Is it too fast? Maybe, but this is the apocalypse. It's love at first sight because you die in a blink. We should at least have a few orgasms along the way. There isn't time to overthink, and after the kissing and seeing him naked, I've lost all my brain cells anyway.

We have this one day together before we get to Dillon, and I want to make it count.

A wave of heat pours out from the roaring fire, and I take a step forward, drawn to how wonderful it feels. Cade joins me by the flames, wrapping his arms around my shoulders and pulling me against his chest.

"You know I won't let anything happen to you," he says. "I don't want to use a gun, but if I have to, I will."

"The real danger might be me," I sigh. "I almost took you down in the river. It's like I was wearing cement boots."

His chest vibrates against me with his laugh. "Please, let's stop it with the drowning talk. I'll find you a life vest somewhere."

"That water is like a million feet deep," I tell him. "And you live by it, right?"

Cade's chin rests on top of my head. "It's a hundred, maybe two in some spots."

"That's like the Empire State building!" I gasp.

"Not even close," he says. "What do you think happened to all those tall buildings?"

"Wait, why aren't we taking care of your bandage?" I ask. "Stop changing the subject."

"It's going to hurt like a bitch," he admits. "I already tried taking it off with water and couldn't get through it."

I suck in a breath between my teeth, knowing he'll likely pass out if it's that bad, but we need to get the filthy water washed out of that bullet hole and pop a few expired antibiotics down his throat.

"So, the buildings?" he asks. "What do you think downtown is like?"

I shrug as best I can with his hold on me. "I don't know. I've been in nature this whole time. Maybe those people were safe. I've never seen a bloat climb."

"You're imagining a King Kong situation."

"It's crossed my mind," I quip with a smile. "Go get the medical supplies and stop stalling. Oh, and see if there is olive oil in the kitchen. It will help."

His warmth leaves, and I almost moan from the loss of his touch. I've fallen hard and fast, and I don't bother to ask myself why. Being with Cade feels right, and it's not just because he might be the last man alive in my age bracket. I'd be lying if I said that wasn't a factor, but I don't need a man to be happy. I could make myself pretty darn happy if given the privacy.

He's kind, brave, and can start a fire without a match. These are all great qualities that have nothing to do with his age or how amazing his body looks naked.

Which is amazing.

A nervous giggle escapes my lips, and the wind picks up outside, whipping a tree branch against the window pane. I jump from the noise, still on edge since our dash to freedom.

"You alright?" Cade asks. He has the supplies and dumps them out on the bed with a deflated look upon his face.

"Just the wind," I say.

"Should we go somewhere else?" he asks. "The bathroom or kitchen, maybe? This is where we'll sleep."

"Nah," I shake my head. "Just move the blankets. I'd rather you be as comfortable as possible."

He lets out a nervous laugh, and I sit down beside him, unscrewing the top of the olive oil and pouring a generous amount on the bandage.

"Will that help to get it loose?" he asks.

The truth is, I'm not sure. I think I saw it on some homestead television show, but it's better than nothing, and it can't be any dirtier than the river water mixed with bloat blood.

"Don't think about all this," I say, waving my hand over the bandage. "Tell me about your home. What's it like? Will I like it?"

"You'll have the best sleep of your life at my house. We have four mattresses that are all top of the line because my dad was obsessed with sleep," he explains. "You know, people spend over twenty years of their lives sleeping."

"Wow, I didn't know that." I pick at the edge of the bandage, looking for the loosest spot and hoping something glides without trouble.

"My parents' bed is some special order hand-sewn crazy thing, but it's amazing. Not that you want to sleep in my parents' bed because that's weird now that they're, oh, fuck."

I've removed the bandage on one side, and Cade bites his bottom lip, the veins in his neck protruding and throbbing. I didn't count to three or give him a warning, and considering he didn't bleed profusely, it's best to get this over with. I get a solid grip and pull off the other side.

"Fucking hell," he grits out. "Damn, are you a sadist?"

"What's that?" I ask.

Cade grows pale, and I'm not sure if it's from the comment or the pain.

"It's someone who enjoys inflicting pain on others," he explains. "And my comment was sarcastic. I know you aren't like that."

"You never know," I say and inspect the wound. It's not that I mean to hurt him, but I need to check this out and see what we're dealing with.

"This looks good!" I exclaim with surprise. "I mean, you've got a really weird piercing if this hole doesn't close up, but that's a cool party trick, right?"

"I can't see it because all I see are stars," he admits.

"Are you going to pass out?"

"No," he says. "I already did that once this week, and there's a limit."

I let out a cackle and rummage through the supplies for what I need. There's an antibiotic rinse, and I think about the suture kit, but decide against it. That's above my pay grade, and it could make things worse.

Getting him cleaned up hurts less than taking off the bandage, and as I work, he tells me about his family and growing up. It all sounds so blissfully ordinary, like something out of a television show. They liked to grill and fish. His dad taught him carpentry and loads of other life skills. His mom sounds kind, and he smiles when he talks about her. There is nothing remarkable about them, but they are astounding to me. Special in their normality.

Once he's re-wrapped and I've popped a few random person's pills in his mouth, I think he'll be as good as new. There'll be a scar to show for it, but no one is unscathed these days.

We relax after rearranging the blankets, not that much of a mess was made, and sit in silence for a moment, watching the flames dance inside the fireplace. Both of us are a little battered and bruised, but we're healing, and that might be the most romantic part of all.

"Cade," I sigh.

"Yeah, babe." He gives me a side look, still trying out this babe monicker.

"Are you super nervous, too?" I ask. "About... I don't know. Tonight."

"And every other night together," he adds.

Night after night, now that's a thought. I don't know if I've ever allowed myself to imagine being with someone forever or having a family that sticks around.

"We don't have to do anything," he adds. "Don't get me wrong. I was going to try, but we don't—"

"But I want to."

He arches an eyebrow and tilts my chin upward with a single hand. "Not just tonight, okay? I mean it."

"Are you asking me to be your girlfriend or something?" I joke.

"All I know is I don't want you going anywhere."

My heart thuds against my ribs, and I can tell I'm holding my breath. Closing my eyes, I try to remember this moment. I believe his words, but life today is fickle and fragile.

No one's ever told me they wanted me to stay for good. I didn't know how much I needed to hear that until now.

Cade's lips are on mine, and I'm on my back seconds later. I can taste the sweetness of his mouth, feel his desire on my hip, and I'm drunk with it.

My shirt rips when he yanks it up my back, and his mouth releases mine. "Sorry," he says. "At least it's not Bobbi's Nirvana one."

I laugh and smack him on the shoulder.

"Who cares?" I pull it the rest of the way, the fabric tearing in a steady stream. It lands in the fire, sending the flames high.

"Oh, no," I gasp.

"I hope they have good insurance," he jokes.

Cade adjusts the wood with a fireplace poker, and the flames die down.

"I promise not to make a mess," I say.

"Don't," he growls, and his lips slide down my neck while his fingers pull down the straps of my bra and expose my breasts. My nipples harden from the crisp air, and I wedge a hand behind my back to release the hook. All I can think about is getting us both naked, even if we have a house fire in the process.

Cade leans back, his eyes gazing at my bare chest. "You are gorgeous."

"I bathed," I say. Instant humiliation takes over, and I fight the instinct to cover myself.

His lips lift in the biggest smile. "Me too. Because you know, I was hoping."

"Me too," I say and reach for the waist of his pants.

CHAPTER
THIRTY

Cade

I don't think I've ever laughed with someone during foreplay. My history isn't riddled with lots of women, but I had a few long-term relationships and a couple of one-night regrets.

They never got me chuckling like this.

This feels surreal, like a dream that's lasted too long, and I don't know if I can wake up.

I don't want to.

"Why are sweatpants so hard to remove?" Myra whines.

She's laughing when she says it, and I hop up and pull down the pants, kicking them free of our living room bed. I grab her sweats by the ankles and yank them off in one swift motion, so fast her bottom bounces on the mattress.

"Wow," she says.

"Impressive, right? I've never tried that move before," I admit.

"No, wow, I mean," Myra rambles. "Wow is all I mean. Just wow."

I can't be sure, but I think she's staring at my dick, which is now at full attention. It's a little larger than normal, but nothing to scare a woman away. Myra doesn't look afraid, but there's something in her expression. I'm starting to read her, though it'll take time to truly understand her. I hope more than anything that we get that time.

We crash our bodies back together, kissing and touching, ravenous and messy. Even though I want nothing more than to be inside her, it's more important to me that she knows how much I care about her, that she feels it tonight.

My lips trail down her neck, enjoying her warm, soft skin, until I reach her perfect breasts.

She giggles when I tease her nipples, taunting them with my tongue and lightly sucking at the perfect peaks. Her fingernails dig into my back, and I hear her groan, feel her body tremble beneath mine before I make my way lower.

"How do you like the smell of High Country?" she asks.

I freeze, my lips just north of her belly button. "What?" I ask and cast my eyes upward. She's breathing heavy, her breasts moving up and down, making it hard to focus on what she's saying.

"There was only men's soap in the bathroom. The closest thing I could find that seemed bearable was called High Country."

"You smell amazing," I say, my focus back on her body.

Her hands fall to my shoulders as she attempts to hold me in place. "Really, because it was like the candle aisle at TJ Maxx in there. Sort of overwhelming and all the fragrances made me sneeze."

My hands wrap around her hips. "Babe," I grit out.

She bites her bottom lip and lets out a "mm-hmm."

"I'm more interested in how you taste."

I spread her legs with my elbows and rest my face between her legs before I let her say another word.

CHAPTER
THIRTY-ONE

It's a good thing I just bathed. Otherwise, there's no way I would be letting this man have his face so close to my lady bits, but the smell of man-soap? It's not what I wanted for our first time.

"Y-you don't have to do that," I stutter. "I mean, if you think you have to or something."

"What man doesn't want to do this?" Cade asks. He leans on his elbows, a perplexed expression upon his face.

I think back to the boyfriend who told me he found it gross, or the one who said that it wasn't manly. One of them is gay now, or I guess he always was gay, but what about the other?

While I'm contemplating all the lies I believed, Cade dives back down, his tongue giving a long, languid lick.

"Oh, wow," I say.

My head lolls back, and Cade takes this as encouragement. He finds the tender spot that, for some reason, a lot of men seem to never locate, even though it's right there, and focuses his attention.

I'm shaking, my legs trembling around his face. He wraps his hands around my thighs, holding me in place and refusing to let me move. I can tell I'm losing control, my hands moving to my breasts and pinching my nipples.

This is shameless, and I love it.

Short soft moans leave my lips, and I spread my legs wider, desperate for his tongue that's putting exactly the right amount of pressure on my clit. A tightness forms in my stomach, the crest of my orgasm threatening to escape.

The feeling rises, creeping through my limbs until it breaks free, and I cry out. My entire body stiffens, frozen in place while the waves of pleasure crash over me, until there's nothing left, and I'm a pile of listless limbs.

Cade kisses the inside of my thighs, his palms running up and down my legs.

"Wow," I whimper.

"You say wow a lot," Cade notices. "Not that I'm complaining."

He crawls upward and rolls next to me, his arms wrapping around my middle while he spoons me from behind. That impressive cock of his, hard and long, throbs against the back of my thighs.

"Are you… happy?" he asks. There's a timidness in his voice, as if he's not sure if that was okay.

"I'm amazing, Cade," I tell him. "I can barely move."

"We don't have to, you know…" His voice trails off.

Oh, but we will. We could die walking out of this house tomorrow. Heck, we could die tonight after accidentally sending smoke signals to anyone within a hundred yards. I'm not dying without Cade, whatever his last name is, having sex with me.

I really need to get better with names.

Finding strength, I sit up, my legs still a little shaky from the orgasm. I push his shoulder down so he's resting on his back and straddle him.

"What's your last name again?" I ask.

Cade smiles, his hands resting on my hips.

"Miller," he chuckles.

The fire warms my back, sending shadows across our bodies. The sun has lowered, making the air around us colder.

In this moment, I think he might be the most beautiful thing I've ever seen. It's not that I'm especially attracted to wounded men or the lack of a good shave, but the way he's looking at me makes my heart somersault. I'm giddy and excited, the entire world around us fading away. Here and now is all that matters.

I give a coy smile, scooting back to get the right angle. "You ready?"

"You can feel that I am," he says.

His fingertips dig into my thighs, and I notice how he's restraining himself, allowing me to lead.

The head of his cock springs up, and I wrap my fingers around the shaft. It takes everything in me not to make a joke about whack-a-mole, even though I know I never have to be serious around Cade. We are people who joke and laugh and, as of tonight, make love.

Cade gives me a wide smile, his eyes heavy and ready for this. Guiding the tip of his cock, I lift to my knees and slowly lower until he's inside me, and I'm filled to the hilt with this man.

It takes my breath away.

His torso lifts, and I'm thrown on my back, his cock still buried deep. The fire burns at my side, and he thrusts, sending jolts of electricity throughout my body. It's a mix of sensations, and the scream I let out is one I never knew could leave my lips.

"Are you," he says, his words breathless between thrusts, "okay?

A sheen of sweat mists his chest, his breath warm on my shoulder as he moves in and out.

"Good," I say. "Oh, really, really good."

His hand reaches behind my head, fingers wrapping around my loose braids and grabbing them tight. My chin lifts, exposing my neck when he pulls just enough not to hurt, but to feel so good.

"I'm close," he grits out.

My hips lift, curving to the right spot because I'm right there with him, our bodies working together perfectly.

He takes the cue, staying deep inside me and rocking until I'm trembling once more, a mess in his arms. It's a good thing he has such a great hold on me because I'm shaking seconds later, and I bite down on his shoulder, a moan escaping that might pique the interest of local wildlife.

I'm an animal, too, and one that is having multiple orgasms.

"I'll pull out," he gasps.

Except we're locked together, our bodies wrapped in such a way that in the throes of my orgasm, I can't let him go. In another life, I may have been excellent at wrestling.

My body convulses, and I feel his cock stretch me as it grows so large it almost stings. Fingernails dig into my skin, my teeth make marks on his shoulder, and I feel it, the flood of his cum barreling inside me.

It's too late to stop, and it's something we should have talked about before, but it doesn't matter now. All that matters is how good we both feel when he relaxes on top of me, breathing heavy with a look of pleasure on his face.

"I'm sorry," he whispers. "That was wrong. I should have controlled—"

"Stop," I tell him, placing my palm across his mouth.

We rest in a tangle of limbs for a few minutes, listening to the crackling fire until I feel that I can move. I scoot out from underneath his hold, and he pulls me close so we're face to face, arms wrapped around each other.

"If you're worried about getting me pregnant, you won't," I tell him.

"They have birth control in that place?" he asks.

It might be a joke, but I can tell he's genuinely curious.

"No," I say and shake my head.

He must see the look in my eyes, the sadness I thought the end of the world had buried, now crawling back to the surface.

The brief, fragile joy of feeling like I finally have a family shatters, leaving only a hollow, aching sorrow behind.

CHAPTER
THIRTY-TWO

Cade

She looks devastated, not the face I want to see ten minutes after having sex. Something simmers beneath the surface, words she wants to say but holds back from me. I curl a loose tendril of hair around one finger and give her the space to speak. That's something else my mother taught me, a lesson which has served me well over the years.

People need a road to travel on, and when it's someone's turn to talk, get out of their way, give them room to go.

"Would it be okay if I didn't look at you when I talk about this?" she asks.

I press a kiss to her lips, then turn, slipping her hand into mine and holding it against my chest.

"This okay?" I ask. "I could go into the kitchen, but I won't smell good when I return."

"You need some High Country soap? You'll smell like you wrestled a pine tree and then rolled in a meadow of manliness," she says, and we both laugh.

"Okay, so I am not someone who will be birthing now or, um, ever. And I usually tell people when I get into a relationship, but we've known each other like three days, and one of them you were unconscious, so…" She trails off.

"You don't owe me any explanation," I tell her and squeeze her hand tight. "We are on the apocalyptic dating fast track. I get it."

"Right. Nothing like global collapse to move a relationship along," she admits.

"Is everything alright?" I ask. "Health-wise?"

"Okay, so this sounds kind of gross, but you did just have your face in my vagina, so I think we've passed the TMI stage. I have Uterine Fibroids."

I was just licking every crevice of this woman and fucking her as deep as she'd let me, so there's nothing she could say that would gross me out. Men who can't handle bodily functions like menstruation and UTIs aren't real men.

"I'm sorry you have to deal with that," I tell her.

"It's okay if you have no clue what those are," she adds.

"I don't," I admit. "Trying to walk the line between supportive and not intrusive."

"You're doing great," she tells me, and I bring the back of her hand to my lips and give her a soft kiss.

She clears her throat and adjusts herself. We are still very naked, so I have to try to stop the rush of blood to my dick. I could easily go another round because her tits are caressing my back, and my ass is tucked against her warm center.

"Please don't get carried away by how sexy this sounds, but they are these noncancerous growths, and they can mess up my uterus. Basically, I can get pregnant, but I never stay pregnant. And I would never even know if I get pregnant, because the fertilized egg can't implant."

"Implant?" I ask.

"Like dig it's little way into my uterus and hitch a ride until it has eyeballs and lungs."

I take in this information, trying to determine how she feels about this diagnosis. She's joking around, but there's always a lightheartedness to Myra, and we're still in that beginning stage where even if things are deep, we might brush it off. This is the end of times after all, and when the absolute worst happens, everything else takes a backseat.

"That sounds hard, and I'm sorry," I tell her.

"Thanks," she sighs.

"And listen, even if you can't get pregnant, it doesn't mean that I had the right to release inside of you like that. There are other reasons to be careful."

"Like diseases," she says. "What if I die?"

"I hear the sarcasm, but I'm still apologizing. And I truly am sorry if being a mom is something you want, and it's out of reach right now. That's not fair."

She takes a nibble of my back before smacking a kiss on the skin. I take it as permission to turn around, and I pull up the blankets, tucking us in for what's bound to be a restful sleep after all that exertion.

We're done with the topic, and I won't keep her talking about something I'm certain upsets her on some level. Who wouldn't feel frustrated if their body didn't work the way they wanted, or they faced a diagnosis that left them feeling out of control?

"We leave when we wake up," I tell her. "Any longer, and we risk the bloats making a circle back."

"How long does it take them to circle where you are?" she asks.

"About three days. Maybe four if they make a stop, but that doesn't happen all that often anymore."

She shudders at my words, both of us silently dwelling on the thought that weighs heavily on our hearts. They don't slow down because they aren't finding and turning large groups of people anymore. After the first two weeks, there was no one left along the route. We can only hope there are other survivors like us, hiding out and staying alive.

"Let's sleep, Cade," Myra yawns. "Big day tomorrow."

Her breathing slows, and once I'm sure she's asleep, I slip from her arms. It doesn't take long, and I give myself a moment to admire how beautiful she looks in the firelight.

I'll need to stay up a while longer. As much as I appreciate the verbal affirmations that she enjoyed herself during our activities, if anyone lives near here, they know our whereabouts.

I grab the handgun and make my way to the corner bedroom. The window on two walls allows for a good view of the community, and right now, I'm worried about neighbors more than bloats.

It's pitch black outside, the sun making its way below the trees and past the horizon. Darkness after the world ended is different. There's a depth to it that my brain doesn't understand. Growing up with streetlights and screens, a television always on, and someone scrolling on their phone didn't prepare me for how completely black the world becomes at night.

The stars usually help, and they're brighter these days, more than ever before. But tonight, with the sky cloaked in thick clouds, not a single ray of light will break through.

Except when I stand in this room, I don't encounter total darkness.

I wonder if he can see me.

The man across the street and three houses down.

He must not care if I see him the way he's standing in the window, a candle held up to his face. There's something deranged about the way he remains there. It's unhinged to make yourself known like that.

I don't recognize the person, not that I would expect to after all that's happened, but I know he's unafraid.

No, he can't see me.

I'm concealed by the dark, but the smoke from our fireplace draws his attention.

I chamber a round in the gun and wait. Ten, maybe fifteen minutes before he steps aside, disappearing from sight.

I check the locks in the house, every window and door, before heading to the main closet, where I know I'll find more weapons.

We'll need them.

CHAPTER
THIRTY-THREE

Cade's sitting on the floor of a back bedroom, his back against the side of a bed. Curtains are drawn, but there's a sliver open, and his gaze remains fixed on the spot.

"What are you doing in here?" I ask.

He doesn't startle, which tells me he was already awake and heard me coming inside.

"Did you sleep in this bed?" I ask. "Were you in here the whole time?"

I'm peppering him with questions, but I don't remember him leaving last night. He's in here wearing fresh clothes with a few new guns next to him.

"I slept enough," he answers. "I'm keeping watch. We have some neighbors."

"Was it the fire?" I ask.

I likely woke the neighborhood with my sex screams, but I'm giving myself the benefit of the doubt.

"People are aware of any changes in their hideaways," he says. "I would notice a single footprint on our property. Anything could have told him we were here."

"Him?" I question.

"Two hims, from what I can tell."

"Maybe they're a couple," I muse. "A happy couple of dudes just wanting to stay alive and garden. Do they have a garden or something like that?"

He stands and turns to face me, a half smile on his face. It's annoying to most people how I look at the bright side all the time, and I wonder if Cade will tire of my happy anecdotes after more than a week together.

We'd have to survive that long to find out, and thinking back on the bloat mountain, sludge river, and now the strange neighbors, survival doesn't look promising. It's a good thing I had those orgasms in time.

Cade gathers his guns, inspects each one, and lines them up neatly on the bed.

"We need to go, but it's a question of when," he says. I wait, watching him let out a long sigh before he continues. "I've thought about this, and if we stay another night, we risk bloats. If we go now, we risk people."

"You think they're dangerous?" I ask. Glancing at the line-up of guns, that answer may be obvious.

"It's a higher likelihood that they'll let us be on our way, but it's a risk. If we encounter bloats, that's certain death."

I place my hands on my hips and huff. "So what you are saying is, we are dag nabbed if we do and dag nabbed if we don't."

Cade nods, his eyes never leaving the guns. "Do you know how to shoot?"

"Not even a little," I admit. "But you know, times are tough. I'll squeeze a trigger if I have to. I've always loved Kill Bill. I'll pretend to Uma my way through it."

"Good enough for me," Cade agrees. "Let's pack up."

We scavenge the place for something other than the dozens of protein bars we brought and find some unopened peanut butter and a dozen more bags of Halloween candy. It's like these people were awaiting a rave of trick-or-treaters at the rate they were stashing choco-late bars.

Candy ran out in three days back at the dam, so I'm happy for a caramel nougat surprise. They have some medical supplies that I'm happy to take, and half a bottle of antibiotics, another great find. I've never been so grateful that no one ever finishes their full supply of antibiotics.

We also accidentally unlatched a sex swing from the ceiling in one of the bedrooms. It came flying down, spinning in place, awaiting an occupant. It's almost enough incentive to stay another night, but we are out of time, and death means no more sex, so we decide against it.

With everything packed, the nerves hit hard. The moment we step outside, we'll be targets in broad daylight. We stand frozen by the front door, bags strapped and stripped to the essentials, light enough to carry, heavy enough to mean survival.

Cade makes it clear that we will be running.

"I will go down the stairs first so I can protect you with my body, but once we get to the ground, we switch," he explains. "My back should be facing them."

"Should we have the guns in our hands?" I ask. "If they're down our pants like they do in the movies, we don't look like much of a threat. But you know, if they see us holding guns, it's threatening. Oh, golly, what do we do?"

Cade thinks on this and agrees we should holster them in some way. He checks the safety on mine about five times before I situate it in my waistband.

"Are you ready?" he asks.

"Absolutely not, but I wasn't ready for last night either, and that worked out."

His face contorts. "You weren't ready?"

"I don't mean like that. I wanted to. Obviously. I just mean, who's really ready? Being naked in front of someone, and legs spread. It's not something anyone is ever prepared for, you know," I ramble. "I'm usually the kind of girl who gets a wax first. I like to be tidy."

Cade puts his hands on my shoulders, and my mouth snaps shut. "Myra," he says.

I nod in response, afraid that if I say one more word, it will turn into a hundred more embarrassing ones.

"We should talk about this later. Do you know the plan? Are you ready to run?"

More nodding from me with a thumbs up, and he turns and opens the door.

Bright light beams into my eyes, blinding me for a moment. He waits for me to move forward, and I take three deep breaths and then one step, giving him the all clear. He sprints forward, and I follow, careful to put my hand on the rail so I don't tumble, but flying down the steps as fast as I can go.

We reach the bottom, and Cade is at my back, his chest almost pushing me forward even though I'm running as fast as my legs will take me. My lungs burn, and I taste copper in my mouth.

We're near the trail now, and in daylight, I spot a parking lot just beyond it. I push forward onto the dirt path, refusing to stray from the plan. The fear of those two neighbors feels almost foolish as my foot slams into the ground, kicking up a cloud of dust. They haven't even opened a window or—

Bang!

I stop in my tracks, hands over my ears, and crouch down. Cade almost knocks me over, but he recovers, twirling around to my other side and grabbing me by my arm to rush us forward.

Bang! Bang! Bang!

My mind can't catch up to what's happening, but I hear the yelling, and then the start of an engine. It doesn't sound like a car, but a motor is running behind us, and as we pass the tree line, I turn to look.

Two four-wheelers lurch forward, their tires skidding against the concrete before gripping hard. The wheels are massive, built for tearing down dirt paths exactly like the one we're running on.

They look human, not that it helps, because these guys do not want to say hello. They both haven't shaved in a month, which isn't surprising, but I don't think they've bathed either. I swear I can see twigs in one guy's hair, and the stains on the other's shirt look like blood. Maybe it's ketchup, but considering it's the end of the world around here, I'm betting blood.

"Cade?" I half scream, half ask.

He pulls me along, and my muscles burn as I try to keep up. "This way," he orders. "Don't look back." We cut through the trees, the parking lot in sight, and I hope he has a plan.

Bank! Crack! Bang!

The neighbors shoot off a few more rounds, their off-road vehicles cracking twigs and slicing the bark of trees right behind us.

"Leave the girl, and we'll let you go, son," one yells.

That can't be good.

I know Cade won't leave me behind. Something in my gut doesn't doubt it for a second, but he's not going to die because of me.

"They're right behind us," I huff out between heavy breaths. Our feet hit the pavement, and I notice what he's after. There are two, maybe three cars that have a door open.

"Just leave me," I tell him.

He doesn't answer, gripping my arm so hard I know it will bruise.

"Those cars will be dead," I blurt out. This is the worst one-sided conversation I've ever had with a man.

One of the four-wheelers screeches onto the pavement, and I jerk my head back. The other appears to be stuck between some trees, tires spinning in the dirt while going nowhere.

"Go for the Jeep," Cade yells.

A shiny black Jeep Wrangler sits in the farthest part of the lot. Its door is open, but so is the rest of it with the top off. I want to ask him if he's sure, but all I can do is hope he knows something more about vehicles than I do.

"All we want's the girl," one guy screams with a country twang. "We'll treat you real good, sugar."

His shooting says otherwise, but these aren't men who care to debate. These are people who let the excuse of the apocalypse make them murderous rapists.

Dark spots form in my vision, my breath ragged and shallow. Not only am I lacking in car knowledge, but I'm far from an athletic person. It's all I can do to get to the Jeep without my body giving out.

As we approach the door, I sort of swan dive into the passenger seat, my legs sticking out the back. Sliding over streaks of black ooze that cover the red leather interior, I situate myself to sit. These people were ripped from their cars while trying to get away. It's tragic, but so is the fact that I just got clean and now I'm covered in bloat guts again.

Cade skids across the hood like we're in an Indiana Jones movie, which would be super hot if I wasn't seconds away from rape and death.

The redneck reaper is only a few parking spots away from us. Cade finds the keys just where he thought they would be, sitting in the ignition, and by some miracle of modern technology, the thing starts.

That's when the unthinkable happens. Instinct takes the reins, carrying me through the next sixty seconds. There's no logic, no plan, only raw reaction. I don't have any other explanation for it.

Sometimes I surprise myself.

Heck, I downright shock myself.

I've always been the type to stick to the corners. Quiet, unassuming, and never rocking the boat. Where I come from, making noise or picking fights is a quick ticket to losing your place to sleep. It's no wonder I never grew the kind of personality that bites back.

Today, I sink my teeth in.

Our pursuer rises in the saddle with a triumphant "Yahoo!" just as I flick the safety off my gun and shoot him.

Shoot him right in the dick.

CHAPTER
THIRTY-FOUR

The engine roars to life.

It was a fifty-fifty shot, but the only one we had. There isn't a chance in hell I'd give my woman to these two hillbilly thugs. I'll have to ram the car in front of us to get out, but this Jeep can handle it.

Bang!

A sharp crack erupts nearby, and I slam the car back into park. What I see next makes no sense.

The driver coming at us crashes, his four-wheeler thudding against several cars lined up in the parking lot. He falls to one side, clutching his crotch and screaming. His vehicle comes to a stop against a mini-van, the engine rolling but taking it nowhere.

Myra turns, her wide eyes meeting mine, the gun clasped in her hands.

"I shot him in the penis," she gasps.

I look at the injured man and back at her a few times, shocked and impressed. His friend, still stuck in the woods, abandons his ATV and starts running toward the scene.

"Good job, babe," I say.

Despite how she probably just saved our lives, a celebration will have to wait. Putting it back in drive, I hit the gas, thankful it's still got most of a tank of gas, and shove a small sedan out of the way before breaking free.

His friend shoots at us a few times, but the distance is too far, and he's a terrible shot. Myra doesn't duck or flinch. She's pointing the barrel of the gun at both men, who continue cursing at us from the parking lot.

It's empty threats. "We'll find you! You can't get far!"

Their voices fade away as I'm still pressing the gas pedal to the floor. It's going one hundred miles per hour before I come to my senses and slow down. We drive another five minutes before I pull over to check on Myra.

I keep the car running when I park and turn to her, checking over her body with my hands. "Are you alright?" I ask. "You could be in shock."

"Right in the dick," she says. Her eyes lock on mine, wide and unblinking. "In the zipper, Cade."

"He had it coming," I say. "You want to hand me that gun?"

"I didn't even think about it, you know," she says. "I was pointing at his gut. Looked like the largest target."

"Let me get the safety on," I say, and take the gun from her.

"I mean, a penis is not a very big target. It's not like I meant to do that," she muses. "Must have been karma. You think it's gone?"

My lips find hers, and she puts her hands on the side of my head and holds me there, enjoying the moment and kissing me back.

"He had it coming," I repeat when we separate.

"For the record," she says with a smile. "Your penis would be a huge target."

"Let's hope it never comes to that."

I know this road, paved right before everything went to shit. Weeds sprout out from the sides, and a few cars sit abandoned along the stretch. It's flat here, and I can see for miles, but it's the woods around us we need to worry about.

"By foot or by car?" Myra asks. She's thinking the same thing I am, curious about what's likely to keep us alive.

"I don't know," I admit. "It's a thirty-minute drive to my house."

"You really went on a long boat ride downriver, didn't ya?" she asks.

At the time, it didn't feel like I went that far, but I was being shoved along by a thousand undead, and time got away from me.

"It's also thirty minutes if we drive the speed limit, which I wouldn't," I add. "But that doesn't change that a loud car would draw attention."

"By bloats and by other neighbors," Myra sighs. "I can't promise I'll be able to shoot everyone's dick off."

I chuckle and take her hand.

"We could fly right past them, but if we get surrounded…" I trail off.

"Right, and if we drive up to the house, we might lead something to Dillon."

"Can't drive the whole way no matter what," I muse. "We're on the other side."

Myra lifts her hands in the air. "Wait just a minute!" She smacks her legs, stretching her neck toward me in disbelief. "We have to cross the river again!"

I might have left that part out, but we couldn't get past bloat mountain, so there was no choice. My plan was to help her swim over until I found out what an epically bad swimmer she was. One problem at a time, though.

"I need a protein bar dipped in peanut butter after that news," she huffs.

I reach for the bag, and she stops me. "I'm being dramatic," she says and smacks my hand away. "Let's save the food. This is fine. Maybe we can blow the airbag on this thing and I can float across like I'm tubing."

"Have you ever gone tubing?"

She squints and shakes her head. "Absolutely not. That's a yeast infection waiting to happen."

Myra grabs a bag and slams it in her lap, shaking her head and huffing.

"Whelp, I think we've got to walk," she announces. The car door opens, and she hops out, turns around, and straps the bag to her back.

"Wait a minute," I argue. "What if we drove part of the way?"

"How many houses run along this river that might have people with working ears?"

She makes a good point. The car is loud and will draw the attention of bloats and other survivors. Both are equally dangerous.

"Okay, it's half a day's walk," I tell her.

"Woods or road?" she asks.

We both say, "Woods," in unison, knowing we're sitting ducks out in the open.

Even though she said no, I can tell she's hungry. She didn't eat this morning out of nerves, and then ran a mile in a dead sprint. I take out a protein bar and dip it in the peanut butter as we walk. When I hand it to her, she simply shrugs her shoulders and takes a bite.

"What do you do all day at home?" Myra asks. "When you aren't out for a kayak, of course."

I'm still on the fence about whether I'm upset about my spur-of-the-moment fishing excursion. It put Dillon in danger, and the idea of not getting back to him makes my stomach turn into knots. Except without that foolish decision, I wouldn't be walking through the trees with Myra. We wouldn't have had last night, which I keep replaying in my head every spare second I get.

"We did a lot of surveillance the first couple of weeks. Watching the comings and goings of bloats and what neighbors we could see," I tell her. "Once we realized they were circling in a pattern, every day was about food. We worked on our garden, but planting season is over for a lot of things, and we didn't have all the right seeds."

"We had some planters on the roof of the dam," she says. "But nothing had sprouted yet. Everyone was too concerned with making liquor and burning through the supplies. It looked like we had a lot in the beginning, but they went fast."

I shake my head. "It's too bad. That place was stocked for a snowed-in winter, and with some planning, it could have been great."

"What's done is done," she sighs. "So, since the garden is stalled, you fish?"

There's a crunching of leaves and cracking of twigs, and we stop cold. Myra gestures ahead, and the terrifying threat reveals itself as a pair of squirrels. We move on.

"We were trying to hunt," I admit. "With a bow and arrow, so we didn't draw attention to ourselves."

"Oh, that's smart. Deer? You should do that."

"It's harder than it looks," I admit. "Not everyone is as good a shot as you."

"I was *not* trying to shoot him in the penis," she growls. "That was an accident."

"Like I said, he had it coming."

"I'm starting to agree," she admits. "I did archery for a few years, you know."

I don't explain that I wouldn't know because we've only been together for less than a week. Instead, I simply say, "I didn't know that."

Myra already seems like a constant in my life, someone I may have just met, but a presence that was always there.

My mother harassed me from time to time about settling down, but it never bothered me that I was in my thirties and single. In fact, it never occurred to me that I needed to start a family. Finding a wife wasn't on my radar.

And then came Myra, and the idea of not being with her forever until my dying breath sounds impossible. Everything was on pause until she came around. The timing is nuts, bloats, and bombs, and bullets in the penis, but I'll take it.

I embrace it.

"I bet I could do it. I could get a deer or maybe a turkey with an arrow," she says, taking another bite of her peanut butter-covered protein bar. "It's Thanksgiving soon, and I did shoot someone right in his tiny penis."

"I bet you could," I agree.

We both know she was aiming for the man's gut, but if she practiced some archery, I think she might be a fair shot.

"What did you do in high school?" she asks.

There's the sound of an engine, an ATV, if I were guessing. It's in the distance, but out there, searching for us. We keep walking, picking up the pace a little, necks craned to listen.

"Swimming," I say, and I hear Myra groan.

CHAPTER
THIRTY-FIVE

Myra

We walk for hours with that sound fading in and out somewhere in the distance. A four-wheeler driven by a dickless man or his bestie, searching for us in these woods.

It's quiet most of the way, both of us on high alert for what could happen, but what choice do we have? There is one thing we could do, but Cade won't. That doesn't stop me from asking.

"You should swim across the river without me," I say.

He falters, his footing catching on a branch by the shock of my words.

"I can't have this discussion with you," he says and marches forward.

"Be reasonable. There's safety on the other side," I say. "Maybe you can find a canoe to push over or something after you cross."

"That river is a mile wide down here," he says.

"I'm never going to make it across," I grit out.

It's been hours of walking, listening to the danger all around us. Combine that with the need to cross a body of water and with urgency, I know I'm going to be the death of this man.

Literally.

"Cade, I'm not something special you have to die for. There is nothing so important about me that you need to sacrifice yourself and Dillon."

That causes a full stop, and he turns on his heel to face me, a look of pure bewilderment across his face. "Do you think there needs to be?"

"W-well, yeah," I admit. "You should have someone irreplaceable if you're willing to die. I'm painfully average. I know it's the end of times, but don't settle."

The words I'm saying kill me a little. I like Cade, and if more than a calendar week had passed, I might even spit out the love word. It makes no sense. I have my full frontal lobe, but these feelings are real. So real that I'm willing to push him to do what might save his life.

Cade looks up to the sky, his Adam's apple bobbing as he takes a deep swallow.

"I can't imagine what it was like to grow up the way you did," he says, and his eyes lower to meet mine. "To have to be some savant or extraordinary to get adopted. Being forced to prove that you're worthy of love."

I choke down the lump in my throat, but the tears come anyway, and I hate myself for still crying over the ghosts of childhood rejection.

Damn him for seeing right through me.

"And maybe you haven't noticed," he continues. "But I am painfully average."

I open my mouth to object, but he puts his hand up and takes a step closer.

"I'm downright boring, and guess what, I never wanted to be anything else," he confesses. "I liked Saturday nights playing cards with my parents, who I lived with. I enjoyed building my house with all my spare time, because I was a LEGO nerd as a kid. I never won a medal in a sport, just felt happy to be there. My income, average. My schedule, predictable. I ate the same breakfast every day. Have for decades. My Saturday morning ritual was to clean out my toolbox and organize my garage."

Hot tears hit my cheeks, my chest heaving as I hold back a sob.

"I like normal," Cade says with a shrug. "I like you. Can we be simple together? Try to garden and maybe figure out my dad's cross-bow. That's all I want. Damn, that would be paradise."

I want to tell him how wonderful that sounds. How miraculous a modest, unremarkable rhythm of life would feel. To sleep in the same bed with the same person, without pretending to be perfect or happy every waking moment, and knowing that it will always be the same path we walk together, a steady hum of days without pretence or fear of rejection.

"You're asking me if you're exceptional enough," he says. "You're fantastic. Funny and kind and hot. I'm the one who doesn't have something special to offer. Just a life. Is that enough, Myra?"

He studies me, curious and confused.

"That would be great, actually," I choke out.

"Just so we're clear, I may be boring — not a catch by some standards, but I'll always be there. Someone you can set your watch to. I just want you, Myra."

He's wrong. He's the best man I've ever come across, but I'm crying too hard to say the words. His arms wrap around me, and I fall into them.

There are too many reasons to count for why I'm crying. We're exhausted, being chased by hillbilly thugs, and I have to get in a river one more time, but I think my tears are ones of relief.

I can be still for once in my life.

"I'm not leaving your side," he repeats.

I nod into his chest, and he kisses the top of my head. "About another hour's walk," he tells me.

"What?" I ask. I was sure he said we had much longer to go when we started. "Your house is that close?"

"No," he admits. "We're going to the marina. We need a boat."

CHAPTER
THIRTY-SIX

Cade

"What if, and hear me out?" Myra starts.

"If you talk about me crossing that river without you, I'm going to spank your bare ass," I tell her.

She flushes and flashes me a quick smile.

"No, sir. What about we go for the little kayaks down there?" she asks. "Now I know you've had some bad experiences with kayaks. I get that, but—"

"It's too slow, Mrya," I sigh.

"But you can clearly see there is no one in there with guns. This is the safer option."

"We have guns," I remind her. "And you're a grade A dick shot."

"True," she agrees. "But what if we leave under the cover of night?"

"We have to go now," I say. "Bloats will be circling my house before dawn. That's the routine."

Her eyes scan the area. We've been hiding behind an old shed for so long my legs are cramping, and I could swear the sound of the ATV is getting louder. The time to move is now.

"Who leaves boat keys in the boats, anyway? This won't be like the

Jeep," she counters. "Now with the kayak, no keys needed. And it's got a nice cubby at your feet for snacks."

"Follow me," I tell her.

She rolls her eyes as I grab her elbow and lead her at a steady jog to the row of bass boats.

"We are always running," she mutters, but I ignore the complaint. Once we're home, I'll keep her in bed for a week.

Our footsteps whisper across the wooden planks, and I cling to the silence like it's a blessing. Keeping to the thick brush has spared us so far, and our stalkers slip out of sight in the opposite direction. I can only pray the distance we've gained is enough and that we're not walking straight into another trap.

The sun sets in a few hours, and this is the only plan I've got.

"Cade," Myra hisses.

We skid to a stop and place my finger over my lips, urging her to stay quiet. She looks panicked, more so than normal.

"I can hot wire it if I need to," I say. "We have a few minutes."

I look at a few of the boats, hoping by some miracle a key would be left behind, but no luck. Myra hisses at me again and points at a few houseboats in the next row.

Squinting my eyes to see better, I find nothing and no one.

"Do you see?" she whispers.

A boat bobs along the bumpers, one that looks a little older and will be easier to start, and I pull on the front ropes and jump inside.

"No," I say and reach a hand out to her. "Come on."

She's frozen on the deck, her gaze transfixed in the same direction. Jerking my head around again, I look, but see nothing. There isn't time to waste, so I rip off the panel under the steering wheel and ask her again. "Please, babe, will you get on the boat?"

Her feet move while her eyes do not. Once she's close enough, I grab at the waistband of her pants and yank her inside.

"They have a garden?" she says.

"Lots of people did," I tell her. The wires spill out, and I rack my brain trying to remember how this goes.

"It looks cared for, especially after that cold snap last week," she says. "And I swear I saw somebody."

"Then it's definitely time to go."

My mind drifts to the task at hand.

Red wire... blue wire... wait, is this red or sun-faded orange?

"Are you sure you know what you're doing, or did you just watch a few YouTube videos about this?" she asks.

"I'll have you know I've seen every *Fast and the Furious* movie," I joke. "That makes me overqualified."

She ducks low, collapsing into a seat, and the boat rocks from the movement. "Did you see that?" she asks.

I peel back the plastic on the wires, finding the ones I need to start the motor. We need a spark to get it going, but not too much, or it will fry the engine. This work is too precarious to look back at an overgrown garden. Yes, I would love some tomatoes right now, but I can't eat them dead.

"We'll be out of here soon," I promise. "Hold tight."

The engine fires to life with a few thuds, and I fly to the back of the boat to unwind the rope.

"Get that side," I order.

Myra stands, her head still checking over her shoulder every few seconds. No matter what she saw, we are about to be away from all of this and safely at my dock.

The boat drifts free, and I give a quick check around to make sure we can reverse and drive out of here without getting hung up. She's back on the ground between the chair and the dashboard, holding herself and looking in all directions.

I hit the throttle, and we rear back from the spot.

"Myra, check the storage," I order. "There are life vests somewhere. Put one on."

The boat scrapes against the wooden walkway as I shift gears. Myra stumbles, but I snag her with one hand. Thank God she's found a life vest, and I hit the throttle and we launch forward.

There are a few turns to get out of the marina here, but the expanse of the river is within our reach. I check the shoreline and scan the other boats, only to find nothing. The motor is loud, and water crashes around the dock with our speed, so I can't let down my guard.

Myra works the clasps of the orange life vest, eager to get it around her chest. They come loose, and she gets it around her shoulders, pushing her arms through. I let out a sigh of relief. No matter what happens, she won't sink to the bottom.

"There," she says, admiring the vest.

"Buckle," I yell at her, and look to my right.

I blink, uncertain if what I'm seeing is real or just another trick of the sinking sun. A man and a boy linger on the edge of a houseboat, the man's hands resting on the boy's shoulders. They're half-hidden by a tangle of wildflowers and tomato plants, red fruit dotting the vines.

This place must be abandoned if that food gets left out in the open without being stolen.

"D-do you see them?" Myra stutters.

We're about to take the last left, and I have to slow the boat down to take the sharp turn. Closer to them at this point, I understand why her voice shakes. This isn't a trick of the light. The boy steps forward before the man can pull him back, and we get a better look.

He's maybe ten or eleven, dressed in matching pajamas that appear clean. He's bald, which was hard to make out at first because his pale skin is riddled with dark lines. Veins of black cover his exposed arms and face, a dark spiderweb of infection riddled across his skin.

The man resembles his appearance, but he wears a ball cap. When we make the turn, our eyes meet, and I notice how the color is wrong, unlike anything I've seen before. There are only grey orbs where eyes used to be, and I speed up once we make the turn, ready to leave this place.

"That's behind us now," I yell over the noise. The tip of the boat lifts with our speed, and for a few seconds, we're flying over the water, our chance to get home within sight.

I picture it clearly, our floating dock with brand new handrails that mom insisted we paint red. A few hanging baskets with dead flowers, but they look alright all the same, and Dillon. He'll come out when he sees me, run through the yard, and start climbing the rocks before he calls me every curse word he can think of, before giving me a hug.

"I'm almost there, little brother," I say to myself.

"Hey, did you buckle—"

I don't get to finish my question before the explosion.

A violent crash slams into us from the left, my ears ringing just before the boat lurches right and tosses me into the water. I spin, my back colliding with the hull, or something just as unforgiving, sending pain shooting all the way to my toes.

I can't move. Every nerve screams as I'm dragged down, pain flooding through me while something pulls me under.

Light filters through the water, and I will myself to swim upward, but my limbs refuse. Only my eyes obey, tracking Myra's legs kicking frantically above.

The sight of her gets me moving, but barely. My left side claws forward while my right arm and leg hang dead weight. I'm torn apart with every stroke, but I keep forcing myself closer.

A shadow drifts across the water, and I realize it's the boat, tilting as it sinks to the bottom.

My chest burns, and the lack of oxygen makes my vision go blurry. I can't swim diagonally to her anymore, needing air right this second.

I'm only a few feet from the surface, air almost within reach, when she slips under completely, arms stretched overhead as she sinks.

In the same instant, an arm plunges down, seizes her wrist, and hauls her out of the water.

CHAPTER
THIRTY-SEVEN

MYRA

Floating is better than drowning.

The neon orange life vest helps with that, but it's also a bright beacon for anyone to target me. I might as well have a disco ball above my head playing rock music.

Floating, however, is not swimming. That is a skill I do not possess and am unable to figure out by the time I see them coming.

Cade hasn't surfaced, and I'm panicking, trying to find him while strangers in a steel boat barrel in my direction.

The pointed tip of our getaway boat points skyward, its back end lowering below the surface, a small Titanic in a doomed mission across the water.

Add to that, my life vest isn't buckled, and I'm hanging on by my elbows, my mouth bobbing in and out of the water while I cough and sputter, trying to get in a good breath. This time, there isn't a layer of bloat blood covering the surface, but the situation still screams death. I'm waiting for the inevitable end, and as seconds tick by, I worry Cade's already arrived.

People already know I'm out here. They're maybe thirty seconds from scooping me up and doing unthinkable things, so I do the only thing I can think of.

I scream my head off.

"Cade!" I yell.

Kicking my legs, I thrash away from the steel boat, screaming and throwing the largest adult fit I can manage without gulping too much river water.

"Cade! Where are you? Please, Cade!"

The boat draws closer, and I see them. My heart fills with dread as I realize I've moved zero feet and Cade is still nowhere to be found.

This isn't how I wanted to die. No one wants their life to end, but there are better and worse ways to do so. Every survivor has seen that firsthand, and turning into an inflated corpse filled with motor oil for blood is the bottom of the list.

Plan B comes to mind, and it isn't ideal, but I had a good run, considering the world ended. If this is it, I want to do it on my terms.

I let go.

Slipping through the flotation device, all the struggle leaves my limbs. I'm sinking, a stone falling at the speed of gravity.

But only for a second.

A hand grabs my wrist, so hard I worry it might snap, and I'm thrust upward, a shock of cold causing me to gasp before I'm hurled into the stranger's vessel, sliding across the hard steel.

"Myra!" Cade yells from behind me.

Twisting my body, I reach for the sound and find him swimming toward us.

Well, sort of.

He's a bit lopsided, struggling with the action and almost treading water instead of the athletic grace of yesterday.

Hands grab at my waist and arms, and I fight them, all while my body convulses from the cold. Being soaking wet does have its advantages, and I slip from their grasp, almost diving headfirst back into the river, but closer to Cade.

"She is being so difficult," a young voice whines.

"Can you blame her?" the other one asks.

Half my torso is back in the water by the time I'm pulled back in, my hair flinging over my head like a shampoo commercial as I plop back down on my butt. The aluminum floor of the boat bruises my tailbone, and I cry out from the sharp sting.

A blast hits the water a few feet from Cade, the spray reaching ten feet high and sending a wave that rocks the boat and scoots Cade closer to us.

"Out there with them, or in here with us?" the man yells to Cade. "It's up to you."

"Cade! Get over here!" I scream. "Oh, mylanta, what is that?"

"It's either a harpoon gun with an explosive tip, or a rocket-propelled grenade," the boy says.

He stands in the boat, knees bent to keep his balance, and I feel my jaw go slack as I look him over. It's the child from before. Pale skin covered in thick dark veins. They pulse at the surface, threatening to pop, but he isn't bloated.

In fact, he's completely normal aside from the infection ravaging his body. Almost cute. Yes, I would define him as downright adorable with his little smirk and Marvel ensemble.

How long can he stay like this? I've never seen anyone last more than a minute.

"Those sound bad," I whimper.

Moving to my knees, I cling to the side of the boat. It rocks uncontrollably, and I'm shocked we haven't sunk in this one as well.

"Cade, my burrito man. You need to get over here!" I yell.

He pauses for a second, the wave pushing him forward, but he isn't moving, a shocked expression on his face.

"It's apocalyptic Batman and Robin or being blown to bits by grenades!" I scream.

Both are terrible choices, but his woman is with the dynamic duo, so he needs to get swimming.

"I like Batman," the boy says. "But it got really dark."

I jerk my head to face him. "How are you calm right now! You're what, ten?"

"Eleven," he says and puts his hands on his hips.

"That's it," the man says.

He gets close enough to grab Cade by the back of his shirt, then hooks his arms under his armpits to haul him into the boat. Cade's raw scream rips through the air, sending a shiver straight through me.

Something is wrong with his bad arm, maybe his leg, too, but the boat swerves to one side, powering through the water before I can get a better look.

"What do you think about Superman?" the boy asks.

Another blast goes off behind us, and I go into a fetal position beside Cade, who is moaning on the bottom of the boat. This must be what shock feels like. I'm aware of my surroundings, but everything is an echo. The world is moving around me, too fast to focus on any one thing. My mouth opens to say something, anything, but I can't get a word out.

"They won't bother us over here," the man says.

I don't know who they are or where here is, but I sense the world spinning around me, the edges of my vision going dark.

"Did you hit your head?" the boy asks.

His face looks out of focus, and I try to sit on a bench, but can't find my balance. Before I can stop myself, I vomit at his feet, which, oddly enough, helps.

"Ewww," the kid says.

"Come on, Scout, she's been through a lot," the man tells the boy.

The boat begins to slow, and I look back at the water. Silver flecks reflect on the river, and I realize they are fish, dead from whatever bomb went off underneath.

"How many of you are there?" Cade asks.

"Wha—" I start to ask, but then I see them, more bloats standing at the dock to greet us.

CHAPTER
THIRTY-EIGHT

Cade

Short or tall, round or thin,
With freckled nose or dimpled chin.
We come together, show you love,
Because every person is enough.

"She's been mumbling that forever," Scout says.

"Give her some time," his father, Link, tells him.

"I've given her three hours and thirty minutes." The kid checks his watch. "Thirty-two minutes."

I take Myra's hands in mine, well, in my good one. I'm more beat up than I'd like to admit, but at least I hurt my bad arm.

My hip isn't great, but it's back in its socket, thanks to Link and one of his neighbors. I passed out from the pain for a good ten minutes, and we need to wait before he fixes the shoulder.

"Myra, babe. I need you to snap out of it," I tell her. She's been coming in and out of consciousness, but her pulse has been getting stronger, and I've watched her focus on my eyes a few times. "Come back to me."

Her rambling stops, and she meets my gaze.

"That was a poem from when I was in the system," she explains.

"That's nice. What makes you say it now?" I ask.

Her eyes dart to the four strangers in the living room of this houseboat. They're in different states of disarray, but all show symptoms of infection. One would pass for a bloat, his body extended to the point where I wonder if he might pop, but he speaks with the words of a scholar.

This afternoon has taken a sharp left, but we're still alive.

"Just thinking about… inclusivity."

"That's a big word," Link says. "I think she's back with us."

"Where is that, exactly?" she asks and raises her eyebrows.

We are on one of many linked houseboats back at the marina. That's how Link got his name, I've learned. He and his son became infected, but never turned completely. He lost his wife, but I didn't ask for more details. We've all suffered unimaginable casualties, and he's still suffering.

When they realized they wouldn't turn completely, they searched the river looking for other survivors.

Most ran for their lives.

We explain this to Myra, who remains silent as everyone chimes in with their story, and she takes it all in, nodding and listening.

"You've been through a lot," Myra says when we finish. "I-I think it's nice you found each other."

"We think there are many others like us," Link explains. "But we can't search much further. We've come across the Cavanaughs a time or two, and that's been a bit risky."

"They have taken a shine to you," one of the neighbors says.

She's an older woman, maybe in her eighties, but there's new life in her somehow. It sparks from her grey eyes, and I can't explain it, but she sounds energetic every time she speaks.

"Which is not a good thing," I tell Myra.

"Who are the Cavanaughs?" she asks.

Link offers us some coffee, and she declines until it's shoved under her nose. The irresistible smell takes over, and she holds the cup close before taking a languid sip, smiling as she swallows the liquid.

"Big family that owns a bunch of land East of the river," Link explains. "Mostly tents and trailers out there, but they live on a hilltop.

All I can guess is with their vantage point and about a million trail cams, most of them figured out how to survive."

Myra gives Link an innocent glance, still confused. "Well, that's good, right?" she asks.

"They're pure evil, honey," the old woman says. Myra extends her hand, but she shakes her head. "I'm Eleanor, and I don't want to risk getting you sick."

"Oh," Myra says, and dips her nose back into her cup.

"It's just not good sort of folk," Eleanor continues. "But they're scared of us, of turning. Milo accidentally turned one when they tried to raid this place, and now they don't cross some invisible border they've set for themselves."

"Milo?" I ask.

Scout points to a deck a few houseboats down, and we all get up and step to a large window to see him. A middle-aged man stands in his boxers on astroturf, a golf club in his hand. He rears back to swing and lets one fly clear across the water. I'm not a golfer, but the air it gets is a thing of beauty to watch.

Scout steps outside and calls out. "Hey, Milo!" he yells.

The man straightens and waves. "Chess?" he asks.

"I'll get my binoculars," Scout screams back.

"We have to keep him at a distance," Link explains. "He turned someone else in the community by accident. Something about his virus is… different, so—"

"You telling them about me?" Milo screams.

"We are," Scout yells back.

"I never mean any harm!" he shouts. "But I am a good guard dog, right?"

Eleanor makes her way outside, her cane clicking on the tile floor. "We love you, Milo!" she shouts.

"She's got a set of lungs," Myra whispers to me.

"Love you, too, Eleanor!" he screams back.

I rub my head and watch the back and forth like a tennis match. The pain in my leg and arm has lessened due to the migraine that formed after all this shouting.

"It's not the best arrangement, but we make it work," Link explains.

The trio continues to shout at each other, Scout dead set on figuring out how to play Uno with binoculars and Milo insisting they try Battle-ship next. Despite the odd and sad situation these people are stuck with, they've made this work, and it's kept predators at bay.

"What does the Cavanaugh family want with us?" Myra asks Link.

My arm rests in a sling, but I instinctively try to reach for her, and I groan.

"We'll need to set that," Link reminds me before turning to Myra.

"They have always been… sort of sequestered to their own area. Most of them are banned from restaurants around here. Rowdy behaviour."

"That's ringing some bells," I say. "Are they the ones that set couches by Center Street on fire?"

"That would be them," Eleanor echoes as she makes her way over to us. She takes a seat and smiles at Myra, and I see how her gums are grey. It's like watching someone in black and white.

"There isn't a day that goes by that one of them wasn't in a drunk tank," Link goes on. "Add in drugs and ignorance. They are just shitty people."

"But we didn't do anything to them," Myra goes on. "I don't know what we could offer."

Link raises his eyebrows and leans back in his chair. "What do they want with you?" he repeats, his voice heavy with warning. "What's the worst thing that you can imagine? Probably that and then some."

Myra visibly shivers and swallows hard while anger flashes through my veins. I don't know them well, but I know the type.

"You'll be safe here, though, honey," Eleanor assures her.

Her palm rises, wanting to tap it on Myra's thigh, but she pauses and closes her fist, bringing it back down to her lap.

"But we can't stay here," she explains. "We have to get home to Cade's brother. He's all alone."

Scout shouts something at Milo, and Link begs his son to use the radio.

Link asks where I live, and we figure I'm a quarter mile away as the crow flies, but getting another boat across this river is dangerous. This Cavanaugh clan has weapons, boredom, and an evil streak.

"They won't risk coming here after losing a few kin to infection," Link reaffirms. "And if they have two brain cells, they might believe you all are now infected, too."

"That's quite an assumption," I say, leaning back in my seat and considering the theory. "It gives us an advantage, but only if they aren't canvassing the area."

Scout's listening to our conversation, and he asks Milo what he can see from his angle. After a few minutes, he reports back that the Cavanaughs are still perched up on the water's edge, playing with fireworks and drinking beer.

"Gives us time to fix that shoulder," Link brings up again.

"What do you mean, fix his shoulder?" Myra asks. "Do you know… what you're doing?"

"In another life, I was a doctor," Link answers. He stands and grabs some things he used for the leg, a mask, and coveralls, two pairs of plastic gloves, but nothing to numb me. "It's just dislocated, like his hip was. Easy fix in the scheme of things. At least it's not broken."

In the span of a week, I've been shot, dislocated my hip and shoulder, and almost drowned twice – maybe three times. Last year, I got the flu and swore up and down I was on death's door. It's funny how perspective is more about convenience than reality.

"Will there be blood?" Myra asks. She points a finger at Link's getup, trailing it up and down. He does appear to be ready for some splatter.

Link shakes his head. "No, but better to be safe. We aren't positive we can't infect someone given the right circumstances, and I'll be up close and personal."

"About that," Myra says. "How do you find yourself in this predicament? If you were a doctor…"

She trails off, the unspoken thing now said out loud. Was this some sort of Agent Orange gone wrong? Does he have a vaccine, but he'll always carry the virus with him? Is this a virus at all?

"I worked in emergency medicine," Link says.

He pulls out a stool and waves a hand for me to come over. I drag my feet but oblige, grateful for the help but dreading the pain. "The best I can tell is this is a genetic response. Those of us like this have built some family trees, and there are loose relations. Third cousins and such. And there's my son and me."

"Genetics?" Myra asks.

I secure myself to the stool with one hand and take in a deep breath. Link nods, and I nod back, a silent agreement that he may commence torture.

"Oh, yes," Link continues. "There are several mutations that have been cataloged throughout our history of viruses."

Their conversation is a helpful distraction, and I focus on the words, the inflection of his voice, and think of how to respond.

"Some people have genes with stronger defense mechanisms, and others can even prevent viruses from invading cells," Link continues, removing my arm from the sling. "There are people with gene variants that change how they respond to vaccinations. That in turn changes how they respond to medications and other viruses."

"So it's a poo poo shoot as to why you aren't fully infected," Myra says.

Scout stands across the room and tilts his head, a perplexed look on his face, while Link chuckles.

"She's not a cusser," I tell Scout. "She means we have no idea why you and your dad are sort of..." My voice drifts off, unsure how to finish that sentence. Link positions my arm in his, twisting his body and telling me to go limp. Easier said than done, but I do my best because once is enough for this fix.

"Like a Marvel character?" Scout says. "Any day now, I'm going to have lasers for eyes."

"That's DC Comics. You're thinking about, FUCK!" I scream out without thinking. A wave of agony flashes through me, so strong my vision goes dark. Blinking a few times, Scout comes back into view, and I hear Myra apologizing for me.

"That was not an appropriate word, but his body has had more than one boo boo," she explains.

"Superman," Scout replies. "You're right. Different universe. I'll take webs then."

Eleanor lets out a throaty laugh, her head whipping back while Link inspects his work.

"Looks good," he says. "But you'll need to keep it in that sling for a week at least."

I thank him, my mind spinning with the next problem we have yet to resolve.

How do we get back to Dillon?

CHAPTER
THIRTY-NINE

Myra

Cade's sleeping, and I hate to wake him after yesterday. That man was flung around like a marionette, and he's finally resting peacefully.

We are staying in an empty houseboat, nestled between Eleanor's and Link and Scout's. My heart breaks for them, but I'm also grateful they are still alive and not rotting from the inside out.

It's a mix of emotions.

There have to be more of them out here, people that are somewhat immune, but never went full-on dark side zombie.

A door opens from somewhere in the house, and a steady thump hits the floor. Eleanor, I imagine by the sound of her uneven footsteps and cane.

"Yoo-hoo," she calls out.

Letting Cade sleep, I slip out of the bedroom to find her.

"Hey there," I say. "Thank you for the accommodations."

"Has he calmed down?" she asks.

Eleanor is referring to Cade's insistence that we figure out how to get to his brother before the sun goes down. We finally convinced Cade that there was no way we could make it to Dillon without running into bloats at this point, and we would need to wait until they made their steady march past his house.

Dillon knows their patterns, too, and he's not stupid. Far from it, and when they fill his streets, he should be hidden away like they always are. Last night was no different.

That buys us a few days to figure out how to get out of here safely, and I'm not counting on the Cavanaugh killers to move from their hunting spot easily.

"He so desperately wants to get home," I explain.

"And you?" she asks, taking a seat on an old leather sofa. "You're always welcome to stay here, dear."

"Thank you," I say. "You all have been very kind."

There's something nimble about her, even with the cane and the way her shoulders slump when she relaxes. Despite her appearance, she gets around well and doesn't appear in pain.

"What's it like being infected?" I ask, taking a seat across from her.

"I don't recommend it, but I must admit, I feel more alive than I used to. The first few days, I don't remember anything, and then, well, when I saw myself in the mirror…"

"Must have been quite the shock," I sigh.

She nods. "I waited for my end, alone. I lived alone before all this, you see, and well, days went on and nothing changed." Her finger lifts in the air, pointing at nothing in particular while she continues the story. "I wondered if I was gone, but my mind was still around. Did I die and not understand it? You can imagine when Link arrived with his boat, I didn't want to talk to him at first."

"He came right up to you?" I ask.

"At that point, he knew the infected didn't attack him or his boy." A faint smile curves her lips, and her eyes dance with the memory. "If I'm being honest, I've been alone for almost ten years, and this infection, well, it hasn't been so terrible for me. I've got company now, and oh my, this is terrible to say."

"No, I understand," I tell her.

"So many people have lost their lives, and I'm here happy that I have a few friends. I'm awful for even thinking it."

"You are not," I insist. "Everyone wants companionship. A family. I know I do."

My voice breaks with the admission, and Eleanor smiles.

"Had you been alone before Mr. Cade came around?" she asks.

I cross my legs and stare out at the water, feeling how empty the world is now. "In a way," I tell her. "I just never found my people, you know."

"Community is important. If you're searching for that..." she trails off.

"It's so nice of you to offer us a home here, but we have to get to Cade's brother."

She waves her hand at me. "It's not that, but I wonder if I should tell you. Some people don't believe them, but I remember Beth from game nights at the center, and she wouldn't lie."

"Beth?" I ask. "Is she someone who lives here?" I stare at Eleanor, waiting for her to clarify.

She shakes her head and shifts in her seat. "There's a group of folks that have been on the river twice that I can recall, looking for survivors," she explains. "One time, an old schoolmate of mine, Beth, was with them."

"Does Link think they are dangerous?" I ask.

"He hasn't said either way, but they aren't afraid of us. They have seen others that are our way, you know." She points to a large dark vein that creeps from her forehead and down her neck. "He's given them some information about the infected patterns in the area."

"Is there a compound or something?" I ask. "Where survivors are safe?"

"Yes, but they keep it close to the vest where that is, and how many of them are there," she adds. "That's why I hesitate to tell you. It's still a risk."

The idea dances around inside my head. I've had a taste of community life, albeit more of a college experiment. Even so, I'm not sure if it's the best thing.

Except Cade and Dillon have been all alone.

They may long for friends and a sense of belonging. If Eleanor has a friend there, the average age won't be nineteen.

"Do you think they'll come back?" I ask.

"They said they would," she says. "Hopefully not when those Cavanaughs are holding camp downstream, but they know the risks. Would you want me to tell them where you are if they do?"

"I'm not sure," I admit. "If you trust them, maybe. I guess so."

Cade can handle strangers, and Eleanor seems trustworthy. She and the others here are the only reason we are alive. I can't see her doing us any harm.

"Hopefully, we get to where we're going," I say, slumping down in the seat. "I haven't a clue how to get to Dillon."

"You're a smart girl," Eleanor says. "Something will come to you."

"I just wish those evil Cavanaughs would leave," I say. "They're probably mad that I shot one of their cousins in the penis."

Eleanor lets out a cackle, and I smile back, a chuckle rising in my throat.

"It wasn't on purpose."

"Oh, yes, I bet it was," she counters.

"Well, shooting him, yes, but not in the penis. And now it's made them furious. They're after us."

"They aren't furious," Eleanor says. "They're bored. This is all a game to them. They want someone to play with."

I sit up straight in my chair, my eyes finding the two-way radio Link has left for us.

An idea spins inside me, a top that refuses to fall. It could be the worst plan ever created in the history of plans.

Or, it could be genius.

There are far fewer people alive today, so where I sit on the ladder to genius is closer to the top than usual. That's something.

I've got to be smarter than the Cavanaughs. They got themselves shot in the penis by a woman who's never pulled a trigger.

"You alright, honey?" Eleanor asks.

"Uh-huh."

My hand wraps around the radio, and it takes me a moment to turn it on and hear the static buzz into my ear.

"I have a thought that might get us out of here," I say. "Do you think Milo would help?"

"Absolutely," she says. "He's a good man."

Swallowing hard, I slide open the screen door and exit to the patio. Milo's sitting out there, leaning back on his wicker furniture, his face pointed toward the cloudy sky.

"Hi, Milo. My name is Myra. O-over," I say.

He's got a fishing pole out in the water, and I watch as he sits straight up from the sound and fumbles for the radio.

"Hey there, speed racer," he says. "How's it going?"

Even from here, where I can make out the outline of his body that's changed from whatever bloat virus touched him some weeks ago, I can tell he's smiling. That calms me a bit.

"It's good because I have an idea," I say. "To help Cade and me get home."

"You need my help?" he assumes. "Give it to me."

"How good is your golf game?" I ask.

"I've got more birdies than a pet store."

I have no idea what that means, but by the tone of his voice, I'm guessing it's just what we need to make this work.

CHAPTER
FORTY

Cade

I don't know about this plan.

"We have another day to think of something else," I tell Myra.

She ignores me, mixing cornstarch and water with black dye.

"Where did you even get all of this?" I ask.

"It's RIT, dear," Eleanor says.

"What?"

"RIT," she repeats louder.

"WIT?" I ask.

"RIT. I'm saying, RIT," she says, slamming her cane down on the floor.

Leaning down, I whisper in Myra's ear. "I'm afraid to ask what RIT is."

"It's dye," Myra answers. "See. It makes bloat blood."

She puts a spoon into the large bowl and pulls it out, letting the dark contents drip from the utensil.

"Needs more cornstarch," she says to herself.

A drill twirls in the distance, and I flinch, which hurts. Half of my body has been pulled and torn, and any sudden movement sends sharp pains through my limbs.

"I think I found the right size bit," Link says. Scout reaches into the bag and pulls out more practice balls. They pour out, bouncing all over the floor, a few landing under the table where Myra works.

"Only two at a time, son," Link says.

Scout nods and scurries around the room, picking up the fallen white globes.

"How are you even going to get the liquid into the golf ball?" I ask.

Myra stands excitedly, and the chair scoots out from behind her, scratching along the linoleum floor.

"Look what I found," she exclaims.

A large turkey baster needle appears.

"Great," I say and shake my head. "You're going to vaccinate practice golf balls with bloat blood."

"Worked with Pete," she reminds me.

"This is different," I argue. "What if they don't get far enough? What if they don't explode on impact?"

"Then we don't go, but it will work," she insists.

Setting down the giant needle, she picks up a large green book. It's faded from age and the sun, and she hands it to me, a proud look upon her face.

"The Complete Book of Golf?" I ask.

"That was my late husband's," Eleanor says.

"That's so sweet," Myra coos.

"He was a bastard who spent more time flirting with the beer bitches on the course than with me," she admits. "But the book's so damn heavy, it flattens my flower petals."

Myra freezes, a nervous smile on her face. "Well, that's very informative," she manages to get out. "You see, Cade, a golf ball weighs about one and a half ounces, while a practice ball is more lightweight. This bloat blood—"

"Cornstarch and water," I correct her.

"Bloat. Blood." Her eyes meet mine, and she raises her eyebrows.

"When it comes to the Cavanaughs, fine. It's bloat blood."

"Technically, we want them to think it's Milo's blood, right?" Scout asks.

"Whatever it is, it will scare the shit outta 'em," Eleanor chimes in.

Link hands her a ball, and she balances it on the table, filling the baster with her mixture. The needle of the baster fits perfectly, and she squeezes the plunger until a drop of liquid bubbles at the top.

Setting the ball on a portable scale, she claps her hands together and exclaims, "Yes! It's one point seven ounces. That's heavy enough to fly where we need it."

"And if it doesn't break?" I ask.

"With the hole and pressure, I think it will," Link chimes in. "We can run a test."

"There's no time," Myra says. "Let's get two dozen of these and get going."

I want to object, and considering this plan is insane, I need to, but the idea of getting home to Dillon nags at me. Bloats passed through the night before last, and he was alone. For the first time since everything went to shit, he didn't have me by his side.

"And if it doesn't work?" I say. "We don't go anywhere."

"What do we have to lose?" she asks. "We'll hang back in one of the boats and chill until Milo gives an all clear."

"Simple enough," I sigh.

"Simple enough," Myra agrees.

"One requirement to try this," I say.

Myra's back straightens, and her eyes light up. "I'm listening."

"Buckle your life jacket this time, will ya?"

Milo's got a Ranger boat that costs more than my house. The engine rumbles, turning over and waiting for fuel to hit its metal arteries. It's likely not his, and neither is our speedboat, but how sad that he can't enjoy it out on the water.

The man is a leper, unable to touch anyone ever again, and he can't have fun catching a few Striper fish?

The radio clicks to life. "You ready?" he asks.

"No, but let's do it anyway," Myra says. "A-and, before you go, we really appreciate this."

Myra frowns, guilt sinking into her expression.

"I'm fast and have a hell of a drive," Milo says. "Wait two minutes and then stay back a bit. Be ready to cut and run if we have to."

Myra nods, and the radio turns on again.

"I can't see if you're noddin', sweetheart. Is that a yes?"

"Yes, over," she responds.

In this wild plan, we never considered how dangerous it would be for Milo. He's a sitting duck out there until he gets a few fired off, and even then, they could shoot him.

The tip of the boat lifts as he flies off into the water, a steady wake left in his path that rocks our boat.

"This will work," I say. I'm convincing myself, knowing Myra doesn't need affirmations, but it helps.

Myra's counting to herself. "One Mississippi. Two Mississippi."

"They are terrified of getting infected, and they know what Milo looks like," I go on.

She's at fifteen Mississippi, and I already know this will be an exceptionally long two minutes. I keep rambling, doing my best to pass the time.

"We just need one ball to crack in their line of sight. They see that black blood, they'll run."

It's been seventy Mississippi's when I hear a gun discharge.

"Go!" Myra yells.

We fall back in our seats with the speed of takeoff, wind piercing into our faces as we round the corner and make it out of the marina. Milo hasn't stopped yet, and a few pops go off close by, but with all the disruption in the water, we can't tell where.

"What's he doing?" she asks.

"Getting close enough."

"That's too close!" she cries.

I know Milo wants to be sure, and he might have a small death wish or think he's invincible. It's hard to know which, but I watch as the boat comes to a sudden stop and he walks out onto the bow where a tee has already been placed.

The Cavanaughs have lined up on their beach, maybe a few hundred yards away. It feels too close, but also so far for a golf ball to travel.

We hold our breath, feeling hopeful and a little stupid all at once. Do we really think that some ooze-filled golf balls might scare murderers away? These men are cold-blooded killers.

Gunfire stalls as Milo gets into his backswing, the ball flying high into the air with a line of black liquid pouring out from the puncture mark. It spins and curves, the fake blood painting the sky before it lands on their beach.

He lines up another, and we watch a Cavanaugh bend down to inspect the arrival. *Whack!*

Another one flies through the air with an arc of black spray, and I see it shatter on their cement dock.

With this landfall, the men go mad. There are a few shots fired, but as the third ball disappears into the sky, they scatter.

"Now!" Milo calls, placing another one on the tee.

I put it in drive and speed around him, Myra waving as we pass by. Another ball flies over our heads, but it lands on a lonely shore.

"Shit, it worked," Myra says.

"You said a bad word," I point out. "You've never done that."

"In the week you've known me," she mocks. "But you're right. I don't do that."

Milo disappears into the distance, and Myra covers her mouth with her hand. "I didn't give him a proper goodbye," she says.

"Yes, you did," I remind her. "We had a whole goodbye tour. I think the goodbyes lasted longer than our stay there."

The surface of the river calms, its water flat and empty, and my eyes search the shoreline. Considering what cowards the Cavanaughs are, they ran back home, which is in the opposite direction.

She turns and sits, and without looking, I can sense her despair.

"I know it's hard," I say. "Knowing you'll never talk to them again. But they're safe, and they have each other. That's something."

Myra doesn't respond, but we aren't far from my house, the familiar flower pots coming into view on the dock. I was wrong about the longest two minutes being before. This time, as we approach my home and my brother, it feels like time is stretching out before us, pulling away with every inch we move forward.

"That's it," I tell Myra, pointing at the tree where I tied up a hammock. It's frayed beyond repair, but we aren't relaxing outside anymore.

She stands, and in that same moment, a gunshot rings out and pierces the hull of the boat.

CHAPTER
FORTY-ONE

Again, our boat has been shot. This time, by something less aggressive, but my annoyance doesn't waver.

Cade pulls at my lifejacket, shaking me a few times.

"It's buckled," I yell over the noise.

The boat is still going, but it's making an awful noise, and the engine roars while one side takes on water. I grab our supplies, wrapping the straps around my arms to keep a hold of everything.

"We've got to get as close as we can." His voice shakes, and I can feel my throat close as I realize the inevitable fact that we're going to end up in the water.

Again.

"I'll swim you in," Cade says. "We're close."

"So, I'm going to be an orange buoy in the water again?" I ask. "The last time, I was an easy target for bloats to pick up."

"They weren't bloats," he says. "They were mostly human. Half bloats."

"Oh, like the half-blood prince!" I exclaim, just as the engine of the boat sputters and dies.

Cade takes a quick look around us, calculating his next move. "I don't know who that is," he admits, gripping the shoulders of my life vest with two hands.

"You don't know about Harry Potter?" I squeal.

He picks me up and throws me into the water, a grunt of agony leaving his lips from the motion. I'm shocked by the cold and his lack of magic knowledge, but it doesn't take long for me to begin my flailing and thrashing.

Think Olympic swimmer, Myra. Stop it.

My limbs calm, and I watch as Cade throws on a life jacket before he jumps from what's left of the boat. There's only a sliver remaining above the surface, which quickly disappears below.

"Good gravy, this river is deep," I sputter, icy water splashing onto my lips. "I could use some Gillyweed right now."

Cade reaches my side, out of breath, still no wiser to my Black Lake references. It's a shame, and if we survive, I'm going to have to find some books. I bet I could recite the first one from memory if it came to that.

"I can swim us to the dock," he says. "Just let me catch my breath."

I take a moment before I crush his ego a bit, and decide honesty might be the best policy. "I mean this in the nicest way, burrito-man, but are you insane? You are very, very injured."

I'm useless in the water, and he's clearly exhausted. Add in the fact that someone's shooting at us, probably a leftover Cavanaugh too stupid to run, and it's starting to feel like all we can do is wait for the death.

"Milo might come looking for us," Cade says. "He might have heard the shot."

"That would lead to infection," I remind him.

Cade lifts his chin, searching for the source of our downfall. "Where are they?" he mutters.

It's silent for too long, only the sound of water splashing on our faces and our ragged breathing. Whoever is out here playing target practice with human lives, they won't stop. These could be our last few moments alive.

"We should kiss," I say.

The deflated look on his face evaporates, a smile breaking through.

"You are so…" he trails off.

I try to shrug in my bulky vest, but it makes me sink a little, and Cade lowers one hand to my waist, propping me up. It's awkward, us bobbing together while I stretch my neck to reach his lips.

"Someone is out here," Cade says. "We need to concentrate."

He kisses me anyway. It's not passionate or filled with heat. That's impossible when there is about a foot of foam between us, but it's what I want to do if this is the last thing I ever do.

"Cade!" A voice rings out, and everything stops.

It's a man, and he doesn't sound too far away. Jerking my head around, I search for the person, but can't spot anyone at first. Whoever it is, they know his name, and it doesn't sound like Milo.

"Cade!" the man calls out again, and we both zone in on the location.

Someone waves at us, and as he gets closer, I notice the person staring at us in disbelief has similar features to Cade's.

"I'm sorry," he screams. "I thought. I-I don't know what I thought."

"Please tell me that's your brother," I say.

"Dillon!" he screams. "Go back to the house."

"No! I think he should come this way and help," I argue. "Dillon! Come back. Hi, I'm Myra!"

Cade's panicked, his features tight and agitated. "He can't be out in the open," he demands.

"I'm out in the open wearing orange," I try to reason with him. "Only deer cannot see me right now."

"Someone shot at us, Myra," he says. "He can't be out here."

There are a few seconds where it clicks that Cade is not under-standing the series of events.

"Burrito-babe," I sigh. "Dillon shot at us."

Cade shakes his head. "That's not possible."

"He's got a gun with him now."

He turns to face his brother, who is desperately paddling our direction.

"Did you shoot our boat?" he accuses.

"I didn't know it was you, and you were coming right for the dock," Dillon explains.

"Seriously, man. She can't swim."

"How was I supposed to know who you were, and that you had someone with you, and that she couldn't swim?" he gripes. "Why would you take her on the water? You never think things through."

Laughter rises in my throat, and after all we've been through and how far we've come, Cade and I are brought right back to the beginning.

"What's so funny?" Cade says, still agitated with his brother.

"Besides the fact that you two are having a silly argument? Do you see our rescue boat?" I point out.

Cade tries using one arm to swim toward his brother, both of them working hard to bridge the gap.

"Right back to where we started," he grumbles.

"I know, right?" I say. "Stop trying to swim. He's getting here fast enough, and the danger is over."

"A fucking kayak," Cade sighs.

"It's the only boat that's survived gunfire," I point out. "A hardy sea vessel."

"Good point," he agrees. "It's slow and awkward, though."

"Well, so am I," I quip. "But I'm still around, too."

CHAPTER
FORTY-TWO

Dillon and Cade couldn't be more opposite.

It's been three weeks since I found myself in their living room, providing Dillon with a long-winded rundown of what's occurred since Cade's failed fishing attempt. River water dripped on their floor while Cade stood beside me, nodding along.

Dillon took the information in like a computer calculating a formula before sitting in silence for a good ten minutes.

Then we all enjoyed a meal of soggy protein bars.

"There's no evidence to think the Cavanaughs know you're here," he mused. "But we should reinforce the barbed wire."

Ah, yes, the barbed wire. I almost plowed straight into it when we first arrived. Running toward the house, joyous to finally find myself here, both men were screaming behind me to stop.

It was a close one.

My survival skills have not improved since then, but I am more aware of our borders.

Lucky for me, in these three weeks, the only body of water I find myself in is a bathtub. I'm relaxing in one this evening as Cade brings in a refill bucket warmed by the fire.

"I'm fine," I tell him. "See if Dillon wants a warm bath."

"He's too busy counting Brussels sprouts," Cade says. "Harvest time finally arrived."

I sit up in the tub and look out the small box window. Dillon is hunched over the garden, plucking out the vegetables and setting them on a towel.

"Yum," I snort.

"Food is food," Cade reminds me.

Nodding, I sink my shoulders beneath the water while Cade pours in another bucket. Warmth spreads from my toes and up my legs, relaxing me, and I close my eyes.

"Link radioed," he says.

"He did?" I question.

Link doesn't call unless there's something to say. Scout, on the other hand, likes to chat once a day. I imagine a young boy might get a little bored, but Eleanor is teaching him Gin Rummy, so he's getting attention.

"He said there are survivors on the water."

The discussion about Eleanor's friend and a colony of survivors has come up a few times, but it's been a source of contention. Between the three of us, we can't make heads or tails of what to do if they arrive.

"For someone who claims he never thinks things through, we keep having the same conversation," I say.

"I give something a lot of thought when it comes to you," Cade says.

His fingertips dip into the warm water, reaching below the surface and trailing up my leg.

"Dillon says we should consider going with them," I remind Cade. "Milo said he'd play a golf game behind us if necessary."

"We're safe here," Cade counters.

"And almost out of food," I remind him.

He raises an eyebrow. "Are you running from Brussels sprouts? Because I'll have you know, when cooked properly, they are delicious."

I splash him with the water and sit up, ready to exit the tub and call Link.

"Where are you going?" Cade asks.

"I'm going to talk to your brother and call the houseboat crew," I say. "We need to figure out what we are doing."

"This group of survivors is staying with Eleanor and Link for tonight. Bloats come by, remember?"

"Oh, how could I forget?" I groan. "Another family bonding night in the basement."

His hand slips over my thigh, resting between my legs.

"We're alone now."

Fingertips slide toward my center, and I lean back in the tub, spreading my legs until my knees hit the porcelain sides.

Cade doesn't need much cajoling, his mouth finding mine while he massages my most sensitive area.

A moment alone is a rare thing after arriving here. Sure, almost losing Dillon made him want to keep an eye on his brother constantly, but sometimes both of them have fallen asleep in the same bed.

It's not the swoony fantasy of romance novels, more snoring and farting than spicy passion. Not that I feel that way towards Dillon. Ew. He's like my brother.

Cade finds my clit, circling and teasing, until I cry out into his mouth.

I'm pulled from the tub, soaking wet and dripping all over the floor. A snap of cold air sends pinpricks over my skin, but I'll be warm soon enough.

"Cade!" Dillon calls from outside. "Can you bring me the basket?"

I groan while Cade kisses my neck, sucking and biting, and ignoring his brother.

"He's going to come up in a minute," I warn.

Cade picks me up, setting me on the bare counter, and I yelp from the cool granite on my bare bottom. He hits his knees, his face diving between my legs. I place my hands on top of his head, fingers sliding through his hair until I grip a handful. Leaning back against the mirror while his tongue knows exactly what to do, Dillon calls out again.

"This harvest is great!"

"Gosh darn Brusels," I moan.

"Ignore him," Cade whispers into my spread legs.

His movements grow faster, purposeful. A rhythm he knows will get me there, and as the heavy feeling in my stomach grows, soft, steady moans leave my lips.

I tug at his hair, just enough to tell him he's got it right while sparks of pleasure shoot through my limbs.

"Cade!" Dillon yells again, but I block him out.

Rocking on the counter, I press my center into his mouth while he sucks my clit until the feeling overwhelms my senses. I'm frozen, back arched, mouth open.

My legs shake over his shoulders, and he doesn't dare move anything but his mouth that continues its assault.

"Y-yes," I say. "I-I, oh-wow."

The orgasm sweeps through me, nipples hard, body trembling, until every part of me goes limp. Dillon's voice is somewhere in the distance, and I try to warn Cade, but I sound drunk, a wilted flower in his arms.

He yanks me down and turns me to face the mirror. There's the sound of his pants hitting the floor while I lean over, my nipples hard against the cool surface.

There's no teasing because there is no time, and when he slides his hard cock inside me, and I'm filled to the hilt, I moan so loudly I'm sure Dillon hears.

"I'm dropping these in the sink. Can you wash them?" Dillon yells from downstairs.

He did not hear me.

Cade doesn't stop, pulling his hard cock out, only to slam it inside again. He places his hands on my shoulders and thrusts while holding me in place. The pace is fast, desperate for release, and I'm loving every second of it.

There's nothing to hold onto as he plows into me, but I find the faucet with one hand and do my best to match his rhythm.

"Fuck, you're so tight," he says.

I'm hoping that means he's close because I can hear Dillon's footsteps on the stairs.

I'm stretched to my limit, the angle of his cock feeling too good, sliding over the spot inside that makes me completely lose my mind. A second orgasm grows, and I can't decide if I should cry out in pleasure or try to remain silent.

Cade can feel the tension rising. His hand reaches between me and the countertop, pinching one nipple, and the sensation makes me whimper in response.

"That's right," he says, wrapping his other hand around the front of my neck, lifting me slightly to standing while he thrusts.

The position is my kryptonite, sending my body into a ball of need. I tremble, reaching for my clit, rubbing furiously to find another orgasm before Dillon catches us.

"Come for me, baby," he demands. "Explode on my cock. You know how I like it."

I do, and the orgasm rips through me while my walls tighten, feeling his warm release while he kisses my neck.

"Oh, n-no," Dillon stutters.

He's somewhere close enough to see this, but I keep my eyes closed, utterly mortified.

"I told you he was in the house," I tell Cade.

"You…" he takes a few heavy breaths, pulling himself out of me. "Did not."

"Well, I did in my head," I say.

Opening my eyes, Dillon is nowhere to be found. Cade hands me a towel and wraps his arms around me.

"He knows we have sex," Cade says and kisses me on the cheek.

"And how we have sex. And where. And in what position," I carry on.

"I'm considering going to the survivors' compound," Dillon yells from down the hallway.

"Oh, come on," Cade hollers back. He storms out of the bathroom, naked as the day he was born, to argue with his brother. "Don't be like that. I thought you were outside."

Here we go.

"You can both stay here, but I think I need to try to meet more people," I hear Dillon say.

I wipe myself down with the towel and consider going back into the tub, but I get dressed instead. Marching out into the hallway, I find Dillon and Cade arguing, Cade still in the nude.

"I agree with Dillon," I say.

"Not this again," Cade argues.

"We can't keep living like this," I tell him. "We will run out of food. The Cavanaughs could seek us out. And poor Dillon, well, he's taking this third wheel thing well, but—"

"I am not taking it well," he interrupts. "I love you, Myra. I really do. You're the nicest person next to Mom I've ever met, but now we have three mouths to feed. No fish. The river's going to freeze over. This is it."

Cade pauses, and I hand him a towel, which he rips from my hand and wraps around his waist.

"I'm going to wash some Brussel sprouts and radio Eleanor," I say.

"This decision isn't made," Cade counters.

"Except it is," I tell him. "I appreciate your thoughtfulness lately, but what does your gut say?"

"To go," he admits before thinking better of it.

Dillon smiles, and I escape the hallway before anyone changes their mind.

"Come on, Dillon, let's go," I say. He takes the hint and skips after me.

"Sorry you had to see that," I tell him, embarrassed.

"I didn't see much," he says.

"But maybe it was a good thing," I add. "It got us to a decision about leaving, pushed you over the edge a bit."

"It wasn't that," Dillon admits. "I decided before I walked in on you all."

I frown, confused, and grab our rain bucket as we enter the kitchen, dragging it over to the sink. Dillon takes a side and lifts it onto the counter.

"What happened?" I asked. "To make you decide?"

He holds up a Brussel sprout. "This," he says.

I wash one off and take a bite of the raw vegetable.

"Makes total sense," I say, trying my best not to spit it out.

CHAPTER
FORTY-THREE

Cade

2 months later

I have never once set foot inside a cave. When videos would pop up about cave diving, I would chastise the idiots who would leave their happy families to go wedge themselves into dark rock, hundreds of feet below the surface.

This cave isn't what I expected.

It's spacious, almost like an open-floor-plan house. Honestly, it's a little too open. Some pathways lead to carved-away spaces, and I'm working on making a few more. Construction is slow with limited supplies, and all the work it takes to run the place, but every day I get up and contribute.

It's a simple routine where I start each morning with Myra in my arms, do some work to make this place safer and better, and then go to sleep with the woman I love.

We're happy in our simple existence, just as I promised her.

Myra and I get some alone time, but for the most part, there's a lot of cave togetherness.

Meal times are a cluster of everyone and more bonding than I can usually handle, but I can tell it makes my family happy, so I'm back in our makeshift cafeteria, looking for Myra.

I find her in the corner with Caitlyn, who looks downright pissed off. This is typical of Caitlyn. She's good to everyone in her way, but Myra might need saving.

"You do not cut your hair," Caitlyn says. She's got a finger pointed at Myra.

"It's not a big deal to me," Myra counters. "It's just hair."

"I don't care if she wants a shorter look," I tell both women.

Caitlyn glares at me and puts her hands on her hips. I appreciate her, and I am sure Caitlyn's objection is for a good reason. Even though everyone in the caves is a decent person, people can take advantage of Myra. She's naturally giving, and others have a tendency to take.

Living here has been an adjustment, and it helps that almost everyone has a *fully formed frontal lobe*, as Myra puts it.

"She was cutting it because someone wants her hair, Cade. They want to make a wig or something. What's next? She flays herself so they can wear her as a skin suit."

"Myra," I lament. "Come on. You have to stop doing this."

"She said she needed it," Myra explains.

I put an arm around her, kissing her head and leading her back to a table. Caitlyn walks off with her man, Riley, talking with her hands, no doubt about keeping Myra out of trouble.

"We talked about this," I remind her. "Before you give anything away, we chat."

"I don't need your permission," she says.

"You are absolutely correct. I don't decide, but you at least give me time to make a case, right?"

She nods, and we sit down next to Dillon. He doesn't give us time to pick up a fork before he's talking a million miles a minute.

"I'm going on a crew to find survivors. I've thought about this, talked with the elders," he says. "I've been studying the lands and maps, and you know how good my memory is. This could help people, and I need some purpose, you know. There's nothing in this cave I'm particularly good at, but I do know how to navigate. I make good plans. Remember when we had to have a blackout for a few hours and I put together the order of things and how to communicate it, and all of that?"

"Whoa. Whoa. Whoa," I say. "Slow down. Let me get a bite."

Dillon swallows hard and waits, his eyes shifting to Myra. I can tell they've planned something. She's to be the supportive sister-in-law, keeping the peace between brothers, I can tell.

"Absolutely not," I say. "Now, everyone eat. I told Riley we'd play cards after, and I'm anxious to win back some fruit."

"You've lost to him at poker the last four times," Myra reminds me. "Maybe just play for fun."

"I'm going," Dillon says. "You don't get to decide."

He looks at Myra and nods, and she nods back, both of them bobbing their heads at each other. It appears Myra's already forgotten her role.

"Y-yes, Cade," she finally stutters. "What Dillon is saying is—"

"No," I interrupt.

"He has more skills than we do to survive out there," she reminds me.

"Name one," I argue, even though he has about a hundred. I'm not sure why I'm arguing so much, but I don't want to lose my brother. We've been safe here, happy.

Right?

"He can swim!" Myra says. I don't remind her that even some babies can swim.

"And I can hunt, and fish, and find food," Dillon goes on. "I could live by myself in the woods for a long time if weather permitted, and you know it."

Dillon is indeed teaching classes on how to start fires and forage for food. Myra helped him with some education basics and understanding how people learn, but he does the content all himself.

"Why are you two always against me?" I say, dropping my fork.

"That's not true," Myra argues and reaches for my hand.

"You were the ones who wanted to come here," I remind them. I already know the battle is lost, but I'll go down bitching about it.

"You will be safe, won't you?" Myra asks.

Dillon smiles and nods. He's getting what he wants without too much of a fight.

I let out a growl and stab a few pieces of food with my fork, but in my heart, I know I need to let my brother go his own way. I have my family to care for with Myra, and he wants to create his own. Maybe that's somewhere out there and not in here.

"You need to remember what kind of people are alive," I tell Dillon. "There are cruel, ruthless men and women who will kill you for supplies."

"Oh, I should ask Caitlyn if I can get you more medical things," Myra says. "You should take my vitamins, too."

"Are you listening to me, you two?" I ask. "And, Myra, those vitamins are for you. I traded cornbread for weeks for those."

She slumps and gives me a lopsided smile. I worry about her in here without sunlight, and our diet isn't exactly full of color.

"Thank you, Myra, but that's not necessary," Dillon tells her. "And, yes, I'm listening. People are awful."

"That's not true," Myra pipes up. "I think there's a lot of kindness out in that world."

"And cannibals, if you ask Caitlyn," I quip.

"I was never heartless or unkind," Myra reminds us. "Neither were our friends in the houseboats. And even Caitlyn would admit that Jim and the others in the retirement community were good to her and that baby they found."

"That's the exception," I argue.

She leans back and crosses her arms at her chest. "Is it?"

"You so easily forget about Lincoln and the Cavanaughs," I remind her.

"I'm saying no matter how many bad people are out in the world, there is just as much good, and that's what Dillon should be looking for. If you focus all your energy on people doing you wrong, that's what you'll see."

She turns to Dillon and places a hand on his shoulder. "Lead with compassion, and you'll be fine. I always was."

I'm speechless because no matter how much I want to continue this argument and scare my brother from leaving, I know she's right.

"Thanks, you two," Dillon says. He's beaming, and I can't help but smile at the guy as he pops up and runs off.

"Admit that I'm right," she says to me after he walks away.

I go with my gut when I respond. "Yes, babe. You are always right."

Her arms wrap around my shoulders, and I feel at peace.

"Do you ever think of leaving?" I ask. "They say fewer and fewer bloats are around."

"I don't really care," she sighs. "Down here, up there. It doesn't make a difference."

"Sunshine could make a difference," I counter.

"I've made a realization," she announces.

"Is that so?"

She takes my face in her hands, and I meet her gaze. "My home is with you. I don't need a place or things. Just us."

Before I kiss her, I remind her, like I do every day. "I'm not going anywhere."

Tips for surviving the apocalypse.

Give what you can, and maybe a little more.

And seriously, learn to swim.

TO CONTINUE READING...

Our Serial Survivors keep on living! Be sure to check out Caitlyn Can't Die, another story in the apocalyptic world alongside Myra. Caitlyn may have survived, but it sucks. Good thing she has grumpy sunshine Riley at her side.

For other works and signed paperback copies, visit www. lizhambletonbooks.com and read below.

The Storm Series is a completed trilogy. It follows Rowan as she navigates a post-apocalyptic future with her twin nephews. She stumbles across an unconscious man, and they create a family together in the chaos of this new world.

The first book in the series is The Third Storm.

The Fate and Flame duet is a completed series set in a future where fated mates are real—and revealed through touch. Emry and Sebastian have built a happy life together, convinced they'll never find their destined matches. But when Emry unexpectedly brushes against Theo, everything changes.

The first book is Twisted Fate.

The Center Duet is a romance set in a dystopian future where marriage is only promised for ten years at a time before you are forced to renew or find a new partner.

The first book in the Duet is The Discovery Center.

Affluence is a dark romance standalone about a woman who comes back to her island job ten years later to seek revenge and come face to face with the man she still loves.

Keep in Touch is a contemporary second-chance romance standalone about a woman who moves to another country. She wants to connect with a pen pal she's kept since childhood, but an unexpected romance blossoms along the way.